EVERYBODY GOES TO JIMMY'S

EVERYBODY GOES TO JIMMY'S

A SUSPENSE NOVEL

MICHAEL MAYO

MYSTERIOUSPRESS.COM

OPEN ROAD
INTEGRATED MEDIA
NEW YORK

Copyright © 2015 by Michael W. Mayo

Cover design by Mauricio Díaz

978-1-4976-6272-8

Published in 2015 by MysteriousPress.com/Open Road Integrated Media, Inc.
345 Hudson Street
New York, NY 10014
www.mysteriouspress.com
www.openroadmedia.com

For Marcia

EVERYBODY GOES TO JIMMY'S

"YOU OPEN A DOOR IN NEW YORK," TINY SAID,
"YOU NEVER KNOW WHAT'S IN THERE."
—Donald Westlake, *Get Real* (2009)

CHAPTER ONE

I'd just got Connie Nix's blouse unbuttoned when the bomb went off.

The sound was hellaciously loud and we could feel the building shake. It went off outside but so close that it seemed to echo in my office. We were stretched out on the divan. Without thinking, I reached for the back of it, but Connie grabbed at me, and we rolled off onto the carpet with me on my back and her on top. We landed hard enough to knock my breath out. She was shaking and, hell, I've got to admit that it rattled me, too. I was so surprised and confounded that I froze for a few seconds and didn't even appreciate it when she tightened her arms around my chest.

About then, I heard hubbub from the bar as my customers herded outside to see what had happened, and Connie shoved herself off me and buttoned up.

Glaring at me, she said, "You see, I told you I don't do this kind of . . . this, this . . . I'm a good girl," as if the blast had anything to do with us.

She kept shooting me nasty looks as she got herself tucked together and bustled back out to the bar. I stood up and decided for the hundredth time that I didn't understand women, and that night, at least, I didn't. Hell, I was young and horny, I didn't understand anything.

Peeking through the blinds down to the bar, I saw the last of the late-night crowd heading out the front door. Connie was talking to Marie Therese.

I straightened the knot of my tie, checked my cuffs, and buttoned my vest before I found my coat and hat and stick. For a moment, I considered dropping the Detective Special in my pocket but decided against it since there were likely to be extra cops about who might not know me. And besides, the weight of the pistol screwed up the drape of the jacket.

I took my time getting ready. Sure, I was curious, but I was in no hurry to see what was out there. I knew what bombs did.

Now, I guess I should explain here that Connie Nix was an adventurous young woman. She got bored with the little California town where she grew up and signed on with this agency that promised they'd find her a position in some rich guy's house, and they did just that. She went to work as a maid in New Jersey at the Pennyweight mansion—yeah, Pennyweight Petroleum—but it turned out to be not what she thought it was going to be.

For openers, old Mrs. Pennyweight was slow to pay, and she worked Connie like a Turk. Then my old friend Walter Spencer, who was married to Mrs. Pennyweight's daughter, got involved in some dicey business that resulted in several bodies that needed to be disposed of. Personally, I was only responsible for one of them, not that it mattered. Connie could see that most of the cleanup would fall on her, so she took me up on my offer of another job and came to work at my speak in the city. If she didn't like anything about the work, I'd pay for her train ticket back to California. That was the deal.

It worked out for a while. Marie Therese and her husband Frenchy found a place for Connie to live and showed her the ropes. Marie Therese and Frenchy had been with the place when I bought it and really ran most of the day-to-day work. Marie Therese was a soft touch for any stray who wandered by, and she and Connie got along swell. Too swell, if you ask me.

You see, Marie Therese decided that I, a mere lad of twenty or twenty-one, needed to be married and set about making plans for Connie to become Mrs. Jimmy Quinn.

Now, I've got to be honest and admit that I noticed how nicely put together Connie was. Her complexion was the sweet color of milky coffee, and she had thick black hair and dark eyes. Yes, I had some ideas about what might happen if she were to be spending time with me at the speak, but I hadn't counted on her being so good at the job. I mean, she took to the work like a lush to gin.

Marie Therese made sure she got involved with the important stuff, like keeping track of inventory, starting with the cigars and cigarettes we sold. Of course, our business was booze, but our take on the smokes was great, and that's what brought her up to my office around two in the morning when things were slowing down. The speak was on the ground floor of a narrow brownstone with the office in the back, up a short flight of stairs.

It was furnished with a wooden desk, filing cabinet, bookcase, table and a rug that Frenchy claimed was a Caucasian from Persia. I bought it from his brother-in-law. A window gave me a view of the bar, but I normally kept the blinds closed. I also had a cabinet where I kept my private stock, a leather chair, and divan. As I remember it, I was sitting with the daily papers at the end of the divan where the good reading lamp was. Connie sat down next to me with a handful of invoices from the delivery that had come in that afternoon—crates of whiskey, gin, rum, and wine; kegs and cases of beer, juices, syrups, seltzer, and smokes—the stuff that Frenchy, Fat Joe Beddoes, and I had unloaded from the truck into the cellar.

She said, flipping through the sheets, "Something's not right with these."

I could tell that she was tired and tense, so I put down the newspapers, turned her around, and started rubbing her shoulders, right up near her neck where she always got tight.

She protested, "Now, Jimmy, don't you start with that, this is important, and we can't . . . oh, yeah, right there . . . that's good."

And before long, we were stretched out, and she was saying, "Jimmy, you know this is wrong. We're not going to do anything here, so you can just stop that." But she kept on kissing me for a nice long time. Things had progressed to the unmentionables when the blast shivered the building and we wound up on the floor.

I checked the bar again and saw that Connie and Marie Therese were still deep in an intense conversation. I found my keys, went out the back door, and unlocked the heavy wooden gate between our loading area and the alley. At one time, that part had been a garden behind the brownstone, but the previous owner had bricked it over and put in the seven-foot wall and gate along with the steel door and the steps to the basement, where we stored our product. As I was locking the gate behind me, a large figure stepped out of the shadow across the alley, and a voice rough with cigar smoke said, "Out for an evening stroll?"

The voice belonged to a cop. His name was Betcherman. He was a detective, and I had no use for him. That night he was puffing on an evil-smelling cheroot. He stood a shade over six-feet and had a narrow face, thin crooked nose, not much chin, and greedy eyes. He put the arm on everyone for free drinks, food, clothes, tickets, this and that. If he thought you were up to anything crooked, he was quick to offer to turn his back for a steep price, and he'd clap the cuffs on you a minute later. Then if you ever called him on it, he'd say that was just the way business was done. He wore loud suits he extorted from cheap haberdashers. Nobody, including his fellow cops, trusted or liked him. He knew he wasn't welcome in my place, so I said, "What's it to you?" and made sure the lock was tight when I shut the gate. I reached into my pocket and slipped my fingers through my knucks.

Before I could take a step, he got in front of me and said, "Hold it there. I'm not done with you."

I told him to go to hell, which was probably not smart, but I was still mad about being interrupted with Connie.

He stuck a hand on my chest and said, "You're not going anywhere until you tell me about the item that was delivered to your speak. I'm in on this deal, see. A piece of it's mine. Give."

"You're nuts. I don't know what you're talking about," I said, and tried to go around him. He grabbed my shoulder, spun me to face the gate and said that he had to find out if I was armed and reached for the pocket where the pistol would be.

He tried to get his arm around my neck, but I twisted back around so I was facing him and crouched. I was too close to use the stick. He grunted and grabbed at my head. I worked my right hand free and hit him hard with my knucks square on his knee.

He howled, spat out his cigar, and staggered back. "You're not cutting me out of this, you little shit," he said and lunged at me again. His knee folded underneath him. He struggled to his feet, cursing me.

"Hey!" a familiar voice yelled from the other end of the alley. "What's going on here?" I heard quick footsteps approaching, and Patrolman Cheeks came to a stop soon enough. Betcherman limped away toward the Broadway end of the alley.

"Oh, it's you, Jimmy. Was that Detective Betcherman? What's going on?" Cheeks was my regular beat cop and a nice young guy. He got a little extra from me every week, and he took special care of my place.

I found my hat and straightened my coat and tie. "I don't know. Betcherman was just talking a lot of screwy talk. Is he working this?"

"No, Detective Ellis is in charge." Cheeks slapped his nightstick in his hand and frowned. He didn't like Betcherman any more than I did.

Light, noise, and commotion were coming from the other end of the alley where he had been posted. We walked back there.

9

When we reached the street, I saw that police cars had cut off traffic to the north and south, and small crowds had gathered at both barricades. There was a big patch of scorched brick on both sides of the alley there. In the dim light of a streetlamp half a block away, you couldn't see much, but that nasty smell was something I knew and hadn't forgot. It looked like whatever it was had exploded about five or ten yards into the alley and blown out windows up to the third floor.

"Anybody hurt?" I asked.

"There's a dead guy up the street," he said, nodding toward one of the barricades. It had to be twenty yards away.

"Something blows up here, and he winds up all the way up there?"

Cheeks shrugged. "I don't know nothing."

That was about all there was to see, so I said to Cheeks, "Tell Detective Ellis to drop by when he's done." And I walked back to the speak.

Cheeks found me a couple of hours later in the cellar, where I was going over the invoices Connie had brought up to the office. He said that Detective Ellis wasn't going to be finished with the bomb and the dead guy anytime soon, and then he said something that just floored me.

"I don't know what this means, but Ellis says you should meet him this evening at six at the Cloud Club. He said you'd know what it is."

It took me a second to make sense of it, then I said, "Yeah, thanks, Cheeks."

It was true that I knew what the Cloud Club was, but I didn't have a hint in hell as to why Ellis would want to meet me there. So I went back to work and worried about Ellis and the Cloud Club, and I remembered the first bomb.

It had been twelve years before, in September, 1920.

I was working for A. R.—Arnold Rothstein—carrying messages, bribes, payoffs, and this and that. On that day, I had a thin envelope—a message, not cash—probably, meant for a captain down at the First Precinct police station. I was almost to Nassau Street, a few blocks up from Wall Street, and I meant to avoid it. There was so much construction work going on down there that even on a good day, the streets were crowded and slow. It was near noon and I was hungry—I was always hungry—when a huge flash of blue light blazed across the building in front of me. Then, before I could even blink against the light, came the sound of the explosion, louder than a summer afternoon thunderclap but sharper and close. As the ringing in my ears grew fainter, I heard something else, a loud crackle that turned out to be shattered glass falling from thousands of windows to the sidewalk. Finally a gray-brown-black cloud of dust swelled up Nassau Street, and I couldn't see anything else.

Too inexperienced to be as scared as I should've been, I turned and charged straight down Nassau to Wall Street to find out what had happened. Coughing against the dust, I ran straight into a guy whose suit was on fire. His face was black, and he bounced off me, slapping feebly at his lapels. People were yelling things like "The Stock Exchange has been destroyed" and "The Morgan Bank is exploded."

When I got down to the corner of Wall Street where Nassau turns into Broad—it was no more than four minutes after the blast, just as the dust and smoke were thinning out and you could see how terrible it was. One car was burning, and another was on its side. I remember seeing a horse with its feet sticking straight up, and there were splashes of red blood and gobs of stuff that turned out to be flesh on the sides of the buildings. The smoke had a nasty chemical smell to it that stuck in your nose and throat, and broken bits of glass were still raining down.

Some people were sitting up or trying to stand, but a lot of them weren't moving at all. The first person I really noticed was a kid, a teenager a few years older than me. He was on his back there in the middle of the street. I could tell by the cap next to his head and the call book still clutched in his hand that he was a messenger, like me, but legit. I could also tell right off that he was dead by the way his arms were thrown out and the flat misshapen mess of his face.

It scared me like nothing else had ever scared me. I realized later that he was the first real dead person I'd ever seen, and as I looked at him then, I understood for the first time that kids like me could die. That's probably when I threw up.

By then, the street was filling up. Men were moving all around, bumping into me and yelling to get the hell out of the way. I stumbled across to the sidewalk and heard an awful sobbing scream of pain and saw three guys trying to pick up a woman who was wedged against a door. When they got her almost upright, she screamed even more horribly, and the men stopped, and we all saw that her arms had been blown off.

I heaved again, and I know now that those probably weren't the most awful things that happened to the people who'd been out on Wall Street at noon, but they were awful enough for me. Even today, that nasty smoky bloody street comes back in my nightmares.

Before long, they got organized and started putting the wounded people into cabs and cars, and we heard the clangs of ambulance bells, and fire trucks showed up. A lot of people were still streaming in to see what had happened. The cops tried to keep them out, and pretty soon soldiers with rifles marched in. They kicked me out, and I remembered that I had a job to do.

When I finally got to the First Precinct police station, I found it almost empty. The captain I was supposed to see was with the rest of the cops back at Wall Street. I hung around for a while, not sure what to do, then went back uptown. I didn't find A. R. until nearly midnight at Ruben's, where he conducted his business in those days. Like everybody else, he was angry, and he said that it was the goddamn Reds who'd done it. It turned out that they put a big bomb on a horse-drawn cart, and the Red who drove it just stopped in the middle of Wall Street right at noon, when everybody was outside trying to find lunch. He ran away, and the bomb killed about thirty people.

Now, the truth is I didn't know who or what Reds were and had to ask Mother Moon. She was the old gal who owned the building in Hell's Kitchen where I lived and sent me out to work for A. R. She explained that there were Bolsheviks and communists and anarchists, and they were all Reds. That didn't help, and so she spelled it out. All of them hated J. P. Morgan and the other bankers and bosses because the bankers and bosses had all the money and ran things. The Reds thought they should have all the money and run things, but they kept fighting with each other. The communists wanted the workers to be in charge of everything, and the anarchists wanted nobody to be in charge of anything. She wasn't sure what the Bolsheviks wanted.

But how, I asked her, was blowing up a bomb going to make J. P. Morgan hand over his money? And how was killing a bunch of regular people going to get other regular people to want to become Reds?

She shook her head. "I don't know. It doesn't make any sense to me either. The only way I know to get money from rich people is to steal it. That's what we do, but we get to keep damn little of it for ourselves after we pay off our bosses, like the alderman, bless his worthless bleeding shit-stained ass. And now I'm tired of talking. Fetch my pipe."

Twelve years later, in the cellar at my speak, I still didn't understand politics. So I decided not to think about the bomb and the dead guy up the street. I couldn't do anything about them. Instead, I went over my inventory again and saw right away what it was that had bothered Connie and, I supposed, had Betcherman in such a lather. We had one box too many. Mr. Smiles, the colored man who delivered our packages with his cart and horse, had sixteen parcels on the inventory sheet he got from the post office, and he'd delivered seventeen. The odd box was a heavy cardboard carton with a return address of Custom Paper Products in Chicago. Typed at the bottom of the label was CONTENTS: SPECIAL ORDER NAPKINS/COCKTAIL, DINNER, DESSERT. The package was addressed to me, Jimmy Quinn, at the wrong address—222 Twentieth Street was a couple of blocks away.

I didn't know anything about any napkins, but figured that Marie Therese might have ordered them. And with the wrong street address, I could see how the guys at the post office might have listed the standard items, then found one more, and instead of adding it to the list, they just stuck it on the cart. Mr. Smiles, by the way, was called Mr. Smiles because he never—and I mean *never*—smiled at anything or anyone. He'd been delivering stuff for businesses in the neighborhood long before I moved in. When I took over the speak, Frenchy explained the situation to me and said Mr. Smiles got a dollar a month from the previous owner and two bucks in December. I told Frenchy to kick in another dollar every month and to tell Mr. Smiles to look after us. Maybe that extra buck helped the package find its way to my place. Maybe not. I'll never know.

That night, I used my knife to slice the twine that was tied around the box and the tape that sealed it.

I didn't find any napkins. Instead there were four long narrow books without titles. The ruled pages were filled with columns of letters and numbers written in such a tight dense hand that I had to hold the books up to the dim light in the basement, and I still couldn't make it out. So I took the box and the books up to my office where the light was better. Sitting at my desk, I read:

GS/CPP 22.55
DT/CSO 20.00
AW/RAK 11.50
OF/WTL .05

It went on like that for column after column, page after page, and loose typed sheets of more letters and numbers were folded between the pages. It meant nothing to me, but I figured I'd best hold onto them and put them in my safe.

Connie made a point of staying away from me when we closed, and left with Frenchy and Marie Therese. I checked the locks one more time and went back to my place at the Chelsea.

CHAPTER TWO

The next evening—a Tuesday, I think it was—I got up, showered, shaved, and put on one of my favorite suits, a nice charcoal three-piece, and finished it off with a patterned blue silk tie. Knowing I'd walk to the Cloud Club, I strapped on my knee brace. As often as not I didn't wear it, simply out of vanity. You could see the outline of it under my trousers and that bothered me. But some days it was necessary.

By six, I was back in my office. I asked Vittorio, the maître d' from the Cruzon Grill upstairs, to bring me a ham sandwich and coffee. Before my eats showed up, Frenchy came in. His wide, dour face was even more fretful than usual. Frenchy, by the way, looks nothing like you'd think a guy named Frenchy ought to look—some skinny number with a big nose and a little mustache and a lounge-lizard line for the ladies. This Frenchy was big and wide enough to put Marie Therese in his hip pocket.

He said, "They tried again after we closed up," and I knew what he meant.

Two nights before, sometime after midnight, I'd been up in my office—alone—when I heard noises out back. I got the .38 out of the safe and hurried to the back door. When I hit the switch for the outside light, I heard more noise, louder. By the time I got the door open, all I could see was some guy's ass and feet as he was going over the gate. Sounded like he landed on his head in the alley, and I know I heard at least two guys running away. I went back inside and told Frenchy about it. He agreed that it was probably just kids, but then the next night, there's the bomb.

So, as soon as Frenchy came in to get ready for the lunch crowd, he checked the alley and the doors to the cellar, and he saw that somebody had been at them. We went outside to look. The steel doors were set flush with the paving stones right beside the back steps. Somebody had tried to break through them. You could see shallow gouges in the heavy steel of the hinges and lock where they'd used a hammer and chisel.

Frenchy said, "I checked the locks and I've been down in the cellar. They didn't get in, didn't come close. I mean, hell, these damn things are as thick as the doors on a safe. You gotta pick the locks or blow 'em up or something. Seems like a hell of a lot of effort to get to a few hundred cases of liquor and wine. Kind of screwy, isn't it?"

I looked at the lock on the back door. No marks there. This guy or these guys had been interested in getting into the cellar, not the speak. And there were really only a few marks on the steel doors, like they were making enough noise that maybe somebody heard them and yelled for them to pipe down. Or they realized that banging on the steel wasn't going to work. Yeah, kind of screwy, all right.

Guys had tried to knock us over before. Twice they'd tried to hijack the merchandise while we were taking it off the truck and had the gate and the doors to the cellar steps open. That's the kind of thing you expect, and we were ready. Both times, as soon as we saw guys coming into the alley, we brought out the shotguns, and they backed off. Frenchy kept a big .45 caliber hog leg under the bar, too. I don't know that he ever fired it at anybody, but he had used it to crack a few heads. And like I said, all that, you expect. To see that somebody had really tried to break in to my place, that made me mad. I admit it may be more than a little hypocritical for me to say that, considering how many cars and trucks I stole over the years for Lansky's bootlegging operation.

But stealing a car that's just sitting there, waiting to be driven away, that's one thing. It's different when somebody's trying to break into your place.

Frenchy went back to the bar, and I went to my office, where I ate my ham sandwich and drank my coffee and worried about people sneaking around, and trying to break in and planting bombs and such.

The evening crowd was wandering in by the time I finished. Fat Joe Beddoes and Frenchy didn't need me, so I told them I was going to meet Detective Ellis, and if I learned anything about the bomb and the dead guy, I'd fill them in when I got back. Connie and Marie Therese acted like I wasn't there.

I went outside and picked up a tail before I'd gone half a block.

He was taller than me, maybe five-foot-six. He wore a dusty-gray canvas jacket with the collar turned up, a dark sweater, heavy laced boots, and a black cap that was real easy to spot. With my stick, I don't walk very fast. It's hard for anybody to stay with me without giving himself away, even on a busy sidewalk, and this guy just wasn't very good at it.

It came to me then, smart guy that I am, that he might have something to do with the bomb in the alley or the half-assed attempt at a break-in. I had my brass knucks in my pocket and wished I'd gone ahead and brought the .38, drape of the jacket be damned.

The guy came up right beside me when I stopped for the light at a cross street, and he absolutely refused even to glance over at me as we waited. He had a pale regular-looking face, kind of gaunt and underfed and in need of a shave, like a lot of guys in those days. Short hair, tiny ears under the cap. I couldn't see his eyes. He kept his hands jammed in his pockets and bounced on his feet, more from jittery nerves than the cold, I judged.

I was giving him a quick sideways look when somebody else bumped into my chest. It was a kid, and I felt a quick quiet hand slipping under my heavy coat. I cracked his arm hard with the crook end of my stick, and his hand jerked back as he ducked away. In the same second, the first guy shoved my shoulder, and both of them cut away in different directions and disappeared into the sidewalk crowd. I did a quick pat down of my pockets and found nothing missing. Wallet, keys, knucks, money clip, pen, and notepad were all where I'd put them. People pushed past me on the sidewalk, pissed that I was slowing them down. What the hell was going on? Smarter pickpockets worked in pairs, so it could have been that they just recognized the Brooks Brothers topcoat and made me for a swell. But I had doubts.

Nothing else happened on my way up Lex to the Chrysler Building. Detective William Ellis was waiting for me in the busy lobby.

He was about thirty and, for a cop, on the small side, five ten or so. His overcoat and hat made him look bigger. He wasn't really a regular at the speak, but I could count on his dropping by once every week or two after midnight. If I was around, I made sure he got a round on the house. Gin. That's what he drank. Took a double measure of the good stuff over ice. If I wasn't there, he didn't make an issue of the gratis business with Frenchy, and he always tipped well, even when he didn't pay. As far as I could see, he was a right guy, but I didn't know him that well.

That evening, he had a troubled, distracted look on his face. I guessed it had something to do with the papers he was examining. When he saw me, he stuffed them into his coat pocket and forced a smile.

"Quinn, good to see you. I've been meaning to stop by. Got a proposition that might interest you."

So this wasn't about the bomb. Then what did he want?

"Here, we'll use this elevator." We had it to ourselves. Everybody else was leaving. "Have you ever been to this place? No? It's something, let me tell you, but first you gotta see this."

We got in an express elevator and went straight up to the fifty-seventh floor. The elevator car rose so fast you felt like it was pushing you into the floor, and it made me a little queasy. Then we had to switch to another car to get to the sixty-first floor. It was empty. I followed Ellis around to one side where we were damn near blinded by the setting sun. "Hold onto your hat," he said as he pushed open a glass door, and we stepped outside onto a long shallow terrace. The wind snapped at our coats, and I grabbed my hat to keep it from blowing away.

Ellis spread his arms. "Look at this. Ain't it something?"

We were near a corner of the building looking south and west, so you could see the city stretching out to New Jersey. I had to admit it was pretty damn impressive, but remember, in those days, I'd never been in an airplane or even up that high in a building. Yeah, I know, the Empire State Building, tallest in the world, was a few blocks from my speak, and I'd never set foot in it. Go figure.

This place was kind of scary when you took a good look at it. I mean, the terrace wasn't that deep, and the little wall between it and nothing at all was no more than two feet high. I wasn't about to get any closer to the edge. The angle really made it hard to pick out any details beyond the shapes of the buildings and the curve of the river, particularly when the sun caught on a bright stainless steel eagle gargoyle. It jutted straight off the corner of the terrace like an insane diving board.

Ellis said, "They're going to put flood lights there on the back of that thing. They're going to point up at the top. Look."

I turned around and peered up at a series of stainless steel arches and dozens of sharp triangular windows. It made me dizzy.

It got to Ellis, too. He said, "Yeah, let's get inside."

We went back through the glass doors, and I thought that

whatever he was trying to do, Ellis had shown me an angle on the city I'd never seen. I realized then that I was a street guy, not a skyscraper guy.

We went up a few more floors and got off the elevator inside the Cloud Club, the ritziest, most restricted speak in town. Rockefellers, Dodges, Nasts, and the like wet their whistles there, or so I was told. It was a private club, open at lunch for members only and closed in the evening. I figured Ellis had invited me there to show off his connections. A place like that, and he could get in after-hours whenever he wanted. Only a big cheese could do something like that, and he acted like he owned the joint. And the truth is I was curious about it.

The club was on two levels with the kitchen on the third. There was a bar on the first floor and a small restaurant above it, crowded with twenty-three tables by my count, six two-tops along the walls and tucked next to the big square pillars, and seventeen four-tops. It was nicely turned out but not the best I'd been in and not that much better than my joint. The bar was done up with dark paneling and thick beams and wood floors, something you'd see in a movie. Like the restaurant, it had a cramped feeling to it. I'm not bragging when I say that my place was more comfortable and accommodating, not to mention a hell of a lot easier to get to.

We took a couple of stools at the bar. A colored guy in a white waiter's jacket was loading up a rack with clean glassware. A white guy in a dark suit was making sure he did everything right, and he looked like he wasn't happy that Ellis and I were there.

Ellis fired up a smoke. He wore a mustard-colored jacket, brown slacks, a creamy-white shirt with a gold collar pin, and heavy gold links that you couldn't help but notice when he adjusted his cuffs. He did that a lot. His tie and pocket square were silk with a dark bronze pattern, and the whole outfit had to cost more than most detectives could afford. The straight cops, the strictly by-the-book boys called him "Dollar" Bill Ellis. But he had friends higher up in the force and a good rabbi looking after him.

Personally, I thought the clothes were a little flashy, but then I was taught to blend in. I also had better taste in suits than he did and I bought the best. But, if you looked at his clothes closely and knew what they cost, then you understood that he was only modestly corrupt. Once you got past that, you saw that he still had a cop's eyes, and he knew you were guilty of something.

He held up two fingers to the sour-looking guy and got to his point. "Have you decided what you're going to do when they end Prohibition?"

So that's what he wanted. The question made me uncomfortable, and the truth was I avoided thinking about it. I told Ellis that I wasn't sure. I guessed I'd figure it out when I had to.

"That's sooner than you think," he said. "Roosevelt's going to get elected next month, and a year from now, booze is going to be legal again. And you know what's going to happen then? You want to sell a drink, you're going to have to buy a license. The word has come from on high. We're going to start closing down places like yours."

I hadn't thought of that, but as soon as he said it, I saw that it made sense. Until then, running the speak had been pretty easy. You kept things on the quiet side so you didn't get the neighbors mad. You paid your beat cops every week, and their sergeant and his captain and your alderman, and everybody was happy. But if the bastards decided to make liquor legal again, hell, that would be an anvil in the ointment.

"At first, it's going to be hard to get a license, too," he said. "I hear they're only going to issue a couple of thousand for the whole city. The big guys like the Stork Club, Jack and Charlie, they've got it all worked out already, but somebody like you with a nice little neighborhood place, maybe it's going to be a little tougher to get on board. That's where I can help you."

Everything he was saying was true enough, but I still didn't want to hear it.

"After you get the license, you're going to have to deal with fire marshals, and the health board, and the alcohol commission, and the nightclub and restaurant commission, and any other goddamn commission they can dream up, and you'll be buying licenses and paying fees and taxes out your ass. An establishment like this doesn't need the kind of help I can provide, but I am making sure they get a friendly fire inspector. I could do the same for you."

The guy put a couple of gins in front of us and took a stool at the far end of the bar, where he whipped out a racing form and studied it.

We drank. It was the good stuff but no better than you could get at my place.

Ellis gestured toward sourpuss and said, "Sid and his bosses have lawyers and other stooges to handle those details, but a working stiff like yourself, that's another story."

He pointed at me with his cigarette. "You know me, Quinn. I'm like you, I go along to get along. You deal with these new guys from the alcohol control board on your own, who knows how much you'll have to duke 'em to make sure you're treated fairly. A man in my position can see to it that the proper consideration is given. Help you jump the line when you need to. Grease the skids, if you know what I mean. I will be your representative with these people, your agent."

"And for this," I said, "you will be paid."

He waved a hand. "That's a detail we'll work out later."

I nodded, not agreeing, not disagreeing. "Let me think about it."

"Lotta guys aren't going to make it. They're selling drugs out of their places, or they're crazy, killing each other over business— you know who I'm talking about, I don't need to name names. Guys like that, I don't want anything to do with them. But you understand how things work, you're a guy that people want to do business with. Hell, everybody goes to Jimmy's. You're what, about a block off Broadway?"

"Yeah."

"That's prime property. If you decide to go legit and work with me, you'll make more money than you're making now. Trust me. People are always going to drink, you can count on that."

Everything he said was right, except "Trust me." The world Ellis was describing was coming, and it was nothing I'd ever known. I was used to bribing cops and buying off party bosses, stealing the occasional car, and selling liquor, not applying for permits. The idea scared me. No matter what Ellis said, I knew it would be a lot easier just to sell out. I had no idea how to be an honest businessman. Still don't, truth be told.

"Ellis, it's comforting to know that you're so concerned about my future, but right now I'm more worried about that damn bomb and the guys who have been messing around my place."

He hadn't been expecting that and turned serious. "What're you talking about?"

I explained about the guys I'd heard two nights before and the guys who'd tried to chisel their way into the cellar that morning.

"I didn't really think much of it at the time, but after last night, maybe there's something else."

"What do you mean? That didn't have anything to do with you. It was at the other end of the alley."

"What about the dead guy?"

Ellis reached into his pocket and pulled out the papers he'd been looking at in the lobby. They were pictures. He put them on the bar in front of me.

There were two shots. The first showed a man on his back. It looked like he was in an alley or next to a building because he was lying on pavement by a brick wall. The picture had been taken from above the guy because you could see the three legs of the big tripod they mounted the camera on. His eyes were open, and his vest was pulled up over his loose shirttail. His legs were folded underneath him. There were a few dark spots that might have been blood or soup on his white shirt but nothing to show what might have done him in. The second was a close-up of his face, probably taken in the morgue. Sharp nose, high forehead, thin hair, dull, dark eyes.

Ellis asked if I knew him.

"Maybe, but he's not a regular if that's what you're asking. Hell, I really can't tell anything from these. He just looks dead."

"He was carrying an Illinois driver's license issued to John Zenger. Looks phony."

"What happened to him?"

Ellis shrugged. "Looks like he was too close to his bomb when it went off. His coat's burnt on the back, and he had two short sticks of dynamite on him. Has Fat Joe thrown out any anarchists this week?"

He sucked hard on his smoke and frowned at the photographs, and it came to me that Ellis was stuck between what he wanted to do and what he had to do.

Being ambitious and not too concerned about strict legality, he wanted to put the touch on me for the licenses and such before I either decided to go it alone or to sell the place. But being a detective, he couldn't have unexplained bodies lying around in the street, and if I happened to know anything about the matter, then he had another reason to make nice.

So I said, "Look, whatever's going on here, if you come up with anything that has to do with my place, I want to know about it first, OK?"

He agreed. We finished our gin and left.

Back on the street, Ellis hailed a cab. I told him that I thought we could maybe do business if he didn't try to screw me over on his end, but I'd still have to think about it because I didn't really know what I was going to do. And that was the truth.

He headed uptown in his cab, and I hadn't taken five steps when a kid stepped up in front of me and blocked my way. He was dressed in work clothes, a lot like the guy who'd followed me. Collarless shirt buttoned up to his neck, thin coat, cap tilted at an angle, thumbs hooked in his suspenders.

The kid gave me a cocky look and said, "Are you Jimmy Quinn?"

I nodded and thought he was probably the same boy who'd tried to pick my pocket on the way over.

He said, "I'm supposed to tell you—" but his eyes went wide as he saw something behind me. It was so dramatic I thought he was playing with me, but he spun around and bolted down the street. I looked over my shoulder and damn near jumped out of my skin. Standing right behind me was an old woman in black giving me the evil eye as hard as she could. Her face was right up next to mine, and her breath was foul. She flicked her fingers at me, muttering something I couldn't understand. I thought it was Italian. I knew she was cursing me and slipped my fingers into the knucks. She glared at me some more, then turned and stalked away.

It took me a few seconds to shake off the chill she gave me. I waved down a cab and thought that the night was getting off to a strange start. I didn't know the half of it.

CHAPTER THREE

It was around seven thirty when I got out of the cab and went back into the speak.

We had seventeen customers—fifteen regulars, and two strangers at the bar—a little light for a weekday night. A couple of Dutch Schultz's guys were in a booth, and Mercer Weeks was at the bar. They had no reason to like each other. I didn't know Dutch's guys by name, but Weeks dropped by most evenings. Weeks worked for Jacob Weiss. In fact, he was Weiss's muscle and right-hand man. Everybody knew that Jacob the Wise didn't do anything until he talked it over with Weeks. Word was about that Dutch was trying to horn in on Jacob's numbers racket. That was their business, as long as Weeks and Dutch's guys didn't try to fight it out in my place. Everybody was welcome at Jimmy's— crooks, cops, citizens, as long as they didn't start anything. No guns, no fights. I nodded to Weeks as I passed him, and he nodded back. He knew the rules and wouldn't do anything. I wasn't so sure about the guys in the booth, but decided that they were just a couple of mugs who didn't know from doughnuts about any plans Dutch might have had, and they weren't going to start any trouble.

I bought the place from Carl Spinoza in January, 1929. I can't say that I really wanted to own a speakeasy, but I couldn't continue doing what I had been doing. That was handling whatnot for A. R. and stealing trucks and cars for Meyer Lansky, as I mentioned. I also delivered booze for Lansky, Charlie Lucky, and Longy Zwillman over in Jersey.

The reason I couldn't keep doing what I had been doing was because you needed two good legs for that kind of work. Eventually, somebody's going to try to catch you, and you've got to be able to outrun him. But on the night that Rothstein got shot, in the autumn of 1928, I tore up my right knee. I've told the story before. It comes down to this. I was where I wasn't supposed to be and got scared and ran away. I ran so fast and reckless that I fell and tore apart some tendons or ligaments inside my right knee.

After that night, I couldn't take a step without a cane or a crutch. Eventually, my knee got stronger, and I got a brace to keep it from buckling beneath me, but my running days were over. As it happened, some associates and I had invested wisely in the 1919 World Series, so when I was forced to find a new line of work, I had the cash to buy Carl out. Spinoza's was a fairly prosperous speak in midtown. Like a lot of places, it was easy to get to, but the booze was rotten. Carl would sell any kind of coffin varnish you could pour into a glass.

When I took over, that changed. I made a deal with Lansky to buy the good stuff directly from him, and Jimmy Quinn's sold the best booze at premium prices. We did great business. Less than a year later, the stock market crashed. Since then, we'd been doing OK. Most months, I was covering my nut and making a little money—not as much as before the crash, but I turned a profit. Like most people, I felt I was damn lucky to have a way to make a living, and I figured that once things turned around, I'd be fine. But it sure as hell didn't get any easier with more and more guys out of work and banks closing and the goddamn government about to force me to become an honest publican.

It always made me feel kind of classy to call myself a publican. Had to look it up the first time I saw it in a newspaper. It's a guy who runs a public house where people can buy booze. Means some other things too, but they don't apply.

The speak was a couple of steps below street level. There was a restaurant upstairs, the Cruzon Grill. We had an arrangement with them. Actually, I sort of owned Cruzon, too. Back in the early days of Prohibition, Carl or somebody, I really don't know who it was, made some adjustments to the cellar with hidden storage spaces and passageways that led out to vaults under nearby buildings, including a church. He kept a lot of his inventory there. You see, back then the cops and the feds actually raided speakeasies. It's crazy, I know, but it happened, and so Carl or whoever stored stuff at different addresses, ones that wouldn't be listed on a warrant, so they couldn't seize the stuff. At least, that's what I heard, and I know a lot of guys thought the same thing whether it was true or not.

It had been years since anything like that happened. I had an arrangement with the local cops and most of the feds. Fat Joe Beddoes somehow knew if strangers who tried to get in weren't kosher, and kept them out. Maybe I lost some paying customers because of my bouncer, but we never got raided.

The speak had been tonied up since I took it over. Nothing elaborate, just new carpeting, wallpaper, plumbing in the bathrooms, tin ceiling, and we cleaned the picture of the naked lady behind the bar. We even put in a little dance floor, and if we ever got around to booking any musicians, maybe somebody would dance.

Connie Nix and Marie Therese were behind the bar whispering to each other and giving me cool disapproving looks.

I took my table at the back. Connie brought me a cup of coffee and the evening papers. Then she handed me a card and said, as properly polite as she could be, that there was a gent at the bar who wanted to see me. It was a personal card, not a business card, and it read: JOHANN KLAPPROTT.

I rubbed my thumb over the engraving. Expensive stuff. I told her to send him over. She looked back and raised a hand.

The two strangers at the bar were watching us. One of them was a big scowling bald guy. The other one picked up a short glass and made his way through the tables. He was a sleek but comfortably plump blond man who walked carefully and carried a Malacca cane he didn't need. He wore calfskin gloves and a dark blue three-piece worsted with the faintest of red pinstripes. It fit well enough to have been made for him. His blood-red tie was tied into a tight walnut-sized knot tucked behind the high collar of his white shirt. He bowed slightly before he pulled out a chair and sat across from me.

His face was flushed, maybe from the cold, maybe from the drink, and he sat just as carefully as he walked, tugging his trousers to maintain a sharp crease when he crossed his legs. He was probably forty or so, with regular features, and he wore some kind of woody cologne.

"Thank you so much for seeing me, Mr. Quinn. I won't take up too much of your time."

He had a slight accent and pale gray eyes. He took out a brushed steel cigarette case but put it back when he noticed there wasn't an ashtray on the table. If he'd asked, I'd have told him to go ahead and light up. I always did. That was good business, and it was just the way things were then. Thinking back on it, I believe Johann Klapprott was the only person who figured out how much I didn't like cigarette smoke. He covered the odd moment by taking a sip of his drink and toasting me with it.

"I was surprised to see that you have Steinhäger," he said. "Very few establishments in this part of the city even know what it is."

"Everything we serve is the McCoy, straight off the boat. Don't get much call for Steinhäger, but we try to have anything our customers want." Steinhäger is German gin. Frenchy probably had to dust off the jug.

"Precisely, and that's why I've come here this evening. Is there someplace where we could talk with more privacy?"

I said yeah and wondered what the hell he was getting at. I got my cane, and he followed me to the hall at the back and up the stairs to the office. I unlocked the door, snapped on the reading light, and sat behind the desk.

"Have a seat. I don't have any Steinhäger here. I could order another from the bar or offer you Booth's."

"No, this is fine," he said and sat on the chair facing the desk. He took out a leather-bound notebook and a little mechanical pencil that fit inside it. When he opened it, I could see that he'd sketched a floor plan of the place. Front door, stairs, coat closet, bar, booths, tables. The lines were straight, and the proportions looked about right.

"I represent a party that is exploring the possibility of entering the hospitality business when the sale of alcohol once again becomes legal. This party is looking at several establishments, including yours, for purchase. Do you have any interest in selling?"

"Not particularly."

"Would you entertain an offer? If not, I will not pursue the matter any further, but I assure you, my client is serious."

"Sure, I'll listen."

He sat back and finished his gin with a long drink. He seemed to loosen up, but that was really just part of his pitch. The guy was a born salesman. "I am reluctant to reveal how much this party is willing to pay, but I can assure you it is an impressive figure. For the right establishment."

"First off, who is this party?"

"Actually, it is a group of businessmen and investors, the Free Society of Teutonia." He smiled and leaned back, and I noticed that he was wearing a silver lapel pin with a black cross, a swastika.

Now remember, this was the fall of 1932. Not to be flip about it, but I didn't know from Nazis. I listened to the radio and read the papers, mostly the sports pages and the comics and the movie stuff and the local news. I knew the Nazis were in Germany, and I knew they had big rallies and they yelled a lot. That was about it. I'd seen some pictures of their flags and banners, but when I saw the symbol on Klapprott's pin, the first thing I thought about was Larry Fay. He was a bootlegger and nightclub owner. He also had a fleet of taxis that everybody knew because they had loud crazy horns and lots of fancy nickel-plated gimcracks bolted to the bodywork. They also had swastikas painted on the door. Larry told me he thought they brought him good luck.

That night, I figured that maybe Fay was part of this Free Society or maybe they were trying to buy out some of his operations, too. If they were serious about getting into the business, that would have made sense.

"OK," I said, "to give us something to talk about, since we're just talking, right, why don't you name a number? That way, we'll know what we're talking about, since we're just talking."

He smiled at my bushwa, but I think that by then, he knew what we were doing. Whether he did or not, he took out another of his engraved cards and wrote on the back of it with his little mechanical pencil.

He put the card face down on the table and slid it across to me.

Poker-faced, I picked it up. He'd written *35,000$* with the dollar sign at the end. It was more than I expected.

"OK," I said. "That's the number we're talking about since we're just talking. What now?"

"Do you wish to continue?"

I nodded.

"Could you give me an estimate of your monthly expenses and receipts?"

"Not without going over the books."

"There will be time for that, I am sure. What is your relationship with the restaurant upstairs?"

"I own the building. Vittorio pays rent—not much—runs the Cruzon, sells wine and beer and drinks from our cellar. And he makes sandwiches for me."

"So the two operations could be combined?"

"They already are, really."

"I visited the restaurant earlier this evening and noted the dimensions. That leaves only the cellar. Would it be possible for me to examine it?"

"Sure."

I picked up my cane and my keys, and we went back downstairs. As I was unlocking the door to the basement, Klapprott said, "One moment, please. I'd like my associate to see this."

He made a curt gesture toward the bar. A few seconds later, the bald guy he'd been sitting with showed up. His associate was a mouth-breathing six-footer with heavy sloped shoulders, a cheap blue serge suit, and a bully's happy eyes. He smelled of schnapps—a lot of schnapps.

He asked Klapprott a sharp question in German. The lawyer shook his head.

I told them to wait there until I got the lights. I took my time and made more noise with my stick than I needed to. I also shifted around some cases and boxes before I hit the switch, and they came downstairs. Klapprott started drawing in his little book while the big bald guy poked around.

The cellar had a low ceiling, bare brick walls, plank floor, and a pungent smell. It was a combination of that raw underground earthiness you get in an unfinished basement along with all the old beer and liquor that had spilled and soaked into the floorboards.

Eventually, Klapprott said, "It's difficult to estimate in this light, but it appears that the cellar does not extend to the street."

"No," I lied. "It used to, but Carl Spinoza, who owned the

place before I did, put in those shelves and walled off that part. But that was before my time. We don't use it now. Hasn't been open for years."

The associate was extremely curious about the shelves on that wall. He kept talking to Klapprott in German. He looked over our beer and ice storage and the dumbwaiter that went up behind the bar, but he kept going back to that one wall of shelves.

I couldn't understand the words they were saying, but I recognized the irritated tone of the associate's questions, the slurred voice, and some angry jabber that didn't sound like questions. Klapprott's responses were short. He was telling the guy to shut up, and the guy wasn't paying any attention. He was getting mad about something.

Finally, he came back and pointed at me and waved his hands around. He edged closer, still talking a mile a minute and looking at Klapprott. He turned away, then swung back around fast, trying to sucker-punch me.

It figured that the big bastard was up to something, but I didn't think he'd do anything like that without Klapprott's OK. Judging by the lawyer's surprised expression, he thought the same thing. But the big shit wasn't as fast or as clever as he thought he was, or as sober as he needed to be.

I brought the cane up with my hands spread and blocked the blow. I jabbed with the hook end, aiming for his throat, but missed and crushed his nose. Blood spurted over his chin and stained his shirtfront. He staggered back and knocked over a case of Scotch. I wasn't stopping until I was sure he'd stay down, so I changed my grip and went for his ribs. I swung hard as he twisted away, and I hit his side. Something crunched. It wasn't my stick. He went down to his knees.

Then Klapprott pushed his way between us saying, "Please, Mr. Quinn, no more. I apologize most profusely. Please let me handle this, please."

It took me a second to calm down. I was still jazzed, and I don't think so good when I'm pissed off. A lot of big guys, particularly drunken big guys, think that they can just take a swing at a little guy and slam him around. Makes me mad every time.

Frenchy showed up at the top of the stairs. I told him everything was OK.

Klapprott turned to the big guy who was still on the floor. He knelt and held a pocket square to the bleeding nose.

After I'd calmed down, I said, "Now you can tell me what you really want in my cellar. And you can forget the song and dance about wanting to buy me out."

"That is the truth, Mr. Quinn, I assure you." He stood up and turned around to face me. "It is not the only reason we came here this evening, but an offer will be made, and it will be legitimate. I do not understand why Luther would act so unconscionably."

His sincerity tugged at my heartstrings. "Sure. Now tell me why you were trying to break in this morning. Was that your guy with the bomb?"

"Really, Mr. Quinn, I can promise you that . . . " He stopped, and I could see the moment when the realization came to him. He whirled around and cuffed the big guy on the ear. He rattled off more German. I caught the word *schisskopf*. They went back and forth for a while, with the big guy sounding a little apologetic but still drunk and stupid.

Klapprott took a long wallet from his breast pocket and asked how much for the Scotch. We settled on three hundred dollars. He counted it out.

"I will not ask you again to excuse Luther. He is an idiot and I will see to it that he is properly punished for his stupidity." Hearing his name, Luther said something sarcastic in German through the pocket square he still held to his nose. Klapprott lashed out with the cane and cracked him across the nose and hand. Luther howled and fell back, more blood seeping from his broken fingers. Klapprott kicked him in the thigh and poked him with the cane. Luther scrambled up the stairs.

Klapprott said, "There is one more thing I feel I must tell you. Even now, matters beyond my control are transpiring. They involve something that is of the greatest importance to me and my clients. You are, I think, aware of it."

His tone turned more serious. "These matters concern an item that belongs to one of our members who has not yet taken delivery. Should this item come into your possession, I strongly advise you not to attempt to keep it from us. That would be a mistake, a grave mistake."

At the top of the steps, Luther waited, bleeding all over the floor and giving me a hard glare until Klapprott cuffed him again. The two of them left, and I asked Connie to take care of the mess on the floor. She made a face but got the mop and bucket.

I went to the bar and told Frenchy to give me a brandy. He asked what the ruckus was downstairs. I told him I was pretty sure those were the guys who had been trying to break into our door. "At least the big one was, not the other guy. They seem to think we've got something that belongs to them in our cellar."

Frenchy said, "That's nuts."

I agreed and carried my brandy over to my table. It took a couple of belts for me to calm down. I finally sat back, hooked my thumbs in my vest pockets, and froze. There was something in the right pocket that hadn't been there when I got dressed. I pulled it out carefully. It was a thick square of stiff folded paper about two to three inches on each side. It sprang open when I loosened my fingers to reveal a light blue envelope from the Hotel Chatham. As soon as I saw that, I thought somebody was playing a nasty joke. Then it came to me—the pickpockets, the two guys who braced me on Lex on the way to the Cloud Club. The one guy wasn't trying to take anything, he slipped this into my vest pocket. So what the hell did that mean?

I opened it and read.

Meet me tonight. —Anna

I couldn't have been more stunned if Jack Dempsey had smacked me in the face. I stared at the thing for a long time and was as confused and hopeful and horny and hot and bothered as I'd been in years.

I only knew one Anna, and she and I had spent maybe the most memorable night of my life at the Hotel Chatham.

But she was dead, or so I'd been told.

CHAPTER FOUR

Every guy who met Anna fell for her, at least a little. Some of us a lot more. I guess I met her in 1925 or '26. I was fifteen or sixteen.

I don't remember exactly what I'd been doing that day, probably delivering payouts to one of the judges. Well past lunchtime, I found myself on Fifty-Seventh Street and I was hungry. In that part of town in those days, there were a few fancy places to eat, places that wouldn't let a scruffy kid like me in the front door. I usually wore dungarees or work pants, shirt and tie, coat and cap—clothes that didn't slow me down and blended in on the street. And I had to look like I belonged in a police station or the Tammany offices, where I was assumed to be some Mick's kid.

Besides the fancy beaneries, there were lots of little places with names like Aunt Polly's or the Kangaroo that were meant for women. I guess guys could eat there if they wanted, but none of the guys I knew went to them, so I didn't either. But that day, my gnaw was so huge I was considering it.

Then I saw a brightly painted sign for the Spanish Marketplace, and a cartoon man was part of the design. A menu was posted by the door. It listed sandwiches and stuff, not the beef and beans you'd find in a place that was just for guys or the waffles and desserts you'd see in woman's place. And, when I looked through the glass in the door, I saw the head waitress, a big busty brunette, who smiled at me. As soon as I opened the door, the smell of coffee floated through and that did it.

It was a hole-in-the-wall place with small tables with candles, striped tablecloths and matching folded napkins, and woven rugs on the floor and hanging on the walls. The big brunette showed me to a table next to the kitchen. I stared at her butt as she walked away. Then the waitress handed me a menu, and I looked up and fell in love.

Now, here's the truth of it. Anna wasn't beautiful. Hell, I guess maybe she wasn't even that pretty by some standards, but if you remember what Mary Pickford was like in the movies then, you know what I'm talking about. She was neither thick nor slim. Just right to me. About medium height, a little taller than me, I'd learn later. Her hair was a little more blonde than brown. She had wide shoulders for a girl her size and a complexion that used to be called peaches and cream with most of the peaches in her cheeks. Her eyes were dark, and when she smiled, she could light up a room. She wore a black skirt and a white blouse with lots of ruffles in front, Spanish ruffles, I guess, and a silly little round cap perched on top of her head.

I don't remember what I ordered or what I said at all, but after the meal was over, when she brought me the bill, I said, "What's your name, when do you get off work, and what would you like to do then?"

She laughed and said, "Aren't you the fresh one? I should slap your face."

"No, you shouldn't. You should go out with me."

She looked around to see if any of the other girls who worked there were listening. "I can't tonight. I'm Anna, by the way"

"I'm Jimmy. How about tomorrow?"

"I don't know."

"OK," I said, "I'll come back and ask you then."

I was there the next day, and I was there the day after that and then, worn down by my persistence, she said yes.

At least that's the way I choose to remember meeting her. I was probably too tongue-tied to say anything the first time I was there and came back a couple of times before I screwed up the courage to say a word.

Anyway, she lived in a yellow brick apartment building up on the Upper West Side near the park. It wasn't much of a building, and she shared her room with three other girls, and they shared the bathroom with three more.

I was doing pretty well, so I took a cab to pick her up. She'd never seen me in a suit, either, so she was surprised when she came out onto the sidewalk and saw that I was presentable and I could afford to keep a cab waiting. She gave me a funny look as she got in and said, "You're going to be trouble, I can tell."

She smiled when she said it, and I fell even harder.

I wish I could remember all the details you're supposed to remember about important moments in your life, but I'd be lying if I claimed to. I remember her skirt as something light, maybe pale green, and a blouse with a tie and a cloche hat like all the girls wore. The important thing is that if she looked good in the silly uniform she had to wear to work, she looked great when she dolled herself up in real clothes.

In the cab, she held her bag in her lap and kept both hands on it. I'd had an idea that we'd go to one of those fancy uptown places, and we actually got out in front of one. But when she saw the kind of people who were going in—guys in tuxedos and women in long dresses and lots of jewelry, she took my arm and said, "I don't think this is such a good idea."

"Whaddayamean?" I said, or something equally thick-headed. "I can afford a meal here. My money's as good as anybody's."

She must have realized then that I didn't really know what I was doing. She was always a couple of steps ahead of me.

She said, "Look, Jimmy, I've been working straight shifts all week. This is the first night I've had off since I can't remember. Can't we go someplace where we can get a plate of spaghetti and a beer? That sounds just swell to me."

And that's what we did. Went down to one of those little joints in the Village, which she thought was neat and crazy. It sure wasn't much like the Spanish Marketplace. The one thing that I do remember is the way she made sure that I left a big tip for the waiter. She explained how she and the other girls got fined if anything went wrong at a table. A broken cup, spoon not in the sugar bowl, guy runs out on his check—she'd get gigged for any of those. Most of the girls had to pay to get their uniforms laundered, but she got out of that by working a second shift in the laundry that the owner of the restaurant ran. Anna had to iron all those Spanish ruffles and striped tablecloths and napkins.

She was working a hell of a lot harder than I was, and she made a hell of a lot less. So when I took her home that night, I decided to give her an extra tip.

We were standing on her steps. She was a step higher than me. She put a hand on my shoulder and said, "I had a terrific time tonight, the best in a long time. I hope we can do it again." I remember her smile, and we agreed to go out again the next week. That's when I slipped a fin into her hand. She knew I'd given her a piece of paper money, but she didn't look at it or say anything. She just tucked it into her pocketbook. It may not sound like much, but in those days, five dollars might have been half a week's wages for a girl in her position.

We went out just about any time she could get a night off, and it didn't take her long to figure me out.

The truth is that I had no real understanding of women and even less about sex. Once, I'd been with a bunch of guys who decided to go to a whorehouse. I was too embarrassed to say no and was terrified by the whole thing. The experience was dark, frustrating, brief, and actually kind of painful. Another night when I delivered the booze to a fancy party up in Great Neck, I met a drunken debutante who got all excited when she realized that I was carrying a pistol. She took me out to a dark corner of the garden and dropped to her knees, unbuttoned my fly, and got off to an enthusiastic start before she threw up on my shoes.

So, while I was stepping out with Anna, I wanted some kind of sexual experience that involved a woman, but I didn't really know what it would be. I did know that I wanted to be with this woman, to talk to her and to make her smile. I couldn't take it much farther than that. I was just trying to show her a good time without making an idiot of myself. As far as money went, I turned over everything I got from A. R. and Lansky to Mother Moon. I'd always squirreled away a little for myself, and since I'd been seeing Anna, I squirreled away a little more, but I never flashed my cash. That was just stupid.

We went to a lot of little restaurants. Whenever she heard about some nutty place from one of the other waitresses, we'd have to go. One place was set up like a miniature golf course, and one was called the Rabbit Hole or something like that, and you had to slide down a chute to get in.

We'd been going out for maybe a month when I learned that she'd arrived in the city from a little town in Illinois five weeks before. For once, we were at a joint that was just a joint, not a circus or a rodeo. She was working on her second schooner. Yes, she loved her beer, and I'll admit that I couldn't handle it in those days. After a couple of sips, I felt like my stomach was all swollen up with gas and I didn't want any more. Not Anna—that girl could put it away all night long. Of course, both of us could eat. We were a couple of real trenchermen with just about any kind of food.

As I recall it, she was working her way through some pickled pig's feet when she asked about my family. I told her that my parents were dead. I lived in a building that was owned by a woman who was my aunt or my grandmother or something. I wasn't sure.

Then she asked what kind of politics I had, and I answered that I really didn't know, but I wasn't a Red.

She agreed and sounded more serious when she said, "I don't

want anything to do with a fella who's more interested in picket lines than he is in me."

"So you're looking for a rich guy?"

"Hah!" Her tone made it clear what she thought of the idea. "Any girl who works as a waitress knows how arrogant and snotty society people can be. I don't want anything to do with them, either. What do you do for a living, Mr. Moneybags?"

"This and that. You could say I'm a deliveryman." That was true enough. The day before, I delivered a couple of bribes for A. R. and a truckload of Canadian whiskey for Lansky.

She teased me. "I thought you were some kind of big shot."

"Nah, I've just got a couple of jobs that pay pretty good."

Now some guys, when they were out with a girl or a bunch of guys they wanted to impress, they'd talk about how tight they were with Legs Diamond or Owney Madden, but the guys who really knew Legs and Owney and A. R. and Lansky, they didn't talk about it much. I waved to the waiter and ordered another schooner for Anna.

It was that night, when we were going home, that we ran into an irate asswipe. Actually, he ran into her, I guess, but it was my fault because I wasn't paying attention to anything but her.

We had our arms around each other's waists, I remember that clearly, and she was giggling into my ear about something. We were near MacDougal Street close to Washington Square. There wasn't much foot traffic on the sidewalk in that neighborhood after dark, and I knew it'd be easier to catch a cab a couple of blocks north.

Then, with no sound or warning, this guy came slamming around the corner and barreled right into Anna. He was about seven feet tall and four feet wide with knuckles dragging the side-walk. All right, he was really just a normal-sized guy, but something had made him so angry he was acting crazy.

He hit Anna and pushed her into me, knocking both of us off-balance. She said something like, "Hey, watch where you're going, buster."

He snarled back in a loud nasty voice, "Fuck yourself," and she hauled off and let him have it with her bag.

Now, this wasn't some swing-like-a-girl tap with her pocket-book. She really got her legs and hips into it, and the bag had a thick metal frame. She caught him on the jaw and snapped his head back. He staggered a step, then bellowed and came right at her. I tried to move between them and got it from both sides. Anna came up short with the bag and clipped me on the ear. The asswipe punched me in the gut and chest.

She was yelling, "Come on, you big bastard!" and he pushed me aside to take another swing at her. I weighed in again, trying to push her behind me. He got serious and jabbed Anna so hard in the ribs that she went down to her knees. He pivoted and put two solid punches into my midsection and went for my head. He kept his fists in close like he knew what he was doing and muttered curses as he pounded me. I got my left arm up over my face, but I still saw stars when he caught me a good one.

It seemed like it took forever for me to get hold of the little .32 Lemon Squeezer I had in my pocket. Even though it didn't have a hammer, it tended to catch on the cloth, and I had to keep my finger out of the trigger guard while I pulled it out. All the while, he was pounding on me, and I sensed that Anna was getting to her feet. Then the pistol came free, and I jammed it into the center of his stomach and shot him.

As the report echoed away, they both stood there, mouths open in shock. I think at first he couldn't believe what had just happened. Anna didn't even know that I had the gun, so she was surprised and quiet, too. For a little while, until she barked a short laugh.

I grabbed her hand and pulled her away from the guy as he stumbled backward, his mouth moving like he was trying to say something. Resisting the urge to run, I walked away quickly. She kept swiveling her head around to look back at him. I pulled her along, pausing to ditch the pistol down a sewer grate and then kept us moving. I couldn't see anybody else on the street.

Her face flushed and she started to yell something but gasped and held her stomach.

I looked back. The big asswipe was nowhere in sight on the dark street. I held her hand and pulled her along, heading north. I was pumped up but knew that I had to force the excitement back down. It wasn't helpful. Somebody probably heard the shot. We needed to get away, and we couldn't look like we were running.

When we'd both calmed down and the nausea had passed, she said, "You don't look so good, Jimmy."

"I look better than he does."

"You think you killed him?"

"Maybe."

"You didn't tell me you carried a gun."

"It's just something I have to do sometimes." Truth be told, I wouldn't have had the Lemon Squeezer on me if I hadn't driven that truckload of booze for Lansky. As for the guy, well, that was his bad luck, I guess.

Before we found a cab, she gave me a strange look that I couldn't read. My pulling the pistol may have surprised her, but I don't think it impressed her, not like the drunken debutante.

Later, in front of her building, she pulled me into the shadow of the front steps, wrapped her arms around my neck, and kissed me harder than she ever had. Her body molded itself against mine. I got hard and she knew it.

"Yeah," she said as she plucked the bill from my hand, "you're going to be trouble all right."

Then came the evening when everything changed. We had been to a place called the Bat. It looked to me like something out of a Theda Bara vamp movie. It had all these thick drapes covering the walls and pillows on the floor and incense and no light. Anna said it was Bohemian. I thought it was scary, and I didn't care for the food, either. But she liked it, or maybe she liked the third beer. Something made her looser and more reckless than she usually was.

It was still light when we left, and she said we should walk through the park, so we did.

I strolled. The Bohemian dinner was still kind of heavy, and I was not in the mood to move quickly. I'd made it through half a glass of beer and still felt bloated. She was just the opposite. To this day, I can close my eyes and still see her that evening, the way the low sun flattered her and cast a long shadow and how she skipped and twirled on the path, running ahead and coming back to grab my arm in both of hers. She tried to pull me along faster, teasing me.

Finally, she said, "I bet you didn't know that I was the fastest runner at North Central Illinois High School. I could even beat the boys. I could even beat the boys on the track team. Nobody could catch me. Ever!"

I burped softly and nodded my head.

"And I'm still the fastest. I can beat you, Jimmy Quinn." She danced right up in front of me and touched the tip of my nose.

I should have agreed with her, or kept my mouth shut. Instead, I said, "No, you can't."

She stopped and put her fists on her hips and said, "You don't believe me."

"Look, you don't understand. I—"

"You think just because I'm a girl, you're better than me."

And that started a long argument as we walked. At first, she wanted to race me right there in the park, until I pointed out that she was wearing heels and a dress. Did she really want to race in that outfit? She didn't. I thought she'd lost interest in the subject, but a few steps later, she said, "We can't do it tomorrow because I've got a long shift and I've got to be at the laundry after that. So it will have to be Thursday, OK?"

"What Thursday?"

"We'll race. On Thursday. I challenge you." She tapped me on the nose again. It was starting to piss me off a little. "Got that? I, Anna Gunderwald, challenge you, Jimmy Quinn, to a race."

I remember her expression, the cocky smile, the sun on her

face, and I fell for her all over again, even harder, so hard I could barely breathe.

I said, "OK, then, I accept. You name the time, the place, the distance. I don't care. Now, what are the stakes?"

That brought her up short.

"Let's talk about this," I said as we continued our walk. "You don't have a lot of money to put up, but I do. So why don't we say that if you win, on the course of your choosing, I'll give you one hundred dollars."

Her eyes lit up, and she tightened her grip on my arm. "And if you win? Not that you will."

"If I win . . . you'll do whatever I want you to do on Saturday night. You cannot say no to anything I ask."

All sorts of thoughts and feelings crossed her face then—greed, worry, fear, confidence, uncertainty, and finally, I think, some kind of triumph. She thought she had me. She turned to face me and stuck out her hand and said, "Done."

She didn't know that I don't gamble.

When I walked up to her building on Thursday afternoon, she and her three roommates were waiting for me on the steps. They were giddy and giggling and trying to act like they were football players or something, and I was the opposing team. About all I could see of what Anna was wearing were her shoes, canvas sneakers. She had a blanket wrapped around her shoulders. She was trying to give me a hard look, like the other girls were, and it seemed less forced on her. She really wanted to beat me.

I was wearing work clothes. Pants that gave me a lot of room and didn't slow me down, and my jacket with the extra large inside pocket for securing payoffs and bribes. It was empty. I'd made my last delivery to an aide in the mayor's office in the middle of the afternoon. And, of course, I had my Keds.

Looking at the situation from her point of view, I guess it made sense. She had raced against other guys before and she beat 'em. I was just a guy who was kind of stuck on her, not very tall, not particularly strong. If I'd ever done any kind of racing, I hadn't mentioned it to her, and since guys tend to brag to girls about things they're good at, I probably hadn't raced.

That was true, I guess. I hadn't raced, but I did run. When Rothstein needed a message hand delivered, he expected me to get there and get back as fast as I could. When I was delivering stacks of cash to cops and aldermen, I knew there were guys who'd try to intercept me. In other words, when it came to running in New York, I was a professional and she was an amateur. If I'd been a gentleman, I'd have told her that. I wasn't and I didn't.

The three girls kept giggling to one another, and I knew they were saying things about me, and that embarrassed me, so I tried not to look at them and focused on Anna. She popped up to her feet and tossed off the blanket. She was wearing a light blue sleeveless V-neck jersey with the letters PHS printed on the front, and loose dark-blue silk bloomers that came to her knees.

I had suspected that she would want to race in the park, and that worried me. I was always a little spooked in the park. Too many trees and it smelled of dirt and horses and sheep. I guessed that it would be more like the rolling hills of Illinois, where she'd grown up. Actually, I didn't know if there were rolling hills in Illinois. I'd never really been out of the city and sort of assumed that there were rolling hills on the other side of the Hudson River going all the way to the Pacific, except for the places where there were rolling deserts that I saw in Western movies.

But no, she said we were going to do it right there. We'd start from her building heading west across Broadway and West End to Riverside Drive, where we'd turn south for one block, then back the way we'd come to Amsterdam Avenue, where we'd turn north for a block and be back at her steps. I guessed it a shade under a mile.

If the people passing by thought that the little group of four girls and a guy was odd, they didn't show it. I took my jacket off, hung it on the metal railing, and rolled up my shirtsleeves.

Anna's face was flushed and bright with sweat. Maybe she'd

already run the course, or she was just excited. She had that same triumphant look I'd seen the other night.

I heard one of the other girls whisper, "There weren't so many people when we worked it out yesterday." And another girl answered, "No, that's good. She's lighter on her feet." I didn't say anything. The third girl told us to take our places and put our feet on a chalk line they'd drawn on the sidewalk.

She looked both ways down the street, raised her hand, and said, "Ready, set, go!"

And we ran.

It was a narrow street with shops on the first floor of most of the buildings, delis, grocers, laundries, lunchrooms, barbershops. There were small trees and newsstands close to the curb. Sidewalk pavement was in fair shape, a bit uneven, and it was about as crowded as you'd expect a neighborhood to be on a Thursday evening.

Annà zipped out ahead and hadn't taken ten steps before she had to work her way between two women carrying grocery bags. I stayed a few steps behind for most of the first block until we approached Broadway. That's where I angled left and cut into the street with the cars and trucks and horses. I was ahead of her before we crossed the intersection and stayed on the other side of the street. There were fewer people around us toward West End where the apartment houses were bigger and fewer still on Riverside Drive with all the big houses.

Part of me wanted to look back, to see where she was, but I knew that didn't matter. I tried to think of her as a thug who was trying to hijack a big precinct payment and kept moving, looking ahead. I watched out for groups of kids and big families. Both were slow, and kids were unpredictable. You never knew what they were going to do. Even three adults who were strolling and talking to one another could jam things up completely. You had to be ready to take an angle across a street, so you needed to know what was coming up behind you.

I was so intent on weaving through the crowd that I almost overran the turn at Amsterdam. But I didn't.

The three roommaters' shoulders slumped when I showed up in front of them. I was still breathing hard when Anna came up Amsterdam less than a minute later. Unlike the other girls, she was surprised to see me.

"What did you do? You cheated, you must've cheated. I didn't see—"

"I passed you in the traffic across Broadway. Stayed on the other side of the street after that."

She was breathing hard through her nose and glaring at me, fists on hips, as she walked back and forth on the sidewalk. The silk bloomers were plastered to her thighs, and the shirt stuck to her breasts as sweat darkened it. Right then, she was the sexiest female I'd ever seen in the flesh. I tried not to stare at her.

A guy walking past gave her a wolf whistle. Anna paid no attention. After a long moment, she got her breath back and wiped her hands across her eyes, wiping away either tears or sweat.

"All right," she said. "You won. I don't know how . . . "

"I didn't cheat."

"I didn't say you did. It's just . . . It's just . . . nothing. You won." Her expression changed, and she actually looked happy. And sexy. "All right. Saturday night." She looked up at the girls on the steps. They were worried for her and gave me more nasty looks. "What's it going to be?"

I had no idea. I had forty-eight hours to figure something out.

Saturday night at eight o'clock a taxi parked in front of her building. The driver rang her apartment. When she came down and asked where they were going, he said that he wasn't supposed to tell her anything. I'd like to think that she was tingling with excitement and anticipation, but I doubt that was the case.

The cab took her to the side door of the Chatham Hotel on Vanderbilt Avenue. That's where she was met by Mr. Stebbins, the bell captain who happened to be a mutual friend of Mr. Rothstein and me. When A.R. happened to entertain one of his showgirls, he often used the Chatham, and I had delivered special tips to most of the guys on the staff.

Mr. Stebbins handed Anna a rose. (That was his idea.) He assured her that many of the hotel's finest guests preferred not to parade themselves through the lobby on the way to their rooms, and the staff was always happy to accommodate them.

He told the elevator boy to take her to the ninth floor, the Taft Suite. When she knocked on the door, I let her in. She wore a light blue dress and a cloche hat. She held her purse in front of her stomach like a shield. I can't say that she looked happy.

Let me tell you about the Taft Suite. Imagine three really large high-ceilinged rooms separated by wide sliding doors. Now, fill those rooms with furniture that was big and heavy and not particularly comfortable, as it turned out. Put marble statues of half-naked people on the marble-topped tables and sideboards. Then hang pictures of racehorses and such in ornate gilt frames on the walls. Yeah, it was pretty god-awful and not cheap, let me tell you. But for one night, it was mine. The truth is that I still didn't know exactly what I wanted to do that night, but I knew that this was the kind of place you did it in, whatever it was.

"Listen," I said to her, "I gotta tell you that I still feel kind of bad about the race and everything. You didn't know that I do this stuff all the time."

"You didn't talk me into anything. I did it all by myself."

"And so now you're here to do whatever I tell you to do, right?"

She stood a little straighter. "Yes, that was the bet."

"OK, I've got things figured out," I lied. "I know, because you've told me about it, that you have to share a bathroom with six other girls. Isn't that right?"

She nodded, looking confused.

"So I want you," I said as I walked across the room and opened a door, "to spend at least the next hour doing whatever it is that girls do in the bathroom."

She snorted a surprised laugh and put a gloved hand over her mouth to smother it.

Now, to picture this bathroom, imagine one of those Turkish baths made of sparkling white tile and with nozzles and fixtures and such that I had no idea what they did, and a bathtub big enough for the twenty-seventh president of these United States when he stayed at the Chatham. Taft weighed in at more than three hundred pounds, and Mr. Stebbins claimed that their tub was deeper and wider than the one Taft had installed in the White House.

So, what was I doing? Looking back on it, I think I just wanted to get Anna naked when I was under the same roof, and then I'd see what happened.

All right, you could say, "Jimmy, why didn't you just get the room, take off your clothes, and hop into the big Taft-sized bed and be there waiting for her to arrive?" I admit that the idea occurred to me, and at first, that was the plan, but when the time came, I chickened out. I was too frightened, too inexperienced, too immature, too whatever you want to call me to carry it off.

And so away she went into that vast bathroom, and I could hear water running for the longest time. Then I turned on the radio, and I don't remember what I listened to, but I didn't really hear it anyway. I was imagining what was going on behind that door. I could see her stripping off her clothes and sliding into that ocean of a tub and pouring in all the lotions and bath salts and potions that the head maid had told me women like. And there was a champagne cooler in there beside the tub, but it was full of bottles of beer.

Some time later, I don't know how long, I heard her. Her voice sang out sweet, "Jimmy Quinn, Jimmy Quinn, Jimmy Quinn."

"Yes," I said, and then I said it again when she didn't hear me.

"Turn off all the lights. Do it now."

Hmmm? I turned off all the lights and stood by the door in the dark. "OK, I turned off all the lights."

"Come in, then."

I gulped and opened the door. It took a few moments for my eyes to adjust. It was dark outside, and the only light came in from nearby buildings, reflecting onto all the tile, and through the perfumed fog, I could see what I needed to see.

She said, "It's steamy in here. Take off those clothes."

I was wearing a suit and tie. I remember how clumsy I was with the shoes, how they thumped on the tile floor. She had moved some towels off a small table and had it up next to the tub with a bottle of beer within easy reach.

The tub was full, and she let herself float up to the surface through the perfumed steam and the faint light, and I saw a woman's breasts and pubic hair for the first time. I think I stopped breathing. I know my knees shook.

She said, "Come here. You paid for this tub tonight. You ought to enjoy it."

Somehow, I managed to walk the few steps to the tub without falling over. I got in clumsily opposite her. She scooted around and floated toward me. When her face was close to mine, I could smell the beer on her breath. "Yeah, you're trouble, all right," she said, though she could probably tell how nervous and scared I was right then. Her hands went to my shoulders and pushed me back against the side of the big tub.

"You know that it's different for girls and guys, don't you? I mean, we could have a real good time right here, but what happens nine months later? A guy can just walk away, but if a girl gets knocked up, she's got to do something. I've seen it happen and I can tell you, it's not going to happen to me, no sir, but that doesn't mean that we can't do other things that are just as much fun, well, almost as much fun."

She moved closer. I could feel her breasts against my hairless chest, and I let my hands glide over her arms.

"You've gone out of your way to show me a good time, and I appreciate it."

She rubbed my chest and arms and kissed me softly, then harder. She wrapped her legs around my hips, and even before I knew what was happening, I climaxed.

"Oh, hell," I stammered, hoping she couldn't see me blush, but I knew she did.

"That's fine, baby, don't you worry. We've got all night, and I know you've got a lot more to show me."

She was right. We fooled around in the tub some more. She finished all the beer, then we dried off with the big white towels and got into the Taft bed. She showed me things that a girl could do to a guy and things that a guy could do that a girl really liked. It was exhilarating and draining and frightening and not like anything I'd ever experienced before.

When I woke up the next morning, she was gone. That afternoon when I went to her building, one of the roommates came down to the street. She had a smirky, sneering look on her face when she told me that Anna had left.

"Her real boyfriend came back for her. He's not a kid like you. He just got out of jail, and as soon as he was free, he flew to her side. So you can just get the hell out of here, boy."

I went to the Spanish Marketplace restaurant, and the head waitress told me Anna had quit on Thursday, before we had our race.

With all that boiling up in my head, I spent the next week or so wandering around in a miserable dazed funk. I think I knew, even then, that whatever had gone on between us wasn't love, not the kind of love that you heard people singing about in popular songs or that you saw in movies. But it had been memorable, and I wanted to do it again. I wasn't sure I believed the roommate, but the simple truth was that Anna was gone and there wasn't a damn thing I could do about it. So I just thought about her a lot every day and wondered about what had happened. Finally, as the memories receded, I realized I'd never understand it. But I never completely forgot her, either.

All it took was a certain kind of horniness to bring back the memory of her in the tub, and whenever that happened, I got a monumental hard on.

It was maybe two or four years after that when I ran into the roommate again. It was late on a Friday or Saturday night. I was keeping watch on a couple of mugs who were moving slots and pinball machines for Longy Zwillman at one of his roadhouses over in Jersey. It was a big loud boozy place where guys fought for the fun of it and banged things up pretty good. There was a steady turnover with all of the equipment. I made sure that all the nickels and dimes made it back to Longy, so I was standing by the open back door, where I could keep an eye on the truck and on the guys who were lugging the stuff.

A girl with a cigarette ankled unsteadily by on the way to the ladies'. She gave me a glance, kept on walking, then stopped and turned around.

"You're him," she said, pointing at me. "You're the guy who beat that girl . . . Anna, at that race, and then treated her to a night at the Plaza Hotel. Boy howdy, did she have a lot to say about that. Yeah, you're him. Well, pal, she's dead. Did you know that? I guess not. Yeah, somebody shot her. Girls like her, they get all the breaks for a while—champagne and big cars and nights of luxury."

Hearing her say that Anna had been killed hit me like a gut-shot, and the world slid sideways, but even then I didn't fully believe it. There was something about the look on that girl's face and her voice that made it sound like a lie. Maybe she'd heard it or maybe she made it up on the spot because she was jealous that Anna got a night of luxury while she got boozy roadhouses. Either way, it still hurt to hear it.

CHAPTER FIVE

Meet me tonight.
—Anna

I was still staring at those words, wondering what they meant, when some guy I'd never seen invited himself to take a seat at my table.

It was a little after eight. Business had picked up, and we had a nice midweek crowd at the bar and in the booths. The place had the happy babble that you want from a good bar—that mix of talk, argument, and drink orders, brightened by a woman's laugh every now and again. I didn't notice the guy at first when he eased himself out of the crowd and approached my table.

He was between twenty-five and thirty, medium height and build. His clothes were well worn, and he looked like he'd appreciate a shave and a bath. When he smiled, he squinted in a sly practiced way. I've seen other guys do that same thing because it works with some women. He said, "Mind if I sit down?" and dropped his butt into a chair before I could answer. He hiked the chair around so he could see the door, put down his half-finished beer, and leaned toward me. He kept one hand in his pocket.

He stared hard at me and said, "You're Jimmy Quinn. I've been told that a fellow can trust you. If you take a job, you'll stick with it. That right?" He had some kind of accent. I couldn't place it, but he didn't sound like he was from New York.

"I'm not looking for work. I've got a place to run."

"This is different. I've been told you can take care of certain things."

"What's your name, pal? I don't do business with people I don't know."

He snorted. "Name wouldn't mean anything to you. I could say anything. I could say I was Jimmy Quinn."

"If you're trying to convince me do business with you, you're making a damn poor job of it."

His expression changed then. He'd been coming on like a tough guy, but it looked to me like he thought of something or remembered something and it worried him. "Look," he said, trying to sound more sincere and leaning across the table, "suppose a guy had a particular item that he needed another guy to hold for him without asking a lot of questions."

"I'm not—"

"Good," he said quickly and slid something small under my hand. He did it as smoothly as a three-card monte dealer. If you'd been standing beside us, you might not have seen it. "This oughta buy me twenty-four hours, and there'll be more later tonight."

He scraped his chair as he stood. The chair caught on the carpet, and he had to grab it to keep his balance. I saw that he was missing a couple of fingers on one hand.

He hurried through the crowd toward the front door, and that's when the strangeness of the whole day caught up with me. What the hell was happening? Something was going on, Klapprott had said as much, and it was something I didn't know anything about. I was a simple saloonkeeper. Things like this didn't happen to ordinary guys like me, but somehow, I was part of it, and that was a damn scary thought.

Frenchy and Fat Joe had their eyes on the crowd and would take care of things if any of the customers got so overexcited that they started fighting or put the wrong moves on another guy's woman. Marie Therese and Connie were still conspiring with each other. I opened my hand and looked at the thing the guy had put on the table. It appeared to be a lumpy brown marble. I put it in my pocket, gathered up the late papers, and took them back to my office. I needed quiet, not happy babble, to chew over the day's events.

Upstairs, I poured another brandy. As I sat, I felt the note in my pocket. I took it out and read it again. *Meet me tonight.*

To hell with everything else. Was Anna there right now? Stretched out waiting for me in that huge tub? They didn't need me for the rest of the night. I could leave. I could catch a cab and be at the Chatham in fifteen minutes. Or I could call and ask to speak to the Taft Suite. Or I could talk to Mr. Stebbins, but no, he'd retired and I didn't know the new bell captain.

If she was back, I wanted to see her, not talk to her on the telephone.

And should I have been thinking about her at all?

What was with Klapprott and the Free Society of Teutonia, whatever the hell that was? If all the other crazy stuff hadn't been going on, I might have taken him up on his offer right on the spot.

Somehow, the whole idea of owning and running a legiti-mate completely legal enterprise just didn't appeal to me. I'd never done anything like that. I'd always operated on the *other* side of the law, but I'd never been that far on the other side. Except for all the cars I'd stolen and the guys I'd shot, most of the laws I'd broken weren't that serious, and I didn't have much trouble sleeping. Early on, I learned that there were a lot of places where cops were being asked to do things they didn't want to do, to enforce laws that made no sense to them. If you approached them in the right way and gave them a little something extra to turn their heads while you were doing something that seemed OK to them, they were happy to go along with it. Ellis understood that. That's why he had invited me to the Cloud Club, to ease me over the line the other way—to make me a law-abiding citizen, but not too law-abiding.

Still, given the state of the country and the economy, maybe the smart move was to take the money and walk away.

I dug around in my pocket and found the thing that the guy had passed to me. At first, I couldn't tell what it was and thought it might be a nut of some kind. Then I saw the number and realized it was a crumpled banknote, a ten-dollar gold spot, maybe the dirtiest ten-dollar gold spot I'd ever handled—and, believe me, I've handled some dirty money. This one was wadded into a tight little ball that seemed almost stuck to itself like it had been dipped in glue. It crackled as I carefully pulled it open with my fingertips, and something fell out onto my desk.

It was a small key with a round brass tag attached to it. The tag had the number *43* stamped in the middle. So did the body of the key. It might have opened a steamer trunk or a lock box.

The bill was more interesting. As I pulled at it, I saw that it was stained red and brown. The red might have been blood. The brown was thicker, like layers of paint. I had to scrape it off with my thumbnail. When I finally got the thing flattened out, it looked like a piece of used butcher paper. After thinking about it for a minute, I put both the gold spot and the little key in my safe and got the .38 Detective Special. It was clean and loaded. Probably a good idea to carry it until this business was straightened out.

Back in the bar, I was thinking that I'd turn things over to Frenchy and Fat Joe and wander up to the Chatham just to see what I could see when Mercer Weeks put a hand on my shoulder.

"Got a minute, Quinn? I need a word with you." He was sitting at a two-top with the Professor. She was a mannish-looking woman who always wore tweed coats and skirts, no matter what the weather, and a beret. She came to my place because she loved nothing better than listening to criminals and lowlifes and cops tell stories of their adventures. She'd hang on every word, and she was usually good for a round or two if the stories were really depraved and lurid. I never heard her called anything but the Professor, and I don't know where she taught, or if she even taught at all.

Weeks was one of those rawboned guys who always seemed too long for his clothes at the wrists and ankles. He had a sharply angled, bony face, and he kept his graying black hair short on top and shaved on the sides. He wore cheap dark suits and heavy brogans. He was the enforcer for the loan-sharking side of Jacob Weiss's policy racket. Word was that Weeks would stomp deadbeats with those big brogans, and after he'd done a job on a guy, there was no cleaning them up, so he bought the cheapest ones he could find and had a dozen shoeboxes in his closet.

At least that's what they said. Personally, I never borrowed any money from Jacob Weiss or anybody else. I've been lucky. At the times when I've had the need for large amounts of cash, I've always been able to steal it.

Weeks and the Professor had nearly empty glasses in front of them. His was rye and ginger. She drank vodka in honor of her Soviet comrades, she said, because she was a member of the Russian Mutual Aid Society, or some such. At the time, she was the only person who ordered the stuff. We got it special for her. She raised a hand to Frenchy to order another round for the table. I figured Weeks must have been spinning quite a tale. Frenchy brought their drinks and a brandy for me.

Weeks took a pouch of tobacco and papers out of his breast pocket and rolled a slow, careful smoke.

"I noticed that a couple of Dutch's guys were in earlier tonight, Lulu and Landau," he said, and I realized he'd had more to drink than usual. "Was it business?"

I shook my head. I'd never seen him like that in my place before.

"They didn't ask you to handle Schultz's numbers?"

"Of course not, that would be nuts."

"You sure? Jacob might be interested in making an offer."

"This street's already taken, isn't it? Somebody's running numbers in the bakery around the corner. I thought that was you and Weiss."

"It is," he said, nodding. "I was just thinking, maybe, you know, something different." It took him a try or two to fire up a kitchen match with his thumbnail to light his smoke.

Nobody ever explained to me why they called it "policy." It was just a rigged pick-three numbers game. I never understood why it was so popular, either, but it sure was. The way it worked was you chose any three numbers and you bet on that combination. Your bet could be as little as a penny. I don't know what the top limit was in Weiss's game. But say you bet that penny. If your numbers came up, you won six dollars. Now, you don't exactly need to be a genius to figure that the odds are 999 to 1, and the payout is 600 to 1.

Of course, Weiss had a lot of overhead. People played their numbers all over the city at shoeshine stands and grocery stores and dress shops and laundries. Jacob had kids who'd go into the tenement apartments where women couldn't get out or didn't want to be seen betting their pennies. There were runners who moved the money and betting slips, and bookies and bankers and shop owners who got their cut. The winning number combination was something that was published in the papers every day and, supposedly, couldn't be fixed, like financial statistics from the treasury, or the win, place, show numbers at a particular horseracing track. I'm pretty sure that Jacob Weiss's operation used three numbers from the stock exchange, but I'm only going on what I heard. I never took part in the racket myself, and things always look different from the outside. But I do know this—Jacob the Wise became a very rich man with his policy business.

Now, everybody thinks that Dutch Schultz and Abbadabba Berman were the geniuses who figured out how to make the odds even better than 999 to 1 by placing heavy bets on particular races to screw around with the results. I heard Abbadabba brag that he'd added 15 percent to their weekly take.

Maybe that's true. I doubt it, but it could be. I also know that Dutch and Abbadabba didn't do anything that Weiss and Benny "Numbers" Rosenbluth didn't do better.

Benny had some way of keeping tabs on heavily played number combinations during the day and then buying or selling stocks to jigger the numbers at the end of the day. According to him, he could bump the odds from 1,000 to 1 to 2,000 to 1, depending. He also had some way of making sure that key people in certain neighborhoods won regularly. These were the women and men that other people paid attention to, so Weiss's game was a hell of a lot more popular than Dutch's.

What it all amounted to was that at the height of the Depression, Weiss's policy operation was knocking down seventy thousand dollars a day, six days a week. That's a hell of a lot of pennies and nickels.

Sure, it cost a lot to keep the operation running, but Weiss did well enough to run a busy loan-sharking business, too. It was a hell of a sweet racket.

I told Weeks that I didn't think there would be much interest in that kind of gambling at my place. "Sometimes guys want to use the room upstairs for craps or poker, but we don't get much call for that either. It's not really big enough." I hoped that would be the end of it. I was ready to go to the Chatham.

Weeks slugged back his drink and said, "Everything's gone to hell since we lost Benny Numbers."

"What?" said the Professor, perking up. "Who's Benny Numbers?"

I'd heard a lot of stories about what had happened to Numbers, none of them from guys that I had any reason to trust, so once Weeks started talking, I sat back and listened and tried not to think about the Chatham. A little anyway.

Weeks had been working for Jacob the Wise for a long time, and he'd never say anything bad about him in public. Hell, Weeks hardly ever said anything. Besides being one of those silent types, he had a funny way of talking slowly through clenched teeth, like every word was painful. Word was that he'd been shot in the jaw robbing a bank with Harve Bailey, and he did have a funny mark near his neck that might have been a scar.

Jacob Weiss was one of those smart guys who came from a respectable family that had disowned him years before he became a hoodlum. They took the money he gave them, but they still disowned him. And they were outraged when Benny Rosenbluth, one of the brightest kids in the neighborhood, from another respectable family, fell in with Jacob. He wasn't related. For some reason, the Jews who worked on the wrong side of the law didn't bring their relatives into the business the way the Italians did. At least, that was my experience, and I worked with a lot of 'em. But, the point is that Jacob loved the kid like the son he didn't have. Benny was a natural for the policy racket. I heard that they called him "Numbers" from the time he was a little kid.

Weiss was married, but his wife disapproved of his work even more than the rest of the family, so he kept company with younger women. And that, as Weeks saw it, was where the trouble started. Spring, a year ago, Weiss went up to Saratoga and came back with the dark and mysterious Signora Sophia on his arm. Weeks and Benny Numbers called her Sugartits.

Weiss followed the routine with her that he did with all of his honeys, but he treated her a lot better. First, he set her up in an apartment, but it was a nicer place than he usually got, in a good neighborhood on the east side. He spent most afternoons with her there, and at night they went out. I knew this to be true because Weiss would sometimes bring his young ladies to my place for a quiet bottle of champagne and a dark corner. But he hadn't been in with this Signora Sophia. I'd remember a Sugartits. Apparently she was meant for classier joints than mine. In any case, Jacob was just nuts over her.

Things were clicking along smoothly enough until Jacob decided that they should all take a trip out west. They'd take the

Twentieth Century to Chicago and then to Los Angeles, where Signora Sophia could play the ponies.

"He'd never wanted to do anything like that before," Weeks said, "but then, she wasn't one of his usual showgirls. She was a pretty classy broad."

"But you called her Sugartits," the Professor said.

"Not when they could hear us," he answered, a little offended.

But even when Jacob first brought up the idea, Weeks knew he couldn't go. First, somebody had to stay there and keep the policy racket going. If Jacob and Benny Numbers and Weeks were gone at the same time, the guys who worked for them would steal them blind, and deaf and dumb and any other way they could steal them. Somebody had to stay, and Weeks was the logical guy.

Second, Weeks said, the train would go through Colorado, and he'd been in on the job when Harve Bailey hit the Denver Mint.

"Sure, that was ten years ago, but it's still an open case, and I've been told that the Colorado cops have made the alias I was using then, so I figure it is not a good idea for me to go back."

At the mention of the Denver Mint job, the Professor perked up even more. "Are you having me on, Mercer?" she said with her back stiff to keep her balance on the chair. "The Denver Mint?"

"Oh, yeah, but the papers got it wrong saying that we robbed the mint. We hit a Federal Reserve Bank truck outside the mint. Old Harve had it worked out pretty good, or so we thought."

As Weeks spoke, his voice changed and his eyes lost focus, like he was talking to himself, or was lost in the memory, or he'd had too much to drink.

He said that Harve Bailey who was, hands down, the best in the business, knew that they made regular cash transfers from the mint to the Federal Reserve Bank once, maybe twice a week. The bank guys didn't have to take it very far, so they weren't as careful with it as they might have been. They were smart enough not to have a regular schedule. It could be any morning of the week. But instead of using a real armored car to move the cash, they'd jury-rigged a truck with a wire cage around the back, and they only used a few guards. As Weeks described it, Harvey's plan was pretty simple.

The mint was a big building, took up a block or so in downtown Denver, and the main entrance was on a big street, Colfax Avenue. That's where they moved the money.

"There were seven of us . . . no, nine counting the women, but they didn't come with us," he said. "We had three cars, a big Buick we were going to use for the job, a backup we had parked close by, and a Ford, our real getaway car that we had in a garage Harve had rented about a mile away.

"The way Harve figured it, the best time to hit them was when the money was being transferred from the mint to the truck. There would only be four guards. There were seven of us in the Buick with rifles, sawed-offs, and pistols. So, we'd drive up beside the truck as the guards came out of the mint, jump out of the Buick, show our guns, scare the hell out of everybody with a lot of shooting, grab the cash, and scram back to our garage."

Things didn't go according to Harve's plan.

It started fine. About ten thirty in the morning, as the four guards came out of the mint and crossed the sidewalk, the Buick pulled up and stopped beside the truck. Six guys piled out. A guy named Nick Trainor led the way, and they started shooting. They hit one guard, but he threw the money back into the truck, and an alarm went off in the mint.

"The money spilled out of the bag, and dozens of packages of twenties were loose in the back of the truck. Me and two other guys went for the cash while one of the guards dove under the truck and another ran back toward the doors of the mint. The guards inside started shooting at him! Yeah, they thought the dumb bastard was one of us and blazed away at him.

"The papers said later there were fifty guys shooting at us and I believe it. Christ, for a few minutes there, everybody with a gun was shooting. We got most of the cash.

"I was the last one into the car, and that's when I got hit, I think. Didn't really realize it at the time. Once I was in, Trainor jumped up on the running board and yelled for the driver to step on it. Trainor was shooting back at the mint when we heard one more rifle shot from the building. He got Trainor right in the head.

"We were able to pull him inside and got the hell out of there. I wasn't hit that bad, but we could tell that Trainor wasn't going to make it. We didn't really think about anything until we had the Buick locked up in the garage and tried to patch him up, but there was nothing to be done. I was OK, more or less. Able to drive, anyway. It didn't take long to divide up the money. Harve said that he'd see to it that Flo Trainor got Nick's share.

"Fifteen minutes after we got the Buick into the garage, all of us had scattered. We had to leave Nick, and I always felt kind of bad about that. Couple weeks later, the cops found him sitting there, frozen solid behind the wheel of the Buick in the garage. They said he'd turned blue. Hell of a thing."

The Professor tried to dig some more details out of him then, and maybe he told her.

I didn't find out because Detective Ellis came up to the table. He looked grim.

CHAPTER SIX

Ellis had a car waiting outside. We drove across town toward the East River and turned south. When I asked where we were going, he just said that I'd see. I didn't ask any more.

He stopped by a dark building on a concrete wharf off South Street somewhere between the Manhattan and Brooklyn Bridges. It was a warehouse with double doors big enough for a truck and a smaller door to the office beside them. Another police car was parked there with two nervous patrolmen standing beside it. What light there was came from the street behind us and a bare bulb over the office door. It was foggy, and neither of the lights did much good.

Ellis asked if the ambulance had been there, and one of the cops said it was on the way. Ellis said, "What about the others?" and the cop said they were inside.

Ellis started walking toward the building. He stopped when he realized I wasn't following. Cops expect to be obeyed. Sometimes they don't get what they want.

"Goddammit, hurry up."

"Why?" I said. "What are we doing?"

"Don't try my patience," he said, getting steamed. "I can make this a hell of a lot harder for you."

I knew he was right, but I still didn't care for being ordered around. The two uniforms were whispering to each other. They didn't like being there any more than I did. Even though I couldn't see the river from there, I could smell the oily mix of salt, creosote, and decay, and I could hear water lapping at something.

Ellis and I went through the door and into a small office that was divided by a waist-high counter. It was open at one end. A gooseneck lamp on the counter provided the only light, and I couldn't see anything else. Ellis went around the counter and through another door. I followed and we came into a passageway with tall shelves filled with boxes on both sides. I could barely make out rafters high overhead. I saw faint light and heard voices ahead of us.

The passage ended at an open loading dock where a guy was holding up a kerosene lantern and looking at us. There was something on the floor at his feet, and a flashlight was moving in the darkness behind him. I could see the dim squares of windows or skylights up near the ceiling.

Ellis yelled out, "Betcherman!"

What's that damn bastard got to do with this, I thought.

He was the guy at the back with the flashlight. I could barely make out his voice. "I can't find the fucking lights or the fucking fuse box."

Ellis stepped closer to the guy with the lantern. "What happened? The lights were on when I left."

"They went out," he said. "Just like that." He snapped his fingers.

He was an old guy with a gray soup-strainer mustache, dark coat, and cap. The night watchman.

"I'm here protecting the scene of the crime while that great lummox blunders around in search of the fuse box and illumination." He turned and yelled toward the back, "To your left, like I told you!"

The flash moved right, then left. A moment later, the arc lights high above us crackled to life and revealed more rows of shelves and pallets stacked with stuff. The guy who'd tailed me to the Chrysler Building was stretched out on his back on the floor. Somebody had worked him over pretty good. Bloody yawning mouth, broken teeth. The rest of it was worse. I fought against sudden nausea and leaned on my stick.

Betcherman walked over. "Why in the goddamn hell did they put the fucking fuse box under a fucking shelf?" The bastard was still limping from the pop I'd given his knee with the knucks. Good.

He gave me a mean look and said to Ellis, "D'ya get anything out of him yet?"

Ellis said, "Do you know this man?"

I was about to answer yes when I noticed his coat. It was dark brown. And he was wearing a white shirt. It was dirty and stained with blood, but the guy I'd seen before had been wearing a blue work shirt. I was more or less sure about that.

Betcherman hiked up his trousers and stomped closer to me. "Then why—" he said but didn't finish his question. The gunshots cut him off.

A short burst of automatic fire came from behind him, where he'd just been looking for the fuse box. I saw the muzzle flash. The shots echoed in the loading dock. Betcherman grunted when the bullets hit. His knees sagged, but he stayed on his feet, pulled a long-barreled revolver from a belt holster, and turned slowly around. Then there was a second burst and a third. I couldn't tell how many of the bullets hit him. Ellis had his pistol out and moved toward the big cop.

Fast as a rat, the watchman scurried between two sets of tall shelves. I wasn't far behind. Somehow the shots didn't sound like they came from a Thompson and that was the only kind of machine gun I'd ever heard. Not that it mattered. The loud rip of full automatic fire is scary as hell when it's coming at you. I gimped back to the passageway where we'd come in and heard another burst that sounded closer. By then, I had the .38 in my hand but couldn't see anything to shoot at.

Betcherman was still on his feet and firing toward the back of the building. I could see blood on his backup near his shoulder blade. Ellis kneeled behind a pallet stacked with cardboard boxes and fired in the same direction. I still couldn't see anyone else. Betcherman slumped to his knees.

I heard running feet behind me. The two uniformed cops, guns drawn, charged past me and blazed away at nothing in particular. It was deafening.

The shooting couldn't have lasted more than a minute or so, but it's hard to judge time in situations like that. It ended when somebody shot out one of the big arc lights. Sparks rained down, and the watchman yelled that we had to watch out for fire. He ran out, whipped off his coat, and used it to douse a few embers that didn't look dangerous, but, hell, I didn't know what was in the place. He was unfolding a fire hose when the ambulance arrived and everything got even more confusing.

Ellis ordered the ambulance guys to stay back until he and the two young cops had checked the building. Everybody was making noise—everybody but me—until Ellis yelled, "Shut up!"

The place got weirdly quiet then. I noticed the gun smoke hanging in the damp air as heavy as the fog outside. Betcherman was on his back in a widening pool of blood. They loaded him onto a stretcher and took him away.

Ellis and the two uniforms checked the building and found an open door that gave access to a walkway and the wharf, so whoever had been shooting at us could have got away by boat, on foot, or in a car. They found shell casings up on a landing and more at the back near a door. It must have taken Ellis more than an hour to get things straightened away.

By then, the place was filling up with cops and another ambulance crew, and a photographer with a Speed Graphic. He got a shot of them taking Betcherman out on a stretcher, and then he set up the big tripod and got one of the bloody body on the floor. I still had no idea why I'd been invited to the party in the first place. A cop I didn't know said that Ellis wanted me held at his precinct house for questioning. He put me in the backseat of a car along with the night watchman.

On the way over, we introduced ourselves. He was Mr. Malloy, Arch Malloy, and he was worried as all hell that this was going to be the end of his job. He'd got it through his cousin, and it would have been a really good job if he didn't have to kick back almost half of his salary to his supervisor and buy tickets every month or so to a longshoremen's ball.

To tell you the truth, I hardly remember what he said then. I was still thinking about the Chatham Hotel.

They put us in an interrogation room and brought us a couple of cups of bad coffee. When Ellis finally joined us, he looked tired and pissed off. I didn't blame him. So was I.

"So," he said to Malloy, "Betcherman told me that you found the body."

The old guy had his answer ready before Ellis finished. "I didn't see nothing, and I don't know nothing," he said automatically, then shook his head and added, "No, I didn't find it. He found it—the cop. He found the guy. I was doing my rounds outside."

"That's not what Betcherman said."

"Well, that's what happened. I cover three warehouses all in a row—115, 117, and 120. I go through each of 'em once an hour. I was coming back to 115 when the cop, Betcherman, stopped me at the door and said he'd heard something and found a body inside. He gave me your number and told me to call you."

I stared at Ellis, and he looked back at me poker-faced. "And why would Betcherman be calling you about a killing on the docks?" I asked him.

"Because Betcherman knew that I know you."

"So?"

Ellis took out a worn, floppy leather billfold and put it on the table. "He found this in the guy's pocket. Take a look."

I opened it, and the first thing I saw was a membership card for the United Association of Journeyman Plumbers, Gas Fitters, and Steam Fitters Union, Local 157.

It was made out to one Jimmy Quinn. He also had a New Jersey driver's license and a New York hack license, both made out to Jimmy Quinn. There was no money in the wallet.

"So the guy's got a bunch of phony papers in my name. Big deal." I tried to sound like it was nothing, but the truth is that it spooked me.

"Why do you think he'd do that?" Ellis asked.

"How the hell should I know? Ask him."

"He's dead."

"Ask Betcherman."

"He's dead, too."

So, somebody had killed a cop. They'd be taking this one seriously. "Look, Ellis, what is this? Why're you busting my nuts about it? You know I didn't have anything to do with this."

"Maybe. It's also occurred to me that maybe there's more you're not saying."

I guess there was plenty more I wasn't saying, but I didn't understand it, and anything I said about Betcherman having been behind my speak would make it that much longer before I could get to the Chatham Hotel.

Finally, Ellis said, "What the hell. You're not going anywhere, I guess. C'mon, I'll take you back to your speak and you can buy me a drink."

Malloy perked up. "You own a speak?"

Connie and Marie Therese gave me strange looks as we came in, Connie in particular. I guess I had been acting a little strange. Malloy was overcome by the sight and smell of the place. He made a careful study of the big nude behind the bar and the labels on the bottles. I told Frenchy we needed brandy and took Ellis and Malloy to my table. Frenchy brought three glasses and the bottle.

Malloy gestured toward the array of bottles. "If only the contents matched the containers," he said wistfully.

I told him that they did. We only served the best stuff.

He tasted the brandy, and his eyes widened in delight. "You are a man to be praised and congratulated for bringing an oasis of true spirits into this benighted wasteland that your countrymen have created. An amazing city this is, combining as it does the barbaric and the sublime."

I asked Frenchy if anything had happened in the last couple of hours that I needed to know about. He cut his eyes at Ellis. I nodded that it was OK.

"The Kraut was back," he said, "the gent, not the big bastard you busted up."

"Did he say anything?"

"No, but he kept an eye on everybody who came in, and he made notes in his little book."

I explained to Ellis that Klapprott was a lawyer who said he wanted to buy me out. Ellis wrote the name down in his own little book. Malloy looked kind of curious when he heard the name, too.

Ellis drank and asked, finally, if I'd seen anything when the shooting started at the warehouse.

"Just the muzzle flash. I didn't see the shooter. Did you?"

He shook his head. "And you've got no idea why the guy would've had counterfeit identification with your name."

"No, and if you figure it out, let me know."

"What about you, Malloy? Has the brandy restored your memory?"

He drained his glass. "No, but I have a strong suspicion that another dram might do the trick."

I told him to help himself and he did. He said, "I didn't see anything tonight, but there have been other nights when my employers, Herr Watts and Herr Schmidt, have told me to stay away from 115. I can't say what goes on there, and I shouldn't even be mentioning this now because you'll question them about it and, for sure, that'll be the shitcan for me."

Ellis wrote down the names and asked where he could find these guys. Malloy said he had no idea. Check with the man who runs the place during business hours. He was the one who'd told Malloy that the owners came around from time to time, and when they did, he should make himself scarce. Ellis said, "Tell me about Watts and Schmidt."

"When they show up, they give me a wave and I go to the other buildings. Within the hour, some other guys join them. There will be three or four cars parked in front of the office. When they're gone, I resume my rounds."

"Anything unusual in the warehouse on those nights?"

"Empty schnapps bottles and beer bottles." He drank and rolled his eyes dramatically. "Oh, I shouldn't have said that, I've shitcanned myself for sure now. Mr. Quinn . . . Jimmy, are you needing an experienced night watchman? An honest man, a man who will hold your interests close to his heart? I suspect I shall be available presently, should you care to avail yourself of my services in such a position."

Yeah, that's the way he talked, and he didn't even need a drink to do it.

After Ellis and Malloy left, I collected my hat, topcoat, stick, and pistol. I told Frenchy to take care of closing up. Connie gave me a strange sort of worried look and asked where I was going.

I told her I had to see an old girlfriend. Sometimes the truth is more convenient than a lie.

I walked over to Broadway and hailed a cab. It's funny. All night, I'd been impatient and wanted people to leave me alone so I could find out if Anna really was back. But now that there was nothing in my way, I almost decided to put it off by walking to the Chatham. I tried to tell myself that I needed time to think it all through, time to decide what course I would take. What crap! I was just scared, as scared as I'd been that night six years before.

But I was also curious and horny, so I got a cab.

The lobby of the Chatham Hotel was empty that late, and the elevator was self-service. I went up to the ninth floor and knocked on the door of the Taft Suite.

For what seemed like a long time, there was nothing. Then a woman said, "Come in." It didn't sound anything like her. I took out the .38 and held it against my leg.

Inside, the first thing I noticed was the smell of perfume, something I didn't remember about her. I don't know how to describe it, but it did what it was supposed to do. I think there was only one lamp on. Other than that, the rooms hadn't changed. Same heavy furniture and drapes, and suddenly it was too warm. I took off my topcoat and hat and saw that the door to the bedroom was open slightly. It swung wider, and I could make out the indistinct silhouette of a woman. She moved and I saw the shape of her figure, the curves of breast, hip, and leg. She took another step and smoothly raised her arm. I saw that she had a little automatic, and she held it in a serious two-handed grip. It was aimed at the center of my chest. She stepped through the doorway into the light, and I could see that it was her. It was Anna, but she was different. She lowered the pistol. I dropped mine back into my pocket.

Her hair was very blonde and bobbed much shorter than it had been the last time I'd seen her. Dark lipstick made her mouth look wider. She wore a black satin robe with red flowers. The deep V of the robe and high heels made her look taller, and she had one corner of her mouth cocked up like she was about to laugh. That image of her standing there, so long and sleek in the loosely belted robe, I can close my eyes today and still see it.

She put the gun on a table and slumped into an armchair like her legs had given out. She said, "Hello, Jimmy. God, you're a sight. It's going to be OK now," and she started to cry and laugh at the same time.

I stood there paralyzed, not knowing what to do and staring at the gaping robe. She was still the sexiest, most desirable woman I'd ever met.

Finally, she said, "I'm sorry, Jimmy. I didn't mean to break down like this. It's just that I'm so goddamned glad to see you. I was so afraid that you wouldn't be here, but you are, and now everything's going to work out, I know it will. Oh, it's going to be swell, Jimmy, and do you know why? Because we're almost rich, goddammit!"

And then she started crying again. Somewhere then I got her some water, and we had whiskey, too. She pulled her robe tight, leaned back in the chair, and crossed her legs.

She said, "I know you want to know what's going on with that note and everything, and I'll get to that, but just look at you. Funny, isn't it, how you could beat me so easy in that race and now"—she gestured toward the cane—"it's just funny."

"Things change," I said. "You've changed." Before, she'd been a pretty girl, but what you really noticed first about her was the bright lively energy. That was what made every guy fall for her at least a little. Now she was beautiful.

Sure, the hair and the lipstick and the perfume had something to do with it. I'm not such a sap that I didn't see that. For a while I thought it was maturity, that she was one of those women who'd always look good at any age. But I've come to understand that what I was seeing was determination.

She stared at me like she was intensely interested in anything I might say or do. She leaned forward in her chair and let the robe fall open again. Yeah, she knew what she was doing.

Then my glass was empty. She got up and refilled it and stayed behind my chair. Her hands came around and loosened my tie, unbuttoned my shirt. She pulled off my suit coat and my shirt and murmured, "Very nice. Top of the line Brooks Brothers. You're spending well."

I didn't turn around, but I could tell she was rifling through my coat pockets. I relaxed and drank, and she went back to having her way with me. Such things may happen to movie stars and millionaires all the time, but they don't happen to guys like me very often. When they do, I try not to get in the way.

She kept talking about this and that. I really don't remember what she said. I remember how she looked and the feel of her hands pulling off my shoes and unbuckling my belt. The brace gave her a little trouble. When I was naked, she said, "Come on, the tub's full. I've been waiting for this for a long time."

The black satin robe slid to the floor, and she stepped out of her heels. I saw that she'd filled out nicely. Her face and breasts were flushed a warm pink, but the rest of her body was milky white. She didn't look like the girl who'd raced me in the street. It was hard to imagine this woman ever doing anything like that.

The white tile still sparkled in the faint light from outside, and the Taft tub was still vast, and the bathroom was steamy from deep water. We sank into it, and she hugged me and whispered, "God, this is the first time I've felt safe in months. It's almost over. If you'll trust me."

Then she showed me how much she'd missed me, and an hour later, in bed, she told me the damnedest story.

CHAPTER SEVEN

Anna said that the story her roommate told me all those years ago was true, or true enough. But the "real boyfriend" who had just got out of jail and flew to her side was actually her husband. Well, almost her husband. There was some question in her mind that the man who ran the Honeymoon Tourist Park actually had the power to marry them, and she had lied about her age, but still, she had a piece of paper. She considered herself married, unless he was locked up, and then she considered herself divorced until he got out. It made sense when she explained it, and we were naked and in bed, so I wasn't asking many questions.

His name was Paul Dombrovsky, but he called himself Pauley Domo because that sounded dangerous. He was five years older than her and came from a better neighborhood in the town where they lived near Chicago. In her eyes, he was mature and handsome, and free-spirited because he stole cars. Unlike me, he stole cars for fun.

Pauley Domo came calling for her one Friday night in a brand new Peerless sedan. He told her he was leaving that very night to go to New York, where he was going to meet his partner and make more money than she'd ever dreamed of. He was also going to become more famous than Charlie Chaplin. Was she ready to go with him? Next stop, Honeymoon Tourist Park.

The partner turned out to be one Morris Untermeyer, an older guy she never warmed up to. He was already in the city casing their first big job. You see, they were hoping to repeat Gentleman Gerald Chapman's famous 1921 heist.

The Gent and his cronies figured out the routes that the mail trucks took from Wall Street to the big post office. They knew that the trucks that left late in the evening carried most of the day's important business—bonds, money orders, securities, and cash. The problem was getting the driver to stop and hand over the loot. Gentleman Gerald came up with an idea.

One Monday night after ten o'clock, he rode in the backseat of a convertible with his two partners up front. They tailed a mail truck north on Broadway from the Federal Building until they reached the right spot, where they waved their guns around and told the driver to stop. When he refused, Chapman jumped out of his car and landed on the running board of the truck. He jammed a pistol into the driver's ear and ordered him to pull over. They broke open the back and waltzed away with more than a million dollars.

That had been five years before. Pauley Domo said the time was ripe to strike again.

"Like most of Pauley's ideas," Anna said, "it almost worked."

Morrie drove. Pauley was up front. Anna was in the backseat and saw it all. This is probably a good time for me to mention that I knew Anna was lying at least a little when she told me these stories. But she also told the truth. With this one, I don't know, maybe it happened just like she said it did.

When they got to the spot where they planned to jump the truck, dangerous Pauley Domo opened the door of their Ford, got out on the running board, and froze, hanging on with both hands. Anna told Morrie, the partner, to get closer. He swerved right and sideswiped the mail truck. They both hit the brakes. Pauley fell or jumped and wound up on the pavement with the stopped truck. He broke an arm and a leg in the process.

Anna and Morrie made it about half a block before the damaged front wheel seized up. Guards from the back of the truck braced Pauley. Cops got Morrie. Anna was too quick for them. She hotfooted it out of there.

They took Pauley to Bellevue Hospital to patch up his arm and leg, booked him at a station house, and then transferred him to the Tombs downtown. As Anna understood it, there was a lot of confusion as to exactly what Pauley and Morrie would be charged with. They claimed that they never meant to rob anybody. But the Ford was stolen, and the cops found a pistol under the front seat. Pauley said he had nothing to do with the gun, and there were no prints on it, but they had him bang to rights on the car. They nailed Morrie on another outstanding warrant, and Anna didn't know what happened to him after that. She never saw him again.

They parked Pauley in the Tombs for six weeks while they decided what to do with him. They finally charged him and found him guilty of interfering with a postal worker in the performance of his duties, or something like that. They sent him up to Auburn Prison for a year. Anna went to work at the Spanish Marketplace, met me and all that. Pauley got out eight months later for good behavior. Straight away, as the roommate put it, he flew to her side, thus ending her divorce. Having had time to think on it, he decided they should go back to the Midwest to continue their crime wave. Minneapolis, to be precise.

As Anna described it, Minneapolis was even more accommodating to crooks than New York. I didn't believe it then, and I don't believe it now, but as she put it, the pols and cops were happy to look the other way for just about anything as long as you could pony up the pelf. She was vague on the details, like you are when you're talking about something you don't want to be talking about.

I got the idea that they arrived in Minnesota with a stake, but it didn't last long, and they weren't able to buy the kind of protection that Pauley had talked about. Eventually, Pauley made the acquaintance of some guys who were more successful at armed robbery than he had been, and he and Anna joined up with them. She said they robbed banks, used car lots, big grocery stores, anyplace that handled decent amounts of cash. When I asked who these guys were, she said the names didn't matter, I wouldn't know them anyway, and they weren't all guys. She wasn't the only woman, and they all helped with something. They went as far as Texas in search of enterprises with more cash than guards. It got harder and harder to find places that were worth the time and expense it took to plan a job and pull it off. Eventually, the gang, if you could really call it that, broke up, leaving her and Pauley with another couple about their age, Vaughn Billings and Hildy Jostic. The four of them went to western Ohio because Hildy had family there. Her parents and her idiot brother lived between Dayton and Columbus on a farm with pigs and chickens. Farming was a front for their real business. The place was isolated, and it had enough buildings and water to handle a dozen or so people. It became a popular hideout for guys who needed to stay out of sight for a while and could pay for a little privacy.

The four of them were casting about for something to do when Pauley came up with another almost brilliant idea.

The most important local bootlegger in that part of the state was a young druggist who'd figured out a way to distribute alcohol legally, or almost legally. No sneaking the stuff in from boats or smuggling it across the Canadian border. He actually owned a couple of distilleries that produced "medicinal" hooch. Some of it he and local doctors prescribed to the locals. Some of it he arranged to have stolen and resold to speaks and regular bootleggers. He was a gentleman from a good family and it was such a sweet setup that he could spend his dough out in the open, and everybody considered him to be a respectable citizen. He didn't hang around with gangsters and low-life hoodlums like me and A. R. and Lansky. Guy's name was Livingston. He supported all the local charities and churches and lived in a mansion in the middle of several hundred acres, where he threw famously extravagant parties.

Pauley Domo poked around and learned that the next one was going to be a fancy masked ball. He also managed to get an idea of the layout of the house and cased the roads around the place. It was common knowledge that Livingston was fond of young women, ten-year-old Scotch, and cocaine. Pauley figured, rightly as it turned out, that a couple of sexy flappers in a flashy car wouldn't have any trouble getting into such a gathering.

So, around eleven o'clock on a warm night, Hildy and Anna breezed up to Livingston's digs in a stolen Model A roadster. They wore feathered masks and beaded dresses so daringly cut that they were both falling out of them. They arrived with several other carloads of bright young things, and nobody said squat about invitations. Anna had objected to the way they were dressed, saying that they looked like cheap floozies, but once they got inside, she saw she was wrong. Everyone was in high spirits by then. One jazz band was playing inside and another one was out on the terrace. Waiters and waitresses carried food and drinks around, and you were never far from a bar. The only thing missing was their host. Anna, being the bolder of the two, led the way, and they found Livingston outside dancing.

They grabbed a couple of guys and maneuvered them onto the dance floor where Hildy managed to bump into Livingston and then apologized for spilling booze down his back. To prove that her apology was genuine and to show how thankful she was for this wonderful party, she wondered if he might want to join her and her friend Anna in a little toot and tickle.

Livingston suggested they repair to his special quiet spot in the garden. Pauley Domo and Vaughn met them on the way.

That part went as smooth as any job Pauley Domo ever pulled. Vaughn stuck a gun into Livingston's kidney while Pauley dropped a burlap bag over his head. They guided their man through a gap in a hedge to their car and sent Anna back for the stolen Model A. She said that was the part that really got to her more than the rest, going back into the party where everything was still going strong. She was sure everybody was looking at her funny, even though she had a mask on. A couple of guys grabbed her and tried to pull her onto the dance floor. She made it out, found the car, and saw that it had been blocked in by another car. She said to hell with it, banged fenders, and crashed out.

By the time she got back to the farm, Livingston had been locked in an outbuilding and the idiot brother had been given the job of taking care of him. They made sure that the brother gave Livingston plenty of food and as much booze as he wanted, figuring that was the easiest way to keep him in line. They never had any thought of killing him. None of them had the stomach for that. Vaughn left to go to a pay telephone at a gas station to call Livingston's lawyer. That's when they really got nervous. They knew this was the hard part.

Vaughn got through to the mouthpiece and told him that they had his boss and he had to get seventy-five thousand dollars. No cops. They didn't want to hurt anybody. Just the cash. Then he hung up and went back to the farm, where they sat down to wait.

The plan was that when the lawyer had the loot, they'd send him to another phone booth in Rike's department store in Dayton where Anna and Hildy would be watching. Vaughn would call the lawyer and send him to a second telephone in a drug store a few blocks away where he'd find a note taped to the bottom of the seat in the booth. The note told him where to make the money drop. Anna and Hildy would follow him from the first department store to the drug store to make sure that nobody else was tagging along. Pauley Domo would be waiting for the money at the drop. As soon as they'd counted the loot, Livingston would be sprung.

The next day, Vaughn called the lawyer, and the lawyer said he had the scratch, but there was no deal unless he could talk to Livingston. Vaughn hung up without answering and went back to the farm. They talked it over and came up with a plan. That afternoon, they put on masks, took the burlap off of Livingston's head, and poured an extra fifth of rotgut into him. Actually, Anna said, he sucked it right down.

After it got dark, they put the bag back on and drove him to the phone Vaughn had been using at a gas station. With a gun pressed against his back, Livingston yelled into the telephone, "Goddammit, give these assholes whatever they want! Just get me outta here."

They took him back to the farm, and the idiot brother locked him up again.

The next afternoon, Vaughn got into the banged up Model A. Pauley, Anna, and Hildy took the sedan they'd driven from Minnesota. It was clean, and Anna didn't want to be seen in the car that might be connected with the party. The women let Pauley off at the spot they'd picked. It was a small bridge on a rural road with woods on one side, where he could hide, and a field on the other. He was to tie a strip of torn sheet to a low tree limb and wait out of sight.

The women went to the drug store where Hildy taped the note to the seat in the phone booth. From there, they went to Rike's. Hildy went inside. Anna waited in the car outside the main door of the department store. She knew what the lawyer looked like. He was supposed to be in a dark brown Lincoln Model L. Around six thirty, she saw the big car pull to a stop, and a man she thought was the lawyer got out. He was carrying a bulging briefcase, and he was jumpy as he looked around on the sidewalk and went into the store. His chauffeur stayed in the Lincoln. Anna waited for what seemed like hours until Hildy came bustling out and got in the car.

She was excited, smiling. "It's gonna work," she said. "He's got the money and he's in the phone booth talking to Vaughn."

The lawyer came out directly and got back into the Lincoln. Off he went. Anna and Hildy followed. Again, everything looked like it was following the plan. The Lincoln double-parked in front of the drug store, and the lawyer, this time without the briefcase, went in and came out a few moments later. He and his driver went off in the right direction. While Anna stayed in the car and looked around to see if another car followed, Hildy went into the drug store and called Vaughn to tell him what was happening. If things had gone bad, Vaughn was ready to get to Pauley before the lawyer got there. It was just getting dark when she and Anna headed for the bridge.

Anna couldn't believe it when they got there and Pauly Domo came trotting out of the woods with the bulging briefcase in his arms and a slaphappy grin plastered across his face.

"We got it," he said as he slid across the backseat. "It's here. The money. It's real. We did it!" And all three of them started yelling.

They were home free. It had worked perfectly.

When they got back to the farm that night, they found the stolen car that Vaughn had been driving parked out front. Anna pulled up next to it. Hildy jumped right out, and somebody shot her. She fell back halfway in the car, legs on the ground, hips on the running board.

It hadn't worked perfectly.

Anna heard a voice she thought was Vaughn's yelling Hildy's name, but it was cut off and drowned out by gunfire. Pauley was yelling from the backseat as she got the car started and jammed it into reverse. She felt bullets hitting the car, and headlights were flashing in her eyes. Hildy slid out as Anna struggled with the steering wheel and fishtailed back onto the dirt track that led to the road. She thought there were two cars behind them and they were still being shot at. She couldn't really remember how she got away from them or even where she went that night. She just drove as fast as she could on the country roads. Hours later, when she was sure that nobody was behind them, she stopped and turned around and saw that Pauley had been hit. She got into the back-seat and found it soaked with blood. She slapped him until he opened his eyes, but he couldn't talk at first.

When he came back to life a little, she told him that they were somewhere near Waynesville or maybe Springboro. He didn't remember exactly what had happened until she told him that somebody, a lot of guys probably, opened up on them. Pauley said that it must have been the idiot brother. It didn't make sense for Vaughn to double-cross them. He wouldn't hurt Hildy. The way Pauley figured it, right after Anna and the others left the farm that afternoon, the idiot brother got into the booze they'd left for Livingston. He'd done that before. Maybe he figured that since they were so close, he could take it easy. Maybe Livingston knocked him out when he came with the booze and food. Maybe they drank more and the idiot brother passed out and Livingston walked away.

He probably got out on the road, flagged down a ride, and got off at the same gas station where Vaughn had been making his calls. Now, Anna and Pauley had been right when they assumed that Livingston wasn't a low-life hoodlum thug like me, but since he was in the illegal booze business, he knew several low-life hoodlum thugs, and he called them instead of the cops. Even before the lawyer delivered the loot, Livingston was making other arrangements.

But at that point, it didn't matter what had gone wrong. They had to get away. Pauley said that he knew of a place where they might be OK. It was a hundred miles or so away in a little town called Wapakoneta. If Pauley was guessing right about Livings-ton, the cops probably wouldn't be looking for them, but they'd have to stay away from places where word might get back to the wrong people, meaning the people they usually worked with. It also meant they couldn't go to any of the doctors or vets who treated gunshots on the QT. They had to get to Wapakoneta.

Anna drove through the night. By morning they were seeing signs for Lima, and Pauley said that meant they were going in the right direction. Anna arranged a couple of lap robes in the back, covering up most of the blood. When they stopped for gas, she told the attendant that her husband was sleepy. It wasn't a lie. Pauley drifted in and out, and he didn't look good. She bought a road map. Late that afternoon, she checked them into the Lake Shore Motor Court as Mr. and Mrs. Bill Angiello. She said her husband was feeling poorly and asked for the most private and quiet efficiency they had. She paid for a week.

When she helped Pauley inside, he was hunched over and limping like an old man. Inside, after she'd got his clothes off and cleaned him up in the tub, she saw that he'd been shot twice in the stomach and side, and there was one exit wound in his back. He felt cold and sweaty. She went back into town and found a store where she bought food, milk, bandages, and newspapers. Following his mumbled instructions, she patched Pauley up. He wouldn't eat anything and didn't even want any milk. Running true to form, she was as hungry as she'd ever been in her life and ate damn near everything she'd bought. There was nothing about Livingston in the papers.

Then, for the first time, really, she looked at the briefcase. It had been shot, too. She figured it was possible that the bullet in Pauley had gone through the briefcase first. Inside, there was the money, some of it loose bills, some rolled up with rubber bands around it, some stiff new bills bound in bank tape.

There in the dim yellow light of the little lamps, with all of the curtains tightly drawn, the door double-locked and a chair wedged under the knob, she sat on the floor and counted, writing numbers on the brown paper grocery bag. It was all there—seventy-five thousand dollars, more money than she'd ever seen at one time, and it all belonged to her and Pauley.

Then it all belonged to her.

Pauley Domo died that night.

She said that she sat up all night with the body and the money. What to do? She wasn't about to give up the cash, and the longer she stayed there, the more dangerous it was for her. She was on her own. She didn't know anyone close who could come to help her. What to do with Pauley? She could try to wrestle the body into the car and bury the body in a shallow grave in the woods, or find a place at the nearby lake where she could sink it. But Pauley was a big guy, and she wasn't even sure she was strong enough to move him.

So, at dawn, she wiped down the room for her prints, stripped off Pauley's clothes, hung out the "Do Not Disturb" sign and drove to Toledo, the closest city with a big train station.

"That's the one part of it that I'm really ashamed of," she said, "leaving Pauley like that. But I couldn't think of anything else to do. I'd earned the money, goddammit. We wouldn't have got Livingston in the first place if he hadn't believed that Hildy and me were really going to put on a show for him, so the money was mine. I was pretty sure that Hildy and Vaughn were dead, and I hoped like hell that the idiot brother was dead. The money was mine if I could hold onto it. But, there I was, a woman alone. As long as I was trying to move the money by myself, I was an easy mark.

"So, what I did was I held onto a little traveling money and packed up the rest real carefully in four wooden shipping crates and sent them on their way."

She must have seen something in my expression because she said, "What? You don't believe me?"

She sat up in the bed and shoved a fist into my chest. "You'll believe it when you see the money," she said.

"I'll see the money?"

"Of course. I sent it to you."

For a moment, I was too flabbergasted to do anything. Then I laughed. "Why the hell would you send it to me?"

She snuggled down, pressing her tits deliberately against me, and put her head against my chest so I couldn't see her face when she spoke. "I know it sounds crazy, and I guess I was a little crazy when I did it, but this is God's truth, Jimmy."

She looked up at me so I could see how godly and truthful

she was. "You're the only person in the world I could trust to help me with this. I know I treated you kind of rotten, and I thought maybe you'd hate me for running out on you the way I did, but we had good times, and over the years, I'd ask people about you. I heard when you bought your place, so I knew you were still around and doing well."

"And now," I said, "there are four boxes being held for Jimmy Quinn."

"Aren't you the clever boy."

"Or for anybody who has papers that say he's Jimmy Quinn."

"What are you talking about?"

"A few hours ago, I came across a dead guy who had a phony union card and driver's license made out in my name."

She sat up fast and said, "Oh fuck."

I was not surprised.

CHAPTER EIGHT

She threw off the sheets and slid out of the big bed. As she picked up the robe, she muttered, "That crazy bitch. If she has . . ."

Then she turned and stared at me. "You know something. What is it?"

"All kinds of strange things have been happening lately. Somebody tried to break into my place. Somebody blew up a bomb in the alley last night. Couple of guys braced me on the street and slipped me your note, and there was a kid on the street who knew my name but a mean-looking old lady scared him off. Then a German came in and made an offer to buy me out, and after that, there was the guy I just mentioned in a warehouse over on the East River, and while I was there, a cop got shot and killed, and after what you just told me, I suspect you know more about all that than I do. I'm missing some details. Why don't you wise me up?"

She stood, fists on hips, robe hanging open. I could tell she was working her way through what I'd said, and it troubled her. After a time, she nodded like she'd come to a decision. She shed the robe, opened a bureau drawer, and dressed—garter belt, underwear, and brassiere. White silk, and new by the look of them. Skirt, blouse, and shoes from the closet. She wasn't trying to be seductive or playful, but I still found it extremely interesting. Buttoning up, she said, "I can't stay here. I'll be in touch. And Jimmy, take care of yourself. There are people who . . ." She stopped and thought some more. "No, just . . . take care of yourself. Now get dressed. We gotta get out of here."

She threw the rest of her clothes into a small bag. I dressed more slowly and gave her a Jimmy Quinn's Place business card with the telephone number.

She unlocked the door and kissed me hard. "You did all right for yourself, Jimmy. I'm glad to see that, really I am. I knew you would. I knew I could trust you. You're a right guy."

I caught a cab back to the speak. As the driver headed downtown, I realized I was still completely confused even though a couple of things made more sense. Whatever was going on with the guys who tried to break in and Klapprott's outfit—that had something to do with the seventy-five thousand Anna claimed to have. That's what everybody was looking for. Maybe it didn't matter if her story about kidnapping the bootlegger was phony, if the money was real. And for now, I could figure that the dirty ten-spot was part of it. And I could figure that Anna needed me to get to the rest of it. Sure wasn't love or sex that brought her back to the Taft Suite, not that I was complaining, mind you.

It was around two o'clock when I got back. The crowd had thinned out considerably. Frenchy was behind the bar, and Connie was sitting at a table talking with Mercer Weeks. That was odd. The three-fingered guy who'd left the key and the dirty money was back at my table holding a newspaper up in front of his face, and Malloy, the night watchman from the warehouse, was at the bar. Frenchy said both of them had been waiting to see me.

I held up a hand, gesturing to Three Fingers to wait, and hooked a stool next to Malloy. He was closer. I nodded to Frenchy. He gave Malloy a brandy.

"Ah, Mr. Quinn, I didn't recognize your name earlier, and that shames me. Your reputation precedes you."

"What reputation is that?"

"Why, as a man who runs one of the finest speaks in the city and keeps company with some of the city's most prominent banditti. Alas, as I predicted not long ago, my previous employers, the Kraut cocksuckers, have shitcanned me." He paused to drink.

"Therefore, I'm thinking that perhaps those unfortunate occurrences at the warehouse earlier this evening might have some small bearing on your fine establishment, what with your name having been brought up in such untoward circumstances. Suppose the perpetrators of those horrors were to attempt something similar here after-hours. Wouldn't you want someone on the premises to dissuade them?"

"*Dissuade?*"

"To advise or urge against. To discourage or deflect. A word not often used in this context, but it seemed appropriate."

"And how would you dissuade them?"

He opened his coat, revealing a Luger in his belt. "The Krauts will never miss it."

He hitched up on his stool, leaned over his drink, and gave me a canny look. "Now, sir, I know what you're thinking. You're thinking, here's this feller that I don't know from Adam's off ox. Hadn't even clapped eyes on him until . . . "—he pulled a watch from his vest pocket—" . . . five hours ago. And now he comes into my excellent establishment and asks for a job. But what do I know of him? First, he allowed two gentlemen—gentlemen of dubious quality but gentlemen nonetheless—he allowed these two gentlemen to be cut down in a building that he had been engaged to protect. Second, he brazenly admits to stealing a weapon from his previous employers. Why would I, or anyone, place such an individual in a position of responsibility?"

I tried not to smile. "Why indeed."

He shrugged. "I have no answer. I was just hoping that such a display of honesty, however uncharacteristic, would be persuasive. The long and the short of it is that I need a job and this is a good place. What do you say, sir?"

"Wait here."

Three Fingers still looked tired and watchful beneath a day's growth of dark unshaven stubble. He put down the newspaper and said, "I told you I'd be back. Things are moving pretty fast now. I don't want to trust anybody, but word is you're OK, so that's that. The thing is, it ain't safe for me on the street anymore. Somebody sold me out."

"You want the key now?"

He said, "No, there's something else that's more important—" But he was interrupted by some commotion at the front door.

I heard Fat Joe Beddoes, using his loud no-nonsense voice, say, "I don't know you, so you're not getting in. Get the fuck outta here, ya jackleg bastards."

There were more loud men's voices from outside. I heard Fat Joe open the front door. I told Three Fingers to wait a minute and went to see if Fat Joe needed help.

By the time I got to him, Fat Joe had gone outside to dissuade the jackleg bastards, and he didn't need me. They'd decided to find another speak. Before I could go back inside, Three Fingers scuttled out past me, my paper under his arm. Whatever he wanted must not have been that important after all.

Back inside, I found that Connie had joined Marie Therese behind the bar. I motioned for Fat Joe to come over too.

"This is Arch Malloy," I explained to them. "Remember when Ellis came in earlier? He took me to a warehouse where Malloy was the night watchman. Guy got himself beat to death there. Turned out he was carrying papers, union card and the like, made out in my name."

Frenchy looked surprised. Fat Joe didn't look like anything.

"And Malloy here got fired. At least, that's what he says. And now he has come here, thinking we need somebody to stay here after-hours."

Frenchy gave Malloy a skeptical eye. Fat Joe didn't do anything.

"Consider this," Malloy said. "Like the unfortunate dead man that was found in my warehouse earlier, the two jackleg bastards you just dispatched truly are part of a larger plot. They are in league with my previous employers to do whatever it is they're attempting to do. Just now, they were testing your defenses. In a couple of hours, after you've closed, they or their associates will return with more mischief on their minds."

Fat Joe and Frenchy looked at each other. Frenchy shrugged.

I briefly considered that Malloy and the jackleg troublemakers were part of Klapprott's business, but no, that was too complicated. They were drunks, and Malloy was a smooth talker with a sense of humor and a stolen gun. My kind of guy.

I said, "Fat Joe, how would you like to earn a little extra tonight? Two's better than one. Keep Mr. Malloy company. One of you can sleep on the divan."

Fat Joe shrugged and said, "Why the fuck not?"

I turned to go to my office and found that Mercer Weeks was waiting for me.

"Quinn," he said, "Jacob wants to talk to you. I've got a cab waiting."

CHAPTER NINE

Jacob "the Wise" Weiss had an apartment on the Upper East Side. The story I heard was that when he first tried to buy it, the owners or the board or whoever was in charge turned him down, either because he was a hoodlum or because he was a Jew. That really pissed him off, so he bought the entire building. Now, I can't say that I know it's true, but I do know there were people on the Upper East Side who didn't care for Jews or hoodlums, and I know that Jacob was rich enough to buy apartment buildings. Maybe not the really big ones, but his was only six stories tall. It was on Fifth Avenue up in the Seventies or Eighties, overlooking the park. In those days though, he didn't look down to see nice big trees and green lawns and such. A small army of guys who were out of work had set up camp and were squatting there. They put up shacks and sheds and tents and turned the park into one of the biggest Hoovervilles in the country.

When we rolled up in front of the building, the doorman recognized Weeks getting out of the cab he hopped to, opening the door and touching the shiny brim of his cap. "Good evening, Mr. Robertson," he said even though it was pushing three in the morning. "How are you doing, Mr. Robertson?" he asked, almost tripping over himself to get the elevator doors open. Weeks didn't use his real name there. Neither did Jacob the Wise.

The walls of the small lobby were done up in long narrow mirrors, both regular mirrors and bronze-colored mirrors and diamond-shaped pieces of polished wood and glass that reflected the light. The ceiling was painted sky blue with white clouds.

Up on the fifth floor, Jacob's place had tall ceilings, a herring-bone pattern inlaid floor, and gauzy white curtains floating in the breeze that came in through open windows. The chairs and sofa were covered with some kind of shiny fabric and looked new. I don't know how big the place was, but I could see two rooms off the main room. It wasn't as grand as Luciano's digs at the Waldorf Tower, but it wasn't hard to take.

Jacob the Wise was staring down at the guys in the park. He turned and looked at me, and I could tell he was angry. I'd never seen that before, and I didn't like it.

I always thought that he and Longy Zwillman could have been related. They were both big athletic guys. Jacob boxed when he was young, before he wised up. He had a high forehead, dark wiry hair gray at the temples, eyes you couldn't read when he didn't want you to, wide sloped shoulders, and big mitts with a couple of split knuckles on the right. He favored nice clothes, not as nice as mine but nice enough, I guess. Longy got his start in the numbers game, too, over in Newark, in the Third Ward. But once Prohibition came in, he was quick to figure out what a sweet racket booze was going to be and went with it. Jacob stuck with policy and money lending. Maybe that's why he and Longy were friendly. They didn't compete with each other. They'd even been to my place with their girlfriends. Of course, that was before Jacob met Signora Sophia Sugartits.

He gave me a hard look. "So, you're finally here," he said. "Weeks, give him a drink."

"Brandy. If it's any good."

Weeks poured. Jacob and I sat in armchairs facing each other. His brandy was crap. I set it aside and rested my stick on my lap across the arms of the chair.

Jacob said, "There was a young fella here yesterday who said he had a story to tell me. For a price. It turned out to be a very interesting story." He paused while he put a match to a fresh Havana, making a real production number of it and creating a cloud of sticky smoke. "I didn't pay for it. I thought about having Weeks beat it out of him, but once the guy started talking, I decided to do it myself." He smiled around the cigar. "He said that my money was in transit, those were the words he used, 'in transit,' and when it gets here, you will take possession. And then today, I got a telephone call saying that you've already got my money—my hundred thousand dollars. I want it back."

The smile disappeared, and he gave me another hard stare meant to be threatening.

I sat back in the chair and rested my hands on my stick. "What the hell are you talking about?"

"According to this young fella, the people who had it knew that it was hot and sold it to you for a penny on the dollar. The ransom money," he said, and at least part of the picture came into focus.

"Ransom money? For who? What? I don't know what you're talking about."

He answered with another hard stare. I stared back.

Finally, he mushmouthed around the cigar, "Mercer, did you see anything?"

Weeks, who was staying away from us over by the bar, said, "No. Nothing's changed at his place. It's just like it was last week and last month and before the trip. If he's got the cash, he's not flashing it around."

Jacob said, "That doesn't mean anything," and blew smoke in my face.

"Who is this young fella? What'd he look like, and why would you believe him?"

Jacob shrugged. "Who knows? It could be true. If you try to lie to me, I'll have Weeks get the truth out of you."

"No, you won't. I'll shoot him first."

Jacob scowled at Weeks. "You didn't search him?"

Weeks was unconcerned. "This is just Quinn, for God's sake. If he shoots me, I'll kill him."

I said, "Jacob, I'm not going to insult you and Weeks by threatening you. That's stupid, and I'm not stupid enough to steal from you, either. You know that. So what's going on? I don't know anything about any hundred thousand dollars."

His big shoulders slumped, like he knew what I was going to say, and he knew I wasn't lying. Well, I wasn't lying about some of it, anyway.

"What do you know about what happened to us last year?" he asked.

"I heard you were taking some time off, a long trip out West. Benny Numbers and some of your guys went with you. You came back a couple of months later without him. That's it. I heard other things from guys who probably didn't know what they were talking about. But I don't put any stock in that. What else is there?"

As Jacob told it, his business had been good. Despite the crash, people still gambled with their pennies and nickels, and because of the crash, his loan sharking was better than ever. He didn't say "loan sharking." I think he referred to it as the "banking side" of his operation. So, he decided, for the first time, to take some time off. He asked his friend, Signora Sophia, where she'd like to go, and she said she really wanted to stay in the city, but if they were going to go someplace, it ought to be someplace warm. He suggested Los Angeles and Hollywood, and that was that.

As Weeks had said earlier in my speak, somebody had to stay and watch the store, and that was him. They had to do some persuading to talk Benny Numbers into the trip. "We can't afford it," he said. "I don't want to leave my fiancée for so long," he said. There was too much to do. Jacob had none of it. He wanted a trip, and he wanted his favorite people with him. He also took bodyguards, four of them. An important man in his line of work didn't go about without protection. Jacob the Wise didn't get where he was by taking unnecessary risks.

So one fine evening in the fall of '31, they boarded the Twentieth Century Limited at Grand Central and headed for Chicago, first class. The whole time they were on that train and the others, Benny Numbers acted like he was back in the basement offices on Grand Street where he kept track of Jacob's business. He brought along four ledgers and a briefcase full of notebooks. At every stop, he hurried off the train and went to the closest telephone to call back and get figures from the guys who worked for him. He could have sent telegraphs from the train, but he said he didn't trust them. It was too easy for other people to get their noses in Jacob's business. For his part, Jacob didn't care. He enjoyed the ride and the company of the Signora.

In Chicago, they changed trains for the Chief to Los Angeles, with a side trip to visit the hot springs and the Hotel Colorado at Glenwood Springs, where Theodore Roosevelt and Al Capone had stayed.

It turned out to be a little burg high up in the mountains. The hotel wouldn't have been out of place in Saratoga Springs. It sprawled out beside a wide warm water pool. They attracted a fair amount of attention when they arrived, maybe not as much as Capone, but with his attentive gun thugs and the tall dark ermine-wrapped beauty on his arm, Jacob was something out of the ordinary. The manager ushered them around to a special private entrance.

Sometime during their first night there, Benny Numbers disappeared.

When he didn't show up for lunch the next day, Jacob sent one of his gunmen to check the room. Ten minutes later, looking sick and worried, the guy came back and said Jacob had to see something.

Jacob and the Signora had adjoining suites, but Benny had made arrangements for the rest of them in less luxurious rooms.

The gun guys were close to Jacob, but Benny had a smaller room in another wing. When they got to it, Jacob found that things had been knocked around, like there might have been a fight, but the bed hadn't been slept in.

Under a hotel ashtray in the middle of the bed was a note, handwritten, barely legible. It read:

> No Cops
> We have yr man and his books
> $100,000 dollars
> five days

Jacob sent his guys to look around the grounds just in case it wasn't what it looked like it was. Nothing. He talked things over with the Signora. She agreed this was very bad and went to speak to the manager for Jacob. Acting like it was nothing serious, she asked the manager if there had been any noise complaints the night before. She was asking because her friend in 115 thought he heard something. The manager checked with the night man. More nothing. Jacob's guys came back empty-handed, too. He told them to check with the lower-level hotel staff to find out where the local whorehouses and speaks were, anyplace Benny Numbers might have got a notion to visit and then found himself in trouble. While they were working on that, he called Mercer Weeks and explained what happened.

Weeks started collecting the cash.

It took four days for him to gather the money and for him and two other guys to bring two suitcases full to Glenwood Springs. They took the same trains to Chicago and Denver, where they bought a Ford and drove the rest of the way. Knowing nothing about the area, Jacob wasn't able to do much during that time. He couldn't tell if any of the other guests or hotel staff or the people who passed by on the street were watching him. Everything looked suspicious.

He and Signora Sophia and the guards stayed close. Jacob

was able to ask around and learned that there was one occasional local, "Diamond" Jack Alterie, also known as "Two Gun" Alterie, who might have pulled a snatch like this one. Alterie had worked with Capone in Chicago, but he'd been kicked out of the organization after making nutty threats when his boss, Deanie O'Banion, got killed. Alterie told the papers that he'd meet the killers at high noon on State Street, where they'd shoot it out. Big Al suggested it might be a good time for Diamond Jack to get the fuck out of town, and he went to Colorado. Several years later, when Jacob went there, Alterie had a ranch and sponsored rodeos in Denver and sometimes showed up in Glenwood Springs. He strutted around with a big Stetson hat that looked like an upside-down umbrella, flashy diamond rings, and two .45s strapped to his hips. Not the kind of guy to pull something like this.

When Weeks got to the hotel, Jacob knew no more than he had that first day. The waiting and the damn fact that he couldn't do anything were making him crazy. Jacob wasn't a particularly emotional guy, but he was choosy about who he worked with. He got to know the guys who stuck with him. He really did think of Benny and Weeks as the sons he and his wife never had. And then there were the ledgers. If Jacob were to lose those and if the wrong people got their hands on them, the whole operation would be in trouble. So all they could do was wait and hope they were dealing with professionals.

Of course, Weeks sweated the bodyguards, too. But these were Jacob's most trusted guys, who'd been with him forever. If something like this had happened at home, more suspicion would have been directed at them, but not this far away, and not when they'd been playing cards with Jacob on the night Benny got snatched.

They didn't hear anything for another full day. By then, Jacob was ready to kill somebody, anybody. The Signora locked the door to her suite, ordered room service, and refused to say anything else. Worried about the warrants that might still be out for him on the Denver Mint job, Weeks stayed in his room as much as he could.

On the afternoon of the sixth day after Benny Numbers had been taken, a taxi driver came up to the front desk with a note for Mr. Jason Wentworth, the name Jacob was registered under. When Weeks found the cabbie later, he said a man approached him at the train station. It was dark, and he didn't get a good look, so all he could say was that he thought the guy was old. Yes, it was strange for somebody to offer him a whole dollar to drive a few hundred yards to the hotel, but strange things happen everywhere, even in Glenwood Springs.

The note, written in what looked like the same crude handwriting as the first, read:

> Bring money to Miner's Camp No. 3 at 11:00
> Wait
> Send the Woman

Nobody liked that last part. The Signora flatly refused to do it, and Weeks backed her up. This was his kind of job. That night, he got directions to Miner's Camp No. 3, a little name on the map that wasn't much more than a crossroads higher up in the mountains about nine miles away. He loaded the suitcases into the Ford and drove off.

He came back the next morning. Nobody showed up. They heard nothing for two days. The next note came in the mail with a local postmark. It said:

> Send the Woman

Jacob, Weeks, and the Signora sat down to talk it over. They tried to persuade her for more than an hour. Finally, it came down to Jacob saying, "I am asking you to do this thing for me. I am asking you as an honorable man. If you agree to do this, I will be in your debt. You can ask anything of me. Anything. Weeks is my witness."

She agreed. Weeks asked if she wanted a gun. She said she had one.

That night, they loaded the suitcases again. She drove away, and that was the last they saw of her and the money and Benny Numbers.

They stayed for another month, generating a wealth of rumors among the staff and guests. Weeks and Jacob bought another car and went to Miner's Camp No. 3, where they found nothing but a few empty buildings. It wasn't even big enough to be called a ghost town. They wandered through all the mountain roads and trails they could find, hundreds of miles, but they were virtually empty except for a few villages and mining outfits. They considered hiring the Pinkertons. But Jacob would have nothing to do with the idea at first. He was afraid that word would get back to the cops. Weeks said that he'd bought the Ford under a false name. It couldn't be traced to either of them, so Jacob agreed. Weeks went to Denver and hired the Pinks but only to search for the car. Not that it mattered. The private dicks came up empty, too.

Then the first big snow hit, and that was it. They packed up and went back to New York. Jacob set about straightening up his policy racket. While he'd been gone, everyone involved from the runners on up were skimming as much as they could. With Weeks gone, nobody had been making their payments on loans. Angry and frustrated at what had happened, they threw themselves into work. They talked about going back to Colorado with more men to search, maybe to find more locals who could help. But without Benny Numbers, the policy business took up all their time and energy, and it had been almost a year since Benny had been snatched.

By the time he finished the story, Jacob was really steamed. Talking about it made him mad all over again.

"Then yesterday," he said, "I'm sitting here, right where I'm sitting now, and the phone rings." There was a phone on the table beside him.

"I pick it up, and this voice says, 'Are you Jacob Weiss?' And I say that I am, and she says, 'Jimmy Quinn has your money' and hangs up."

"You said *she*, so it was a woman."

"Yes, an old woman. She was hoarse, whispery, hard to understand, and that makes two people putting the finger on you." He jabbed the cigar at me.

"And you believe them; you think I've got your money?"

"We don't know." Weeks came over to stand by Jacob. "But this is the first thing we've heard. So somebody knows something, and you're in on it."

"OK, let me ask you something—did you check out this guy Alterie who worked with Capone?"

"Yeah, but there was nothing to him. He spends his time playing cowboy."

"Then, as I see it, you've got two possibilities. First, one of the locals had been waiting for somebody like you to show up, somebody with money who won't call the cops. He snatched Benny Numbers and killed him. Then he killed the Signora after she delivered."

They stared at me, looking grim. This was nothing they hadn't considered.

"Or, this is a deal that Benny and the Signora cooked up together, and now they're whooping it up with your money in Paris or South America or somewhere, and somebody else is pulling your leg, saying that I'm in on it when I've never been west of New Jersey."

At that, Jacob shook his head. "No, I know Benny and Sophia. If there was anything going on between them, I would know. I was too close to both of them not to know. And besides, the way Benny worked, he didn't have time to fuck around. And Sophia— I gave Sophia everything she needed."

I rolled my stick and said, "Tell me about Signora Sophia." I thought I probably already knew a lot about her.

When I said her name, Jacob's expression went soft for just a tiny second. But as soon as he started talking, he closed back down and tried not to let anything show in his face or voice.

He met her at Saratoga Springs, at the races. Now, you've got to understand that being seen at the races was quite the big deal for New York society folk. Jacob had been going ever since Rothstein opened a casino there back in the '20s. As a runner for A. R., I was strictly a city kid and never went out of town with him, but I heard it was a real elegant joint. Must have been, he had to pass out fifty thousand dollars a year in bribes to the local bosses to keep it open. Jacob and A. R. got along pretty good because Jacob didn't gamble. He just enjoyed Rothstein's company, and like Longy Zwillman, he wasn't competition. I think Jacob and A. R. liked to watch all the swells playing the tables at A. R.'s place, knowing that sooner or later, they were going to be handing over their money. A. R. once said to me that every game is fixed, and when you own the house, the fix is locked in. A. R. also told me more than once that the people who lost their dough at his place were dubs and dumbbells. I guess Jacob probably thought the same about his customers. Like I said, they were pals, and after A. R. got killed, Jacob still went to Saratoga Springs. Signora Sophia was staying at his hotel.

She was a brunette Garbo—silent, cool, and glamorous. She dressed in dark colors and usually wore sunglasses. She ate alone, and Jacob watched dozens of guys get the brush-off. Everybody had stories to tell about her. Some said she was a white Russian countess whose family lost everything in the revolution. Or she was an Italian duchess whose husband was killed in the war. I don't know what Jacob said to get on her good side. He didn't give away any details, but he persuaded her to join him for dinner one evening, and they ate together that night and the next night and the next.

It turned out that the stories about royalty were bunk. She told him she was a widow from Wisconsin. Her husband had been in the war, but when he came back, he wasn't the same, and two years ago, he had shot himself. She came to that hotel because they spent their honeymoon there, and that was why the management made an exception to their policy about not allowing single women. As for the other stories, she knew about them and didn't discourage them because they made her sound exotic, and she guessed they kept some of the Lotharios from pestering her.

Jacob said, "I knew she wasn't cheap. From the first time I talked to her, I knew that. She had taste. Her clothes and jewelry were the best, and she knew how to order from a good menu, but she wasn't one of those society broads who look down their noses at you."

She told him it had taken her a long time to get over her husband's death, and now she was determined to start again. She didn't know what she wanted to do, but she wasn't ready to go back home and she'd never seen New York, so she was going to begin there. Jacob said he was just the man to squire her around the city.

And that's how she wound up in a swank Park Avenue apartment.

"We were happy," he said. "The 'Signora Sophia' business, that was a joke. When we were alone, I called her Soph. She knew about me, what I do and that I was married, and she didn't care. I didn't care about the secrets she kept from me."

Sometimes she'd be gone for hours or overnight. She said there was another part of her life that she couldn't tell him about. It wasn't another man, she swore that, or a drug habit or anything like that. It was something she deeply believed in and that she had to do. She looked him straight in the eyes and said that she knew how he felt about her, and she felt the same about him. She knew that if he ever caught her with another man, he'd kill them both. She understood it and said that he'd better remember that she would do exactly the same if he took up with some flapper.

"OK," I said, "you set up housekeeping here. Tell me something—this trip out West, was it her idea?"

Jacob puffed on his stogie like he was getting mad. "No, we had to talk her into it. What's with all the questions?"

"Benny Numbers?"

"No, like I said, he wanted to stay here and work. We had to drag him along."

I rotated my stick in my hands and looked over at Mercer Weeks, who'd moved to lean against the mantle and was following everything we said. He had his works out and was rolling a smoke. I asked if he had any ideas.

He finished making his cigarette. "What you said earlier, I guess. Figure somebody on the staff told somebody else when some well-heeled guys from the east were passing through. The reservations were under aliases, but somebody could have figured out that we were the kind of guys who weren't going to call the cops. That would explain them knowing we'd need five days to get the money."

The tip of Jacob's Havana glowed like a hot cherry. "Enough with the fucking questions. Now we get back to the point. People say you've got my money. What's going on, you little punk?" He leaned forward and blew more smoke.

I was already pissed off, and that did it. I choked up on the tip end of the stick and flicked the crook with a snap of my wrist. It missed Jacob's nose by inches and knocked that goddamn cigar right out of his fat mouth. Both he and Weeks were so surprised, it gave me the moment I needed to stand and pull the .38 out of my pocket. I didn't point it at anybody. Weeks stayed where he was. If I'd hit Jacob, he'd have torn my head off, but he knew Jacob was out of line calling me a punk.

"All right, goddammit," I said. "I know you're mad about your money and your woman and your business, and you think I've got something to do with it and you want to take it out on me. Well, you're not. Stay right there, Weeks, I will shoot you."

The cigar was burning a hole in the herringbone wood floor.

"Like that guy said, strange things happen everywhere. There's a guy I saw in a warehouse a few hours ago. He was carrying papers that said he was Jimmy Quinn. Maybe he's the Jimmy Quinn you want to be talking to, but it won't do you any good because he's dead." That surprised and worried them. "If you want to talk to me again, you know where my place is."

I put the gun back in my pocket and walked out.

I wish I could say that I turned my back and showed them my ass, but I backed out, keeping my eyes on both of them. I may get a little reckless sometimes, but I'm not stupid.

CHAPTER TEN

I had Jacob's doorman call a cab, and as I waited for it, I realized I was hungry, so hungry it was painful. I hadn't eaten since my ham sandwich the evening before. So instead of heading back to the Chelsea, I told the driver to take me to an all-night place I knew on Seventh near Times Square. It was still dark when I got out of the taxi. I bought the early edition of the *Times* and the *Mirror* from a couple of kids on the sidewalk. As I was paying, another cab pulled up, and the guy who got out was careful not to look at me. He wore glasses, a cheap brown suit, poorly knotted tie, and a wrinkled shirt.

Inside, I took a booth and ordered three over easy, rye toast, a glass of really cold milk, and a side of salami. When the waitress brought my coffee, she said they were out of salami. Who ever heard of such a thing? I switched to pastrami.

I went through the local section of both papers quickly, but there was nothing about a cop being shot in a warehouse. Detective Ellis was tight with most of the police reporters. If he asked them to sit on a story, they probably would. For a little while, at least. Long enough for him to learn what Betcherman was up to and how bad it would look for the department if it came out. Until then, Ellis would keep it on the quietus.

How had it gone at the warehouse? Betcherman told Ellis that Malloy, the night watchman, found the body of the guy who'd been carrying the phony papers with my name. But Malloy said that it was Betcherman who found the body while he, Malloy, was outside. If that was true, maybe Betcherman had the fake cards all along or took them after he killed the other guy. But why would he do that, and what was he doing in the warehouse owned by the Germans in the first place?

The waitress brought my plate, and as I ripped into my eggs, I tried to figure out where Anna fit into whatever the hell it was that was going on. I first knew her as Anna Gunderwald, the bright beer-loving teenager who wanted to explore the city and race the fastest boys. And then she turned out to be Mrs. Pauley Domo, Midwestern bank robber, gun moll, and kidnapper. And then it seemed likely to me that Mrs. Domo had become Signora Sophia Sugartits, the dark, silent, mysterious Wisconsin widow. I didn't know how or why, but somehow, with her, it made sense. And now she said there was a sizeable amount of cash floating around, somewhere between seventy-five and a hundred thousand dollars, depending on which story was true, with my name on it, and a lot of interested parties who wanted to get their hands on it.

Sopping up my eggs with good rye toast, I understood that there was a lot I didn't know, but Anna had sounded so certain, so confident when she said she'd sent the money to me that I had the feeling that part was true. At least I couldn't see how she would have anything to gain by lying about it. But why? Forget the nonsense about my being the one person in the world she could trust. Why would she send it to me?

But, if she did, then I had a pretty good idea of where it might be.

The eats revived me. I paid and left a hefty tip. Back out on the sidewalk, I couldn't see the brown suit. I headed west. When I turned on Eighth, I thought I saw the guy half a block back, but the sky was just starting to get light. After that, he stayed mostly out of sight. I didn't get another look at him until I stopped at a newsstand for more papers and saw a quick reflection in a plate-glass window. He was still the better part of a block behind me. What to do?

If I was right about the money, I wouldn't be able to check on it for another hour or so, anyway. And I worried that the bad brown suit was part of a team. Even if I thought I'd shaken him, I might not be unobserved. So I decided not to try to lose him and climbed the stairs at the Forty-Second Street station of the Ninth Avenue el. I waited in the middle of the platform and saw him again as he topped the stairs and turned away. It wasn't crowded that early. I didn't see him get on the train.

I didn't see him when I got off at Twenty-Third Street and went back to the Chelsea either. By then, the night had caught up with me, and I was yawning.

Tommy, the nightman, was still behind the desk. His normal expression was a queasy little smile that suggested something nasty. He sounded even oilier than normal when he said, "Good morning, sir. I think you should know that you have company, and the young lady is scrumptious, if you take my meaning."

That was his favorite phrase, "if you take my meaning," and I never understood why he was like that. Even then, the Chelsea had a reputation as a place where anything goes, but we also had a fair number of proper older ladies, women who had been there a long time. Sure, there was a lot of screwing and drinking and drugging, but most of the people who lived there didn't make much of it and stayed out of your business. Tommy acted like a horny kid who was sneaking into the burlesque show.

Going up the stairs to the third floor, I figured he meant that Anna was waiting in my room, but the moment I opened the door, I saw that was wrong.

Connie Nix was asleep on my bed. I shut the door quietly. This was another first.

Until now, whenever I suggested that we retire to my place, she said that it wasn't right for a respectable single girl to go to a man's hotel room. To which I replied, "Huh?"

But here she was. Maybe mentioning an old girlfriend wasn't such a bad idea. She was on top of the covers and had her big coat over her like a blanket. Boy, she looked sweet, scrumptious, even.

I took off my coat, sat in my chair, and left the lamp off. There was just enough light coming in the crack between the heavy drapes. I put my right foot up on the ottoman, rolled my pant leg up, and unbuckled my brace. It had begun to chaff, and it felt great to be able to flex my knee. It felt so good I took off my shoe and flexed my toes.

And so I was sitting there with one shoe off and one shoe on when I heard somebody putting a pick to my lock.

Right off the bat, I did the wrong thing. I should have grabbed my .38, but instead, I took three fast steps to the bed, grabbed Connie by the shoulders and pushed her down between the bed and the wall. Everything that happened after that is kind of confusing, and I know all this isn't right, but it is how I remember it, and this is as true as I can tell it.

Connie yelled really loud when I shoved her, and at the same time, I heard footsteps outside on the wrought-iron balcony. Right after that came the snap of the door lock opening, and then I thought about the pistol in the pocket of my coat neatly folded over the chair by the desk. My stick was there, too. I reached into my pocket and slipped on the knucks.

The door banged open against the wall, and I could see two guys bulling their way through. They looked like big guys. They probably couldn't see me in the dark as well as I could see them, so I tried to jump off the bed and roll across the room to my stick, but my knee gave way, and it turned out to be more crawling than rolling. About then, the window shattered behind the curtain. I made it to the desk and reached for my stick when hands grabbed me from behind, yanked me up, and somebody else started punching my face. I got smacked pretty good before I got one hand up around my head. Connie was still yelling. A brief flash of light cut through the room, and then it went dark again. I still sensed motion near the window. Really, all I was trying to do was to keep from being hit.

The hands that were holding my shoulders were pulled away. I twisted against them and saw two guys fighting in front of me and, I think, another guy behind them going for Connie. I was fumbling for the stick when I heard a loud rip and the drapes came loose. Morning light flooded the room, and finally I could see what was going on.

Two big guys, at least one with a knife, were wrestling right in front of me. As I watched, they went after each other viciously, arms in close to their bodies, both grunting and fighting for the knife.

Another guy was on his knees on the bed. He was trying to pull Connie up from the floor by her hair. She grabbed one of his hands and pushed away from the wall. His hand came down in front of her mouth, and she bit him as hard as she could. Blood flowed. He howled.

The two guys grappling in the middle of the room stumbled toward the broken window and fell to their sides. A fourth guy appeared from underneath the curtain that had fallen over him. It was the cheap brown suit. He took one look at the guys fighting in front of him and went right back out to the balcony.

I felt for my stick, grabbed it, and edged around the two guys on the floor to get to the bed. The guy there pulled his hand away from Connie's bloody mouth and slugged her. I got the crook of the cane around his neck and jerked it back with both hands. He landed on his back with a strangled scream. I got on top of him and pulped his face with the knucks.

The grunts and curses coming from behind me got more intense. I saw that both guys were smeared with blood, and so was my carpet. They were on their knees, barely moving but straining against each other until one of them stopped moving and collapsed against the other. The second one let go, and the first fell on his face and was still. I couldn't see the knife. The guy on his knees tried to get up, but I rabbit-punched him twice with the knucks. He went down and was quiet after that.

My room looked like hell.

Connie was on her knees on the bed, more angry than scared. She said, "You've been trying to get me up here for weeks. I finally show up and you kick me out of bed. Goddamn, what's a girl got to do?"

I'd never heard her curse before. Working in a speak will do that, I guess, or just being around me.

"Are you OK?"

She wiped some of the blood off her mouth, made a face when she saw it, and then spat on the guy on the floor. I got her a damp cloth from the bathroom. She cleaned up, told me I needed to do the same, and went to work on me. I had a bloody nose and two cuts near my left eye, one above and one below. She wasn't nearly as gentle and careful as she could have been and said I looked like hell.

I asked if she wanted to talk to the cops. "They'll be here pretty soon. I think it'd be better if you stayed out of it."

She agreed. I helped her into her coat, covering up most of the blood on her dress, and said, "Go down to the desk. Tell Tommy that I said he should give you a room. I'll be there as soon as I can."

"What the hell's going on, anyway? Who are those guys?"

"I don't know."

"I know it's none of my business, but do they have anything to do with your old girlfriend?" She sounded hurt or jealous, I couldn't tell which.

"Probably. Now, go. No, wait a minute. Here, put these in your purse." I gave her my .38 and knucks.

She got away before the crowd gathered in the hall. A few minutes later, I heard an ambulance outside, and then the guys in white showed up. They decided that the one guy was already dead. They turned him over and put him on a stretcher. He'd been stabbed and sliced so bad it made you sick to look at him. The other guy, the one I'd knocked out, had been cut pretty bad, too, so I guess they both had knives. He was still alive when they carried him out, but they said they didn't think he'd make it.

The guy who attacked Connie was in a bad way. I crumpled part of his windpipe with my stick and made a mess of his face. They said he'd be fine. They cleaned my nose and cuts again and taped them up nice before they carried out the two wounded guys and the dead one.

The truth is, they were working on me when the uniformed cops showed up. I said they might want to call Detective Ellis because these guys might have something to do with a homicide he was working.

Ellis got there twenty minutes later. He was pissed.

I told him some of the truth. I'd just got home. Was about to turn in when I heard somebody picking my lock. Before I could do anything they had the door open. One of them jumped me. While that was happening, a couple of guys broke in from the fire escape. You could see how they tore down my curtains. After that, it was confusing. They fought each other. One guy went back out the window. That's about it.

Ellis gave me a cop's cold, level stare. He knew I was lying, but, really, could he have expected anything else? Neither of us was fooling the other. He was wearing the same clothes he'd had on earlier at the Cloud Club and the warehouse, and he hadn't slept either. But nobody had been punching him in the face so, for once, he looked better than I did.

He lit a cigarette and used my blood-soaked rug as an ashtray.

"OK," he said. "Here's how it goes. Two nights ago, a bomb goes off half a block from your place, and there's a fresh corpse in a nearby alley. Coroner says it could be that he planted the thing and was too close when it went off. We're still not sure about that. And sometime last night, another man is beaten to death over near the East River docks with counterfeit papers made out in your name. Yeah, we checked, they're fake. And somebody's waiting up in the rafters, and they shoot a cop. Now four guys take it upon themselves to attack you here."

He paused, smoked, flicked ashes, and went on. "This doesn't add up, but you're in the middle of it. Explain it to me so I understand."

I found my missing shoe and sock under the desk and put them back on. "I can't explain it, Ellis. The simple truth is that I never saw those guys before. The guys who broke in here and beat me up, I don't know who they are either."

"And if you did, you wouldn't tell me because you'd take care of it yourself."

There was no need to agree with something that obvious, so I asked Ellis about Betcherman. "I got the idea from Malloy that there was something not completely kosher about him. If Malloy really was outside when Betcherman found the body, maybe he had something to do with it."

Ellis got his back up. "Detective Betcherman was an outstanding police officer. He will be missed—"

"Can the hearts and flowers, Ellis. He was bent. Find out who he double-crossed recently and you'll probably find your shooter. Here's something else to think about. Remember when we first got to the warehouse? Where was Betcherman? He was up on the second level in the back looking for the light switch or some such. Then he came back down to where we were. Where did the shots come from? The second level in the back where he had just been."

"Yeah, I'm working on that," he said, impatient to change the subject. "But back to the matter at hand. One of the witnesses here said that you had a woman here in your room."

"All right," I said. "You got me. It was your girlfriend."

He took a swing at my head, but I ducked and stifled a laugh.

A little later, with a quickly packed bag, I unlocked the door to a room on the fifth floor. It wasn't as big or as nice as mine. Just a bed and two chairs with a small table between them. My knucks and .38 were on a bedside table. Connie Nix was asleep in one of the armchairs and woke up right away. I was more than halfway sure that she'd be ready to take me up on my offer of a ticket back to California. I sat opposite her and explained that I'd talked to Ellis and he wasn't happy with what I said, but I kept her name out of it. "I also told him I don't know what's going on, but that's only half true."

"Is this something illegal that you've cooked up? Marie Therese says it's not, but she won't say anything bad about you."

I had to think a second before I answered. "It is illegal. I guess. I didn't start it, and I don't really know how or why I'm involved, but as they say, my name has come up. It boils down to this—there's a hundred thousand dollars, or maybe seventy-five thousand in cash floating around town, and it's got my name on it. At least that's what some people think, and they're willing to do whatever they need to do to take it. That's what just went on in my room, and, somehow, Jacob Weiss is involved. Do you know who he is?"

"Sure, Jacob the Wise. He runs the numbers. I never win. Marie Therese won five dollars about a month ago. Second time."

She was picking things up. "Did you know that he shelled out a hundred thousand dollars to ransom his accountant, Benny Numbers, who got kidnapped out West?"

She shook her head and gave me a quizzical look. "No, I heard Benny ran off with Jacob's mistress, and he killed them both, but I didn't believe it."

She got up, tossed her coat on the bed, and walked around behind my chair. Her hands came around and loosened my tie and pulled it off. She took off my coat and tossed it onto the bed over hers. Then she started rubbing my shoulders. I guess she could tell I was tired and tense, and her fingers dug in up near my neck where I was really tight.

"Poor Jimmy," she said. "All he's trying to do is sweet talk his waitress into the sack and bombs blow up and guys bust into his room."

She came around the chair to face me and got on my lap, her legs straddling mine, stretching her skirt tight across her thighs. She put my hands on her hips and when I moved them higher, she pushed them back down. "What's a girl to think about something like that?"

She leaned in and gave me a long serious kiss that started soft and warmed quickly.

I didn't know exactly what was going on, but I understood that Anna-Sophia-Sugartits was a professional at this kind of thing and Connie was still an amateur—an enthusiastic amateur, but not in the same league. And where, you ask, was Jimmy Quinn on that scale? Somewhere behind both of them, to be sure.

As Connie kissed me and pushed my hands down again, I realized that she wasn't ready to go as far or to be as persuasive as Anna had been, but right then, that wasn't important.

Like I said, such things may happen to millionaires and movie stars all the time, but they don't happen to guys like me, and when they happen twice, you just appreciate every second of it.

Believe me, I did.

118

CHAPTER ELEVEN

Mr. Quinn,
If you wish to continue our discussion of last evening, please
join me downstairs. There are additional matters of mutual
profitability that we might wish to consider.

Johann Klapprott

That was the note, written on thick textured stationery. Tommy from the front desk handed it to me. There was a Germanic-looking JK engraved in one corner. Boy, that was my week for fancy invitations. Get your name associated with a big stash of cash and everybody wants your company.

Tommy whispered, like it was a special secret, "This gentleman arrived in a Cadillac Phaeton."

I could tell I'd just gone up in his estimation if somebody was calling for me in a Phaeton.

Connie was asleep, on top of the covers and under her coat. Yeah, she was still a good girl, maybe not quite as good as she'd been before, but still good, dammit. I'd had my catnap, shaved and showered, hoping that the sound of the water might wake her up and tempt her to join in, but it didn't. I was almost dressed when Tommy knocked on the door.

"He's in the lobby," he said, suggesting that I was some kind of low-class dickweed to keep such a fine Phaeton owner waiting. "What do I tell him?"

I thought a bit more. "Tell him I'll be down directly."

By then, Connie was awake but groggy at the edges. She sat up, pulled the coat up to her neck, and said, "You're going to have a mouse under that eye."

She got up off the bed, gave my mouse a kiss, and took over the bathroom. I told her I'd see her that night. She didn't answer.

I finished dressing with a fresh shirt, a deep-red silk tie, knucks, pistol, and stick. I was wearing a light gray suit, one of my best.

As I was leaving, I realized that sometime in all the commotion downstairs, I'd lost my hat. I stopped at my room on the third floor and saw that the cleaning crew was at work. The hat was on the desk, where I'd left it.

In the lobby, Klapprott was chatting with a couple of older ladies, and judging by the way they smiled and giggled, he had turned on the charm. He wore a black pinstripe three-piece, red-and-black striped tie, and spit-shined black shoes. He had a calfskin glove on his left hand and held the other along with his decorative stick. When he saw me, he made excuses to the happy ladies and extended his hand. No gent would shake hands wearing gloves.

Smiling like sunshine, he said, "Mr. Quinn, a pleasure to see you. Again, allow me to apologize for Luther's behavior last night, though I hardly need to. Few men have handled him as efficiently as you did. Though, perhaps"—he gestured toward my bandaged face—"someone else was more successful."

"Yeah," I said. "I'm a popular fellow. Something about me just attracts attention. I wonder what the hell it could be."

"What, indeed? Perhaps we could discuss it over coffee. I have some outside. Shall we?"

Out at the curb sat a nicely turned out Caddy with the top down. A guy held open the door to the backseat for us. He wore a simple dark suit, not the full chauffeur's getup, and black gloves. I'd never seen him before. He got into the driver's compartment, maneuvered the long car into traffic, and turned south. The backseat was more luxurious than my room upstairs, even before the fight. There was a wicker picnic basket on the floor.

"Do you mind if we drive while we talk?" said Klapprott. "Perhaps I am overly suspicious, but I would like to be sure that our conversation is completely private. I have reason to believe that I have been followed recently."

"There's a lot of that going around."

"And we could do worse than touring the city on an autumn morning such as this, could we not?"

It was a good fall day, still cold even though the sun was up, and I remember his conversation, part of it anyway, as being genuine. The driver knew the city, and we meandered down toward Battery Park without stopping too often in the early traffic. Actually, the truth is I usually wasn't up at that hour, so I wasn't familiar with the traffic and I wasn't behind the wheel in those neighborhoods very often either, so what did I know?

"Have you thought about my offer?" Klapprott asked.

"Not really," I said. "Since you went to all this trouble, I thought you'd want to talk about the money." He gave me a look of phony befuddlement, and I said, "Don't say 'What money?' You'll disappoint me."

He chuckled. "You're right, of course, but I must add that my interest in your establishment is completely genuine. This really is a matter of two birds, but my first concern is the fifty thousand dollars."

"Fifty thousand? All right, tell me about it."

"It is an inheritance. A new member of the Free Society, a particular zealous young man from Chicago, wishes to donate it to the organization. His name is Justice Schilling, and he is a younger son in a large and fractious family. He was always his grandmother's favorite, and when she died, she left him the largest portion of her estate. While his parents, uncles, and brothers received property or real estate, his bequest was cash. I assure you he has all the documentation to prove his claim. He had received the money and contacted our organization when his sister simply stole it. And for reasons about which I can make only the most insubstantial conjecture, she sent it to you, Mr. Quinn."

"She sent me fifty thousand dollars? That's some story."

"I must admit that, at first, I did not believe this young man, but as I said, he has proof and he gave me this."

Klapprott fished a folded bill from his vest pocket. It was a ten-dollar gold certificate, stained with some kind of brown wax. He said, "I see by your expression that you are familiar with this sample. Excellent. You have accepted delivery then?"

I let that pass and said, "I've heard a lot of stories. Why should I buy this one?"

"When you hear what this young man has to say and you see his documents, I have no doubt that you will accept the legitimacy of his claim, and, of course, you will be compensated, well compensated. If you are amenable, we could speak with him now. Would that be convenient? It won't take long, no more than an hour, I assure you."

I shrugged. "All right."

He tapped the back of the driver's compartment with his cane and coughed out a few curt words in German. Settling back in his seat, he produced a green thermos bottle and two silver cups from the picnic basket. He messed with pouring coffee as he spoke. "In your office, I noticed that you read a great many newspapers, so perhaps you know something of the changes that are going on in Europe these days. Tell me, please, what are your politics?"

"I'm a saloonkeeper. Anything that lets me do my business and make a decent living is fine with me."

"Excellent," he said, clapping me on the knee. "That is precisely what the party is attempting to bring to Germany." He handed me a cup of coffee and poured another for himself.

"A toast," he said, holding up his cup. "To our mutual good fortune. You will find this somewhat unusual. It is a special Austrian blend not often found in this country. The flavor you will notice is Prussian cinnamon."

It was strong with a bittersweet edge not to my taste, but I sipped it to be polite.

"Tell me, what do you know of National Socialism, the Nazi party?"

"I've seen the little guy with the Charlie Chaplin mustache, and I've read a few things in the papers, but I don't know anybody overseas, so I don't pay much attention."

"The newsreels make us look like crazed fanatics, but that is not the case. For years, there has been so much anti-German hysteria."

"Yeah, the war had something to do with that."

I thought he'd be insulted, but he wasn't. His expression became grim.

"I know exactly how stupid that war was. I was right there in the middle of it. I know the fools who ordered us to go up out of the trenches. The politicians, the priests, the bankers, the industrialists, the newspapers, the professors, all the bosses, they lied to us. They lied to get us into it, and they lied about the conduct of the fighting. It was a horrible, wasteful war, so terrible that there can never be another. We veterans understand that. You may have read about the mutiny at Kiel that helped to end it. It was primarily an action by sailors and naval officers. I was in a position to take a small part, but by then it was too late. They forced us to accept a peace that has been more damaging than a true military defeat."

By then, I think he'd forgotten that I was sitting next to him. And, to be honest, I've got to admit that I can't really remember everything he said, but I do remember his tone and his emotion.

"Even so, we might have survived all that, but then the goddamn French occupied the Ruhr and everything went to hell. Nobody had a job. Our money was worthless. As bad as things are here, you can't imagine what it was like in Germany. But now we're changing that. We want stability, a return to simple values and simple truths. We want an economy that is fair to everyone, not just the ones at the top. The first slogan you see on the wall in any of our party offices reads simply, 'Freedom and Bread.' That's what we're working for. It really is that simple.

"We want to put Germany back together. Return the economy to its former strength and then become self-sufficient. We have no wish and no need to conquer anyone. We certainly don't go around like anarchists, throwing bombs. Ours is a movement of the young people. Herr Hitler is many things—a visionary, a man who can inspire a nation and revive the middle class. He's only forty-three years old. That may seem old to someone as young as you are, but in Germany we have a tradition of allowing senile old men to tell us what to do. Herr Hitler will be different, I promise you that. More coffee?"

He poured more. A sniff told me it hadn't got any better. I didn't touch it.

"No one will give us a new Germany. We must create it ourselves. We want to give the German people a new ideal. We use the language and music of the military because that is what the average German is used to hearing. It gets his attention and it works on his emotions, but those of us who are doing the real work don't need all of the Sturm und Drang.

"The talk of racial purity is exaggerated and, besides, much of it comes from America. Have you read Grant's *The Passing of the Great Race*? No? I'll loan you my copy. I'm sure you will find it illuminating. I know that some Jews put loyalty to their fellow Jews above Germany, but any Jew who is a good German has nothing to fear from us. If you listen to Father Coughlin on the radio, you understand what I'm saying.

"The Communists, anarchists, and Reds—they're another story. I've seen what they can do to an organization, the way they can destroy from within and the cowardly tactics they use with their bombs. There will be no place for them in a new Germany. If we're going to go to war with anybody, it will be those bastards."

By then, I couldn't understand him. The car stopped. Klapprott got out and another guy, somebody I'd never seen, got in. Klapprott said something to him, tipped his hat to me, and walked away. I tried to say something but couldn't make my mouth move. Like the greenest clodhopper that ever fell off the turnip truck and stumbled into a clip joint, I'd let him slip me a Mickey.

If I'd drunk much more of that goddamned Prussian cinnamon, it would've knocked me out. That's what a Mickey is supposed to do. As it was, I was so dizzy I could hardly sit up. My hands and arms got tingly and flapped around like flippers. When I tried to speak, the sound that came out was a kind of groan, not words. I didn't black out completely, but I couldn't focus my eyes or my attention. Everything became kind of liquid. So did I.

I don't know how long we were in the car. I do know they stopped and put the top up. When they did that, I knew I should try to get out. I managed to get halfway off the seat and slid to the floor. They left me there. One of them went through my pockets and took the .38. He missed the knucks. I heard them talking more German, and I tried not to go under. Bad things happened to guys who got taken for a ride. How bad was this one going to be?

The car stopped again, and some time later, the driver got out. Feeling was coming back to my arms and hands, and I thought I might even be able to get to my knees. I waited and thought that I smelled saltwater and creosote and understood that I was probably back at the warehouse. Made sense to go back to a familiar spot to do the dirty work. My guts turned to water.

The driver came back and started the engine. A moment later, I heard a rumble and felt it through the floorboard. When the rumble ended, the car rolled forward a few yards into darkness. More rumbling ended with the crunch of heavy doors rolling shut against each other. There was more talk I couldn't understand,

and as the jungle juice wore off, I realized things had gotten quiet. If the cops had finished their work and let the warehouse open for business, Klapprott had probably sent everybody home.

When they dragged me out of the car, I didn't resist or even look at them. It was easy to stay limp. Too easy. They left me lying on an oil-stained concrete floor and snapped on a light. I saw a wooden table and a wheeled office chair. Most of the loading dock was dark.

It was quiet for what seemed like a long time, and finally I heard more men speaking German, and a few lights came on. Rough hands hauled me into the office chair, and a couple of beefy-looking guys in worn-out, fraying suits used a roll of friction tape to strap my forearms to the arms of the chair. When I looked at them, I let my head wobble and my eyes roll. They argued in German about what to do with my feet and wound up taping my left ankle to one of the chair's little wheels and my right to the table leg. One of them noticed my brace then. They talked about it, and from their tone, I think they decided that I wasn't going to be running anywhere, so they didn't need to worry about me.

They left me alone, and my eyes grew accustomed to the dark. I could make out the hallway that led to the office and part of the warehouse floor with shelves and pallets. I was at street-level. Most of the storage area was behind me. Over the next twenty minutes or so, six more guys wandered in. Like the first two, they were big, thick-necked, and thick-shouldered, blond and balding, wearing clothes that were a long way from new. Four of them brought grinders of beer. Two drank from flasks. They polished off the beer fast enough and a couple of them went out for more.

They lazed around, smoking cigars and cigarettes. Once in a while, one of them would walk over and give me a thump on the head, and the others would laugh. I had no doubt they were looking forward to working me over. I didn't look directly at them. I let my head loll and tried to act like the knockout drops were still working. I was also twisting my arms and legs to test the tightness of the tape. They hadn't stripped off any of my clothes, so I had some play in my arms. I could push them forward several inches. Given a minute or so to twist and tug, I might have been able to pull my arms free from the coat sleeves, but I didn't think any of these guys were going to give me a minute. Since they hadn't been as careful with my legs, I thought I might be able to get the left one loose from the chair wheel. With a little leverage, I might move the table with my right. It wasn't that heavy. But it wasn't going to do much good against six Kraut bruisers.

That time in the warehouse stretched out in an acid combination of boredom and fear. It ended when another guy came in from the hallway and the six bohunks sat up straight. It was Luther, Klapprott's number one thug, the big shit that I'd gone a round with in the cellar of my speak. He looked nasty and happy to see me, tied down as I was. The moment I saw him, I realized it was likely that I'd die in that warehouse. That sobered me. I tried not to let them see it, though if they'd looked, they would have seen sweat on my forehead. Luther had small bandages on his nose and hand, and he held his left shoulder stiffly. He barked some kind of order, and the other six stood up. He was carrying a red leather case with a leather handle. It sounded heavy when he set it on the table beside me. I glanced at him through half-closed eyes like I was still goofy.

Luther said something to the youngest of the thugs and pointed at me. The kid looked confused and worried. Luther backhanded me across the chops. I moaned and drooled blood.

The kid stood in front of me and haltingly said, "You will say to us what is the money."

I stayed stupid and moaned again. Another guy came around from somewhere behind me and threw a bucket of water right in my face, half of it going down my throat. My eyes sprang open and I coughed, and they knew I was back among the living.

The kid said again, "You will say to us what is the money."

There was some more back and forth in German, and finally one of the older guys challenged Luther. Seemed to me there was some question as to who was really in charge. It ended when the older guy said to me, "Where is the money? Tell us and this will be over." It came out something like "Ver ist duh moony?" He went on, "If you do not tell us what you know, Luther will cause you great pain."

As he was asking it, I was thinking that if I told them where I thought the money was and I was right, then they'd get it, then come back and kill me. If I was wrong, they'd come back and pound me some more.

Something about what he'd said in English caused a lot more talk in German with most of them chiming in. While they were yakking away, I caught some movement behind them and saw someone peek out of the hallway, someone with a soup strainer mustache. Arch Malloy, maybe. Whoever it was, he ducked back so quickly I couldn't tell anything more about him. I tried like hell to convince myself it was Malloy.

I knew I couldn't play dopey anymore, but I didn't have to say anything. I spat blood on the floor and stared at the older guy. He didn't like it.

Luther shoved him aside, gave me an open-handed smack, ripped my tie off, and tore open my shirt. He took off his coat, revealing a big shoulder holster with a broom-handle Mauser under his arm. He clapped a clammy hand across my throat to hold me still and hit me hard in the stomach. It knocked the wind out of me, and I sprayed his face with blood. He cursed and smacked me again, then he went for his red case. He barked more orders.

The older guy said, "He has a device, a—" He stopped, searching for a word. "A machine that explodes dynamite. It is an electrical."

Luther was screwing two long wire leads to terminals on a box that was just bigger than his fists. It had a T-shaped handle on top. Luther said something more, something the older guy didn't like, and held out the wires. The older guy took them unhappily. Luther kept talking and indicated that he should hold them to my chest. As the older guy took a hesitant step toward me, Luther gave the handle a sharp twist. The guy froze with a grimace on his face, yelled, and threw up his hands. That jerked one of the wires off the detonator—if that's what it was. Luther laughed like hell. So did some of the others.

The older guy was steamed and ripped into Luther with a rush of German. I couldn't understand a word, but I knew "Go fuck yourself" was part of it. The two of them stood chest-to-chest for a short moment until the older guy broke it off and went up the steps to the hallway and out. Luther said something nasty to his back and looked to the others for support. Most of them nodded in agreement. Whatever they were saying, I didn't like it.

I liked it less when Luther turned back to me. He took off his coat, loosened his tie, and rolled up his sleeves. He reconnected the wire to the detonator and tried to get one of the others to take the wires. They laughed and backed off.

Luther called the first kid over again, and he went back to his broken English. "You will say to us what is the money."

I shifted my feet a little to get them underneath me and sat up. Luther was glad, I think, that I didn't answer. He rushed right up into my face, trying to make me flinch back. When he got close, I jerked forward. I couldn't stand, but my hands had enough play under the friction tape to stretch to his belt. I grabbed it and pulled. He lurched into me. Recalling what Connie did, I went for the closest vulnerable spot and bit down as hard as I could on his nose.

He howled. I bit down harder and ground my teeth and twisted my neck. Somebody started shooting.

I wish I could tell you I remember details like the savage taste of his blood, but I don't. I remember how great it felt to hear the gunshots. If the other Nazi thugs had guns, they'd show them off, and these guys didn't. That meant whoever was shooting was on my side. And when Luther rolled off me, there they were—Arch Malloy and Mercer Weeks.

Malloy fired twice at the ceiling, and most of the Kraut thugs, led by Luther, ran to the back of the warehouse. Mercer Weeks came down the steps to where I was. Four of the biggest guys fanned out in front of him, ignoring Malloy.

I've never seen anybody do what Mercer Weeks did then. Too experienced to hit a guy with a bare fist, he worked with knucks on one hand and a length of pipe in the other and those heavy brogans on his feet. He was long and rangy, but somehow he made himself compact. I watched him cut down three guys, sliding through the brawl like smoke. I never saw the pipe raised. I never saw the fist cocked. Three of those big beefy guys went down in less time than I can say it. The fourth ran.

Weeks pulled out a folding knife, sliced through the tape, and said, "You sure find your way into a hell of a lot of trouble, Quinn."

Weeks said he'd been following me in his car since I left Jacob's apartment early that morning. By then, we were upstairs from the speak in the kitchen of the Cruzon Grill. Vittorio did a good lunch business and didn't want us to take up a prime table. Besides, the way I'd been beat up and drenched and had my shirt torn, I'd scare the paying customers. So they made room for us in a corner of the busy kitchen. I had a ham sandwich and coffee. Weeks and Malloy had rib steaks, fries, and beer. A good lunch was the least I could do for a couple of guys who'd saved my ass.

As Weeks made his way through the meal, he told me the guy in the brown suit and glasses had been waiting for me when I got in the cab outside. Actually, Weeks spotted the guy and his partner behind us when we went up to the East Side from the speak. On the way back downtown, Weeks followed them following me to the diner in Times Square. After that, when I got on the el, he guessed that I was heading home and beat me back to the Chelsea. He was there to see the two of them sneak up to the wrought-iron balcony and break in through the window. Weeks didn't know anything about the other guys who picked the lock and came in from the hall, but he did see the brown suit come hustling back out of the window a minute or so later. He waited in his car through the ambulance and Ellis and the cops and finally, a couple of hours later, the arrival of Klapprott in his Caddy Phaeton. Then he was behind us on our little drive down toward Battery Park and, it shames me to admit, he was witness to my humiliating Mickey Finn.

Here's where it started to get interesting. Weeks saw them drop me at the warehouse, and he watched the guys who were working there clear out. When the first of the Kraut thugs showed up, Weeks decided to call the speak to find out if they knew what I was up to. Frenchy answered and said he'd just got off the line with an unnamed party who told them he was holding me and would trade me for the fifty thousand dollars that was hidden in the cellar. Frenchy had two hours to deliver the money. Frenchy and Weeks talked it over and came to the conclusion that the whole thing could be a trick to get them out of the speak. Remember, neither Frenchy nor Weeks knew who Klapprott was. Not then. They'd seen him, but Frenchy hadn't heard his voice and Weeks didn't know his name. Weeks told Frenchy where I was, and Malloy volunteered to help while Frenchy and Fat Joe stayed at the speak.

After Weeks had gone through that for me, Malloy piped in, "Describe this Klapprott character."

"About forty," I said, "natty dresser, blond, pale eyes, carries a Malacca cane. Both times I've seen him, he was wearing calfskin gloves."

Malloy nodded. "He's a partner, a 'silent' partner they said, in the group of Germans that own the warehouses. He's been around now and again."

"Ever see him with a big lug, name of Luther? He's a lush, and he doesn't have a nose. Well, he did until about an hour ago."

"Most of the guys who worked there were big, and they were all Krauts—not that I hold that against a man. And as I told you, it was not completely out of the ordinary for the management to tell every man jack of us to vacate the premises for an hour, and I mean that day or night. You see, those three warehouses are about as busy at night as they are during the day. It's true that I've not worked at any other warehouses, and I didn't work at that one for very long, but it struck me as odd. And something else that struck me was that there seems to be an unusually large number of small items. You think of a warehouse as a place that holds vast numbers of this, that, and whatever, but Number 115 isn't nearly as large as Number 117 and Number 120, and I seldom saw items that couldn't be handled by one man or two at most.

"So it's good that I'm done with the place, assuming, that is, I am once again employed."

Having just pulled my ass out of the wringer, he chose a good time to bring up the subject. I said, "Come in around four thirty. Frenchy will show you the ropes. And you'd best bring the Luger."

I turned to Weeks and said, "Mercer, let's talk in my office."

Downstairs, I found a note from Marie Therese on my desk. It said, *Anna wants you to know she is at the Lombardy, Suite 512.* I could tell she had been pissed off when she wrote it. I sat down and worried that I was walking around in a torn shirt and blood-stained suit. The idea of changing clothes again—for the second time that early in the day—really pissed me off. The ruin of a good suit by a couple of Kraut asswipes pissed me off even more.

Mercer Weeks spread out on the divan, pulled his works out of his pocket, and rolled a smoke. "Curious, isn't it," he said, "that this fellow Klapprott thinks you've got *his* money."

"His story is that it's an inheritance that was stolen from some kid who wants to donate it to this outfit Klapprott runs, the Free Society of Teutonia. They've got something to do with the Nazis over in Germany."

"What the hell does that mean?"

"The guys that were working me over—the guys that you and Malloy took care of—they were Krauts. All I know is they think I've got their money, and Jacob thinks I've got his money. That's one part of all this, right? But there's something else you're inter-ested in and for that, I'm the man you want to talk to."

Weeks looked baffled. I turned around to the safe behind the desk and dialed the combination. The package was on top. I took it out and put it on the edge of my desk close to him. "I think this is yours."

He shot me a suspicious look through the smoke and touched the open flap of the cardboard box like it might explode.

I said, "You can see that the wrong address is on the label. I don't know how long it was at the post office before Mr. Smiles brought it in. That was the day before yesterday."

He took out one of the ledgers, and when he saw what it was, all the color drained out of his face.

"Sweet Jesus, Benny's books." He put down the ledger and took out everything else in the box. It was nothing but books. He riffled through the pages and the loose sheets of paper inside. When he looked up at me again, his voice was hoarse and hard. "What do you know about these, Quinn?"

"Nothing. Until last night, when Jacob told me the story about Benny being snatched, I didn't even know he kept books like these. I didn't know what the hell they were when I opened the box, much less that they had anything to do with you. The Chicago address, the stuff about paper napkins, I don't know what it is. Do you?"

Weeks sagged back on the divan, and his face softened but only for a second. Then he said, "OK, this means there is a chance that Benny is still alive. After all these months, I don't know how the hell that could be, but maybe he is. And that's what's important to me and Jacob. We need Benny more than we need the money."

That much I'd figured out already. It didn't take a genius. "Maybe I've got a line on the money, too, I can't say. Hell, I really can't say anything. None of this makes a damn bit of sense. Can you and Jacob trust me?"

He smoked and thought for a long time before he said anything else. "I guess we've got to. You've been straight with us so far. You insulted Jacob, but maybe he had it coming, and that's not important, anyway. Benny is important, you got that? Our operation is nothing without him, and you're going to see that he comes back."

"Weeks, I can't . . ."

Ignoring me, he gathered up the books and the box and went to the door. He stopped and turned around before he left. "Jacob needs to know about these right away, but we'll be keeping an eye on you. Don't fuck this up."

His seriousness was not lost on me. But the first thing I needed to do was to find out if the money was where I thought it was. After that, well, we'd see.

And let me take one second here to say something else. In the years that have passed, the things that happened in the warehouse that morning have become famous. All right, a little bit famous among the low-life thugs in a few disreputable neighborhoods, and I need to set things straight.

According to some versions of the story, I bit Luther's nose completely off and spit it out. That could be true. In all the excitement, I honestly don't remember. But other people, a lot of other people, say that I bit Luther's nose off and swallowed it. That's not true. Not at all. I'd remember if I ate it. Yes, my face and mouth were bloody, but that was because they'd been slapping me around. So, for the record, I did not eat his nose.

Having something like that in your reputation isn't flattering, but it does cause some guys to be careful when they're around you, and that can be useful.

CHAPTER TWELVE

After Weeks left, I bent too close to shut the safe and noticed the dirty ten-spot and the key with the brass tag. Three Fingers had been in last night and said he wanted it, but he vamoosed before I could get it. With all the business about Jacob the Wise, I'd forgot about Three Fingers. But now I had an idea about what it might be, so I slipped it into my vest pocket and locked up.

I found Fat Joe sitting at my table reading my newspapers and smoking a cigar. I said, "That piece you keep in the coat closet, I need it."

He didn't look up from the paper. "Suppose I was to have a fucking emergency."

"This is a fucking emergency."

He grumbled some more, went to the coat closet, and came back with something hidden in his massive mitt. He passed a little Smith with a two-inch barrel to me under the table. I put it in my coat pocket and told him to tell Frenchy to bring his truck when he came in. We might be needing it later. Before I left, I said, "Come to think of it, we could have more fucking emergencies. Best be prepared."

Back at the Chelsea, I found that my room was still a wreck, so I grabbed a clean shirt and another suit, a navy three-piece, and went up to the room on the fifth floor. Connie was still there. She'd showered and the room was sweet with the perfume of her soaps or whatever. She wore a navy blue skirt and matching coat over a white blouse. She looked great. She took one look at me and said, "Jesus wept and shat, somebody beat you up again? Sit down." The speak was having a terrible influence on her.

She still had the tape and bandages and set to work on my mug for the second time, and she was none too gentle about it because she was mad at me. "What's going on, Jimmy? I want you to tell me the truth. Don't give me the soft soap with some story about an old girlfriend. You owe me that."

I explained that Klapprott had the idea that I was holding fifty thousand dollars that belonged to him. He tried to snatch me to get Frenchy to fork it over, but his thug Luther had different ideas and was working me over when Mercer Weeks and Malloy came to the rescue of my sorry ass.

"I have no idea why he thinks this money is his or how he found out that I had anything to do with it. Hell, I don't even know why I'm involved, but you're right, I owe you that."

I remembered what Jacob had said about trying to persuade Signora Sophia or Anna or whoever the hell she was to deliver the ransom for Benny. *I am asking you as an honorable man. If you agree to do this, I will be in your debt. You can ask anything of me. Anything. Weeks is my witness.*

"If you think it's time to catch the train back to California, I'll buy the ticket and help you pack. You see, this isn't over, and it's probably going to get nastier. I'm tired of people following me and pounding on me and knowing more about what's going on than I do. If this money everybody talks about really exists, then maybe I've got a line on where it is. That's the next step."

"Fine," she said with a smile. "I'll help."

I spent another five minutes explaining why I had to do this by myself. It did no good. Hell, I might as well admit it. I've always been attracted to strong-willed women, and I've seldom been able to get them to do what I want them to do. A contradiction that comes with the territory, I guess.

When I went to change clothes, I saw that the light gray suit was ruined, and that pissed me off even more. I was down to my skivvies before I noticed that Connie was directing her complete attention to something outside the window. My near-naked condition made her blush. If I'd been more of a gentleman, I guess I'd have gone into the bathroom or something, but it was too late for that.

"OK," I said, tying my tie, "I expect there's going to be somebody outside watching for me, and they'll follow us. We'll let them, and then we'll shake them. After we've done that, we'll find out if I'm right about the location of the loot."

I checked the straps on the brace, opened the gun to make sure there was an empty chamber under the hammer, and put on my coat. I looked pretty good as long as you didn't notice my face.

"Without being obvious about it," I said, "you're going to be on the lookout for this guy or these guys that will try to follow us."

"Where are we going?"

"We'll start uptown." On the way out, we stopped at my room, and I got some cash from the lockbox in my closet and stopped again at the front desk to use the phone. I called the speak.

"Frenchy," I said. "Got some business to take care of, so I'll be late getting in. . . . Connie's with me. . . . No, it doesn't mean that. . . . " She rolled her eyes. "Did Fat Joe tell you about the truck? Good. . . . No, I'll tell you later, I don't know yet. Bye."

Outside on the street, I hailed a cab. As we were getting in, Connie said, "There are two guys watching us. No . . . one guy and maybe a kid."

"Workmen's clothes? Caps?"

"Yes, they're getting into a car."

The cabbie said, "Where to, Mac?"

"Plaza Hotel, around back on Fifty-Eighth Street, and there's a guy following us." I turned to Connie. "In what? What kind of car?"

"I couldn't tell. It's black."

The cabbie checked the mirror and said, "Yeah, I've got him."

"There's an extra buck in it for you if you lose him." I held up a bill, and he hit the gas.

If I was halfway right in what I was thinking, these guys were from out of town. They didn't have a chance of keeping up with a well-trained native. We had a wild ride up Sixth Avenue, bouncing around the backseat. The hack juked through the traffic just like I used to on foot, leaving a chorus of angry horns in our dust. Connie was sure we were going to die and grabbed me and held on as tight as she could. I thought that was pretty nice.

My idea had been that if we couldn't shake the tail before we got to the rear entrance to the hotel, we'd get out, go through to the lobby, and slip the bell captain a bill to jump the cab line before another car could get around the block. But that wasn't going to be necessary, so I told the cabbie to take us back to East Thirty-Fourth Street, and we wouldn't need the speed demon act.

"What act?" he said and hit the gas.

At Thirty-Fourth Street, I gave him a tip that doubled the fare, and he roared off. Connie asked what we were doing.

I put my arm around her shoulder and said, "First, we're going to go around the block to make sure nobody else is following us." We ambled and turned around three or four times until I was sure we were on our own.

"OK," I said. "Over the past few days, I've heard a lot of stories—knocking over the Denver Mint, kidnapping a bootlegger, a trip out West, a stolen inheritance. I don't know how true those stories are, but for now, let's assume that there's something behind them, right?"

She nodded reluctantly, probably thinking I was a little nuts, but I didn't mind. It was a nice afternoon on the cool side. I was walking with a pretty girl and, for the moment, nobody was trying to beat me up.

"Now, we've got Jacob and Weeks saying that they forked over a hundred grand for Benny. I believe that. I believe it because they've got the money and because Benny is that important to their business.

"And I've got Anna, this old girlfriend who's not really an old girlfriend, saying that she sent seventy-five thousand dollars to me from Toledo. In four boxes, by the way. For now, we won't try to figure out why she would do something as crazy as that. But why would she lie about it? She didn't ask for a loan. In fact, she seems to be pretty well set up. I don't think she was trying to impress me, so again, let's assume it's true. There's probably a connection between the two stories, but, for now, we won't worry about that either. Instead, we're going to think about how she did it. How did she send four boxes from Toledo to New York?"

Connie shrugged her shoulders. "Post office?"

"Nope. That." I pointed my stick at the red and white diamond sign above the door of a storefront across the block:

RAILWAY
EXPRESS
AGENCY

You saw their green trucks all over the city. The Railway Express was kind of like the regular mail, but they had to accept anything you could ship on a train. I'd never done any business with them, but I thought they were more secure than the regular mail. Assuming that Anna wasn't traveling by car and she wanted to keep a large number of bank notes safe, shipping them by train was maybe her best bet.

Connie and I went inside and had to wait on line for one of three clerks. It didn't take long.

When we got to the counter, I asked a tired, bored-looking guy if he had anything for Jimmy Quinn.

He moseyed back to a set of accordion files on a shelf and went to the Q section. He came back with several sheets of smudgy gray carbon paper stapled together. I could see a big square block stamped across the front: HOLD FOR with my name written beneath it.

"Sign here. Need to see your ID," he said, passing a form across the counter.

I showed him my driver's license, the only official paper I carried, and scrawled my name.

"What is it?" I asked.

He looked at the bottom of the sheets and spoke slowly, sounding out the first word. "Yampah Hot Springs Mineral Water. Four crates."

"Where's it from?"

"Denver."

"Can you deliver it to an address here in the city tonight?"

He shook his head. "Tomorrow, day after more likely."

A sign on the wall behind him said they were open until nine. "We'll pick it up later," I said as he handed me the carbons.

"Take these to the desk around the corner."

"One more thing. Do you have any storage lockers for rent?"

He shook his head. "Closest are at Penn Station, and you might try the new bus terminals. I hear they got 'em too."

As we left, I thought for the first time that those crates might really be stuffed with cash. Damn, I could take Frenchy's truck and load it up and drive away a rich man, maybe with Anna, maybe with Connie, maybe by myself. I know that a lot of guys have had such ideas and given in when they've had the opportunity. Maybe some of them even got away with it, but I knew better, and it wasn't really a serious temptation, just a wild hair that could get me in a lot of trouble.

Connie was thinking the same thing. She had a bright dreamy look in her eyes, and I could almost see cartoon dollar signs floating overhead. She sobered up pretty quick and said, "Do you think those crates really do have money in them?"

"We'll find out soon enough, but there's another matter we've got to take care of."

I explained about Three Fingers. She said, "Yeah, I saw him at your table."

"Yeah, that guy. He gave me a ten-spot to hold something for him for twenty-four hours. It's a key with a tag and a number. Might open one of those lockers you can rent for an hour or a day. I think it would be good to know what it is."

We walked a few long blocks west on Thirty-Fourth Street, then down to Thirty-Third and the big stone building that took up the whole block. We crossed Seventh and went through the doors to the wide staircase that led down to the main concourse. Connie grabbed my arm tight, and as we went down the stairs, she held back, surprised and a little scared at the size of the place. She'd only been in the city for a few months. We hadn't stepped out very often because we were working so hard. With the ridiculously cheap prices we charged for the good booze we sold, the joint was open just about every hour that we thought we could sell a drink. If we decided to close for a Sunday, I mostly went to the movies or walked or slept in. I knew Marie Therese had shown Connie around, but that day with me was her first look at Penn Station. From the outside it was a massive spread of granite walls and columns. Inside, it was glass and girders and streaming afternoon sunlight. It almost made you dizzy because it was so big, but then you got swallowed up in the tides of people hurrying to catch trains, and if you didn't move as fast as they did, you were in the way, and they'd knock you down and not look back.

Connie made me stop on the stairs while she drank it all up.

"Wow," she whispered.

The truth is, I walked or drove past it every week, but I didn't go into the place very often myself, and I had to agree. It was worth a *wow*.

They'd moved the information booth to the center of the main level since the last time I'd been there. Once we found it, they told us there were three places where we could rent storage lockers.

One of them was at the Pennsylvania Motor Coach line, right there in the station. The keys there didn't match the one back in my vest pocket. Neither did the other two. Back at the booth, they came up with a list of the other bus stations. There were nine more. The truth is, I didn't know from buses. The whole idea of a bus that would take you from, say, Chicago to New York was new. I'd seen them around in the streets, but I'd never been on one.

Most of the bus companies were within a few blocks, so we didn't need a taxi or a trolley. We just started with the closest and worked our way out. As we were leaving the station, I got a strong sense of somebody watching us. I stopped and turned around at the top of the Seventh Avenue stairs, and there below me was a huge open area filled with people who were paying no attention to us. Connie asked what was wrong. I told her, and she said she felt it too. We stood there staring down for a minute or so, maybe longer, but we were wrong. Nobody was following us. Not then.

The closest terminal was owned by an outfit called Nevin. It was right across the street. There was a second Nevin terminal a block away on Thirty-First near Sixth. No lockers at either. They did have lockers at the Herald Square Terminal and the Public Service Terminal near the library, but they weren't the right kind. We had a short slog over to Forty-Second Street.

I felt eyes on the back of my neck again, but that was still just nerves. Both Connie and I were short enough that we were submerged in the thick slow crowd. I grabbed a handful of the back of her jacket with my right hand to keep us from being separated. I had to work to keep up with the foot traffic because with the stick, I was slow, and Connie was gawking at all the burlesque shows and dancehalls and the guys with sandwich boards for cheap Chinese joints and street preachers telling us we were going to hell. At night, the lights and the neon made the street dreamy, exotic, and sinful. In the afternoon, it just looked dirty and tired. I don't think she saw it that way.

The Dixie Hotel fit right in at Times Square. It had been open for about a year and had already gone bust, but it was still open.

The Central Union Terminal was directly underneath, so it was easy for people to find, I guess.

There was a ramp leading down from the sidewalk to a crowded waiting room. Two sets of doors, one on our left and one across the room, were marked To Buses. Connie saw the sign for the women's across the way and said she'd be right back. As I went to the ticket office, I tried to look for familiar faces, but the place was too busy. I asked the guy at the ticket window about storage lockers. He said they were in the baggage room on the Forty-Third Street side of the turntable. I asked what the turntable was, and he said, "That way," pointing to the far set of doors to the buses.

I went through them and saw what he meant. Two ramps went up to Forty-Third Street. On my level was a big metal turntable, more than thirty feet wide. As I stood there, a bus came down one of the ramps and stopped in the middle of the metal plate. As soon as the bus rocked on its brakes, the turntable rotated a few degrees and the bus pulled into one of ten slips that branched off of the hub. I guess it was a good way to maneuver a lot of buses and people in a limited space, but it stank of gasoline and exhaust. The baggage room was straight ahead through a glass door. Inside, I saw that a guy working behind a counter handled the big suitcases and stuff. A bank of smaller coin-operated lockers stood against one wall. Bingo.

Number 43 was padlocked. I asked the counterman what that meant. He checked a clipboard and said it was past due by one day. It'd cost four bits to get the lock off. I gave him a buck for another day. He took off the padlock and went back behind the counter. I opened the locker and found a banged-up valise filled with wadded dirty clothes. I poked gently with my pen for a few seconds, then closed the bag and put it back. Three Fingers might have had a fortune in emeralds at the bottom, but I wasn't about to go rooting around through his skivvies to find it.

About then, another bus came in, and I heard them making announcements in the waiting room. People were pushing through the doors, and I had to go against the tide to get back into the waiting room. Connie was standing outside the door of the women's looking for me. Three Fingers was behind her, scanning the crowd. If he'd seen her, it didn't look like he recognized her. He knew me right away, and by the surprised look on his face, he wasn't expecting to see me.

After that, everything moved fast.

They made more announcements, and it seemed like everybody who'd been sitting on the benches picked up their bags and headed for the doors. Three Fingers took a step toward me. Connie saw me and headed my way. Somebody bumped into me hard from behind and pushed on past me. It was the boy, the same boy who'd stopped me outside the Chrysler Building. He ran straight at Three Fingers and swung at him with something, a knife or maybe a razor, that drew blood. Three Fingers screamed "Fuck!" at the top of his lungs, and that made everybody stop and stare at him. The boy turned back toward me and ran like hell. All that happened right next to Connie, and she stood there, shocked, with her mouth open. Three Fingers cursed again and ran past me, following the boy back through the doors to the buses. I stuck with them.

People were lined up for the bus in the closest slip. They yelled as the boy pushed his way through and dashed out onto the turntable just as another bus on the opposite side backed out of a slip. The kid was fast, not as fast as me in my prime, but he knew his way around, and Three Fingers had trouble staying close. People were yelling at the bus driver to stop, and he did. Right in the middle of the turntable, like he was supposed to do. It rotated and I lost sight of them, but I knew what the boy was up to. As soon as the turntable stopped with the bus pointed at the ramp, he jumped in front it and charged up to the street. Three Fingers was right behind, running hard. The bus driver stopped and laid on the horn. I got onto the turntable just as it jerked into motion, and I staggered against the side of the bus and braced myself with the stick. People were yelling even louder. More horns blared, and it took me several seconds to figure out which way I needed to go to get back to the ramp. By the time I got to it, I could see Three Fingers up on Forty-Third Street. I gimped up the ramp, sure that I'd turn around and see the grille of the bus bearing down on me, but I made it to the street.

The kid turned like he was going to go after Three Fingers again, when a high-pitched piercing whistle cut through the traffic noise. The boy stopped and then ran toward the sound. The whistle had come from a hired car that was pulling away from the curb. As the boy ran for it, the back door opened, and he jumped in.

By then, the car was no more than ten feet away from me. Tugging the door shut was the crazy old woman who'd scared the boy away from me before, the same old woman who gave me the evil eye. Anna was next to her.

And sitting on Anna's lap was a fair-haired baby girl, two or three years old, maybe more. The two women were so intent on helping the boy get into the car that they didn't notice me. But in that moment as the car went past, I got a good close look at them, and I could see the resemblance that the three of them shared. The older woman must have been Anna's grandmother or an aunt, and the little girl had to be Anna's daughter. I thought I could see something of the teenage Anna in her face.

But no matter. As soon as I saw her, one part of this screwy story made sense. I knew why Anna had come back to New York. To get her little girl.

CHAPTER THIRTEEN

It was about four o'clock when Connie and I got back to the speak. We only had a handful of customers, so I bought a short round for the house and kicked everybody out ten minutes later. Marie Therese locked the front door and put up a sign that said we were closed for a private party. I went upstairs and told Vittorio that we had to shut down that night. He could stay open if he wanted to, but the cellar was locked. He said I was putting a hell of a crimp on his business and decided to close early, too.

Back downstairs, Marie Therese, Frenchy, Fat Joe, and Malloy wanted to know what was going on. Without getting into detail, I explained that there were rumors about some hard cash floating around, maybe as much as a hundred thousand bucks, with my name on it. Maybe it was even true, who could say? And I knew that four crates had been sent to me and were waiting to be picked up at the Railway Express Agency. I was going to get them and I'd need help, but none of them had signed on for this kind of work.

There was a good chance somebody would try to take them. If anybody wanted to bow out, I understood.

Fat Joe said, "Sounds more interesting than the usual Thursday-night bullshit," and everyone agreed.

"OK," I said, "but you need to know this, too. If this money is real, it probably belongs to Jacob the Wise."

"So," said Fat Joe, "are you going to fucking give it back to him if it's got your name on it?"

"I don't know. Let's get it first."

We decided that Marie Therese and Connie would stay at the speak and be ready to open the gate as soon as we got back.

Frenchy's truck was an old Chevrolet with a flatbed and cab he made out of wood. It was parked in the alley out back. He drove. I was in the cab with him. Fat Joe and Malloy rode in the back with a hand truck. Frenchy had the hog leg he kept behind the bar. Neither of us knew if it still worked, but it made a fine club. Malloy had his stolen Luger, and Fat Joe had a riot gun under a tarp. I knew that if we got into a gunfight on Third Avenue, we were screwed, but having come this close to whatever was in those boxes, I wasn't going to let go of it easily.

As Frenchy turned out of the alley, I thought I saw one of the guys in work clothes who'd been following me the day before on my way to the Cloud Club. A block farther on, I was sure I spotted one of Klapprott's thugs who'd been in the warehouse that morning. Hell, if we'd gone another mile, I'd probably have seen Santa Claus.

Afternoon traffic was slow by then, so it took a while to get to Thirty-Fourth Street. Frenchy double-parked outside the Railway Express office. Fat Joe told Malloy to get the hand truck, and the three of us went inside. I gave the four carbons to a guy behind a counter toward the back of the place. A few minutes later he came back carrying a wooden crate about twelve by twelve by eighteen. By the way he was straining, it was pretty heavy. He dropped it with a heavy-sounding *thunk* on the counter, and pulled a cart out from under the counter for the others.

As the guy had told us earlier, the shipping label said Yampah Hot Spring Mineral Water, but it didn't feel like liquid when I picked it up. It was solid—no sloshing, no bump of bottles—and it was heavy, damned heavy. The label read:

HOLD FOR: JIMMY QUINN
NEW YORK, NEW YORK

The guy brought out three more crates, same size and weight. When we got all of them loaded on the hand truck, I told Fat Joe to quit being a dick and roll it out to the flatbed. He was the only one of us big enough to handle it. The boxes filled most of the bed, so Fat Joe and Malloy sat on them.

The drive back seemed to take much longer. Of course, now that we had those boxes that were full of something, we were on a keener edge. I could see that Frenchy was extremely interested in everyone and everything on his side of the truck—cars that pulled up even, guys looking at us from the sidewalk. I was doing the same on my side. Nothing happened until we were almost at the mouth of the alley, and then there he was again, Johann Klapprott. He sat smiling and smoking a cigarette in the backseat of his Phaeton. When he saw me, he tipped his hat.

Fat Joe noticed him and said, "Isn't that the Kraut cocksucker? Want me to kill him?"

"Not yet."

Frenchy slowed to turn at the alley. Connie saw us and swung open the heavy wooden gate. Frenchy pulled past it and backed in. Connie closed and locked it behind us. We opened the steel door to the basement and took the boxes down one at a time with the hand truck. By the time we finished and locked up, the evening dark was settling.

We had to move several cases of product to make room for the four boxes on a counter in the center of the cellar. Everybody crowded around, and even though we were trying to act like we didn't feel it, the idea of money excited us, even Fat Joe.

The crates were nailed shut, and it took some work with a pry bar to get the top of the first one off. Inside was a bright yellow squarish shape tied up with rough hairy hemp rope. Frenchy and I tried to pull it out, but the fit was so tight that Malloy and Fat Joe had to hold the sides of the box while we lifted.

The yellow squarish shape was oilcloth, the kind they used to make rain slickers. We cut away the rope, found an edge of the oilcloth, and pulled it away. It came loose slowly because the oilcloth was stiff. When we finally got it unwrapped, we saw that the oilcloth had covered a solid rectangular block of brown wax. It looked to me like the oilcloth had been put inside the wooden box and then about an inch of melted wax had been poured in. We could see the faint numbers and designs of ten- and twenty-dollar bills embedded inside like they'd been placed there in thin layers of money and brown wax, money and wax, money and wax . . .

Marie Therese scraped at it with a thumbnail and muttered, "Papier-mâché."

Fat Joe said, "This is fucking nuts."

Maybe so, I thought, but it's not a bad way to disguise the stuff. The color was close enough that the markings on the bills seemed to blend with the wax.

Malloy pulled out a penknife and worked at a corner, scraping away slivers of wax as he pulled at a bill.

Marie Therese and Connie put their heads together and said that Malloy's method would take forever and would be hell to clean up. Marie Therese said, "Put it in the dumbwaiter and send it up to the kitchen. Maybe we can put it in a big sauce pan and melt it."

"Or," Connie said, "hot water. Put it in the sink and pour boiling water over it."

Malloy said that would clog up the pipes and certainly piss off

Vittorio. Fat Joe suggested melting it with a blowtorch, but Malloy said that would burn the money and maybe the brown stuff, too. Then Frenchy said that Marie Therese and Connie had the best idea of using hot water, but instead of doing it in the sink, they should put it in a big galvanized tub.

They were loading it into the dumbwaiter and I was trying to open the second box when somebody started pounding on the front door and we all stopped, like we were kids doing something dirty. Marie Therese went upstairs and yelled back that it was Detective Ellis. I told the others to go ahead and work on the thing in the kitchen but not to make much noise. We didn't want Ellis to know anything was going on.

"And remember what I said," I told them. "There is a good chance that this belongs to Jacob the Wise, and if you try to steal his money, he and Mercer Weeks will not rest until they have tracked you down. Do you understand that?"

They nodded but they didn't really agree with me. Malloy said, "Looks to me like someone might already have removed some of these bills. Who could say, really, if a few more were to become separated from their waxy imprisonment?"

"Be careful," I said. "No more than twenty apiece." That meant they'd take fifty, if they could get it loose.

I went upstairs, let Ellis in, and we went to the bar. He'd had time to change clothes, and he looked better than he had that morning, but he was steamed. Even after I poured him a gin, he was steamed. He kept his hat and overcoat on and glared at me. The entire time we were talking, he paced up and down the bar, hardly ever sitting down.

"Tell me about Justice Saenger," he said after he knocked back the drink.

I poured a second drink and said, "What's that, a judge?"

"It's a name. He's the guy whose trachea you crushed."

Trachea? I'd have to look that one up in the dictionary.

"The guy in your room this morning, the guy who was going

after Connie. Yeah, I know she was there, don't bother to deny it, and I'll need to talk to her."

"She's not here," I lied. "What about the other guy, the one who got stabbed?"

"He died. We don't have any leads on him or the other one, just Saenger."

"I told you, I never saw him before, never heard of him."

Ellis said, "He's not talking either, and he probably won't. Doesn't look like he's going to make it. We got his name from an IWW card in his pocket. Chicago chapter."

"The guy in the warehouse had the look of a working man, too. So we've got Wobblies and Nazis."

"Don't joke. This looks worse than it did when the wops were killing each other, not that you'd know anything about that."

He was talking about some business that took place the year before when a couple of Italian gangs tried to get rid of each other and, in the process, take over Charlie Lucky's operation. I played a small part in settling their hash, but that's another story.

Ellis went on. "This time I've got five bodies in the last twenty-four hours, one of them a cop."

"Five?"

"Yeah, the guy who planted the bomb. The guy in the warehouse with your ID, Detective Betcherman, and the two guys who knifed each other in your room at the Chelsea."

"But you're only worried about three. The guys in my room did each other, and we don't even know their names, so to hell with 'em."

"Three's enough. The men upstairs want an arrest soon, and it's my nuts in the crusher. You're going to help me on this whether you want to or not."

I surprised him by agreeing right away. "Right. I've got a couple of things you need."

You see, even though those of us in the booze business had working arrangements with a lot of cops, when it came to other crimes, mostly when we killed or shot each other, we didn't talk to the law, we settled it ourselves. Ellis understood that, and that's why he thought he'd have to get tough and lean on me to get any cooperation. But Klapprott and his goons—I didn't owe them a damn thing.

"First, Betcherman was in this up to his eyeballs. You know that. Find out what he's been doing for the past week and month, find out who he's been dealing with and you'll find somebody who's in on this. You see, there's something you may not know. The night the bomb went off, Betcherman was here. Ten minutes later, he was in the alley at this end."

Ellis gave me a cold stare. "Betcherman told me. That night. Said he was in the neighborhood and heard it."

"Did he tell you he tried to put the arm on me about some deal that he was part of? No? What were his words—'An item was delivered to your place. A piece of it's mine.' That's what he said."

Ellis ignored that and said, "I've heard there was some sort of disturbance at the Kraut warehouse this morning."

"Yeah, I was there. Some guys took me for a ride. They had the same idea that Betcherman did—but they were more specific. And they're working for this guy Klapprott who maybe owns the warehouse. He's also in charge of some outfit called the Free Society of Teutonia that's got something to do with those Nazi guys over in Germany. He's got this goon named Luther who was the guy in charge when they snatched me. They did it because they thought that I know the whereabouts of a certain amount of cash money, a large amount. Did you hear that, too?"

He stopped walking and paid more attention. "Maybe."

"And maybe you heard of some other party that came up missing a certain amount of cash money last year."

He tried to hide his surprise and said, "Are you talking about Jacob Weiss?"

"What do you know about what happened to him and Benny Numbers last year?"

"Not enough. I've heard a lot of stories. All I really know is that they went on a trip and nobody's seen Benny since. Lot of people say he ran off with Weiss's woman."

I thought about everything Jacob had said and how much I could repeat to a cop. Not much. "It boils down to this. Somebody snatched Benny, and Jacob shelled out a hundred thousand dollars to get him back. After that, nothing. No money, no Benny. But now, somebody is telling Jacob that the money is here in the city and that I've got it. A lot of other thugs and lowlifes seem to think the same thing, maybe even the guy with the dynamite, but that's neither here nor there since Weiss is involved."

Ellis agreed. To keep his numbers and loan-sharking operations running, Jacob made payoffs and kept secrets and did favors for some of the most powerful men in New York. He had guys in his pocket everywhere: the mayor's office, D.A., council, police department, and probably other places I didn't even know about. Ellis knew that a detective who brought Weiss's name into a case was doing himself no favors.

"It was what, two nights ago, we were talking in the Cloud Club, just a couple of guys, the proprietor of a fine speak and a moderately corrupt cop. That hasn't changed, and once this matter has been cleaned up, we'll be in the same situation. So for now, I have decided to take you up on your offer, if it's still on the table, of helping me get through the tricky parts of dealing with the city government when booze becomes legal again."

"So, Jimmy Quinn is going to go legit."

"I didn't say that. I said the speak would be legit. And there's something else I think I can do. If things work right, you can clean up Betcherman's murder tonight and keep Jacob's name out of it."

His face lit up with hope and then immediately darkened. He didn't believe me.

"You need an arrest. Maybe we can pin something on that bastard Klapprott, if nothing else. Interested?"

He waited a long thoughtful moment before he agreed.

"OK, can you arrange for the Cloud Club to be open for a small private party later tonight?"

After Ellis left, I tried to sort out what I knew and what I guessed.

I knew that Anna had sent what looked to be a large amount of cash sealed in wax. She sent it from Colorado. It was likely that she was the one who sent me Benny Numbers' ledgers. But she mailed those from Chicago. Klapprott said that Justice Schilling, his guy who claimed the money, was from Chicago. Justice Saenger, the guy who attacked Connie in my room, was from Chicago. Two names for the same guy who was trying to be tricky. The ten-dollar bill that Three Fingers gave me to hold his key came from Anna's waxy money.

Anna had a daughter. Maybe while Anna was in Colorado and Chicago, her daughter was here in New York. Jacob said Signora Sophia had a secret side to her life. That could have been the little girl.

It was time to ask her about it, so I went back to my office and found the telephone message about her hotel.

CHAPTER FOURTEEN

The lobby of the Hotel Lombardy was a lot swankier than the Chatham.

When I left the speak, I walked back to the corner where I'd seen Klapprott. He wasn't there. Still, I hailed a cab and told him to head uptown and make sure nobody was following us. He managed it without as much drama as I'd had that afternoon, and twenty minutes later, he let me off on East Fifty-Sixth in front of the hotel. I told the deskman my name and had him call Room 512. He gave me the eye over my bruised and battered phiz but let me go upstairs anyway.

Anna's digs turned out to be a suite, a damned big one with thick carpets, classy furniture, and a nicely stocked bar. Anna looked great. Twilight suited her. Her hair was fixed up, and she wore a knockout of a tight silk dress, so deep red it was almost purple. It had long sleeves and an Oriental collar high on her neck. She frowned when she got a look at my mug. "What happened?" she asked.

"It's been a busy day. I could tell you about it better if I had a drink. The label on the rye looks to be genuine. Let me have a dram with a splash of soda."

I settled on the settee while she did the honors. She made mine a double. Most of hers came from the siphon. Given the situation, I understood.

She sat close, her thigh rubbing against mine, and leaned closer. She took my face in her hands and kissed me hard. Then she pulled back and traced the bruises and cuts on my face with her fingertips. "I guess it was wrong of me to get you involved in all this, but it's too late for regrets. I'm glad I did it. I knew I could trust you." She gave me her most sincere unblinking soulful gaze.

"Of course you can," I lied.

"I didn't mean to give you the bum's rush this morning, but you surprised me when you said that anybody who claimed to be you might be able to pick up something addressed to you. Everything's been so crazy that I had to make sure it was still OK."

In other words, I thought, she picked up on the hint that other parties had their eyes on her score and might have found out that she was at the Chatham, so it was a good time to make herself scarce.

I took a sip of the drink. It was the McCoy, not some doctored crap. I wondered what and how much I should tell her, what I owed her, and what she owed me. She was probably thinking the same things, but then she was always two steps ahead of me in that department. I couldn't come up with a useful reason to mention seeing her and the little girl that afternoon, or that I had taken possession of her waxy loot. We'd get around to those soon enough.

"I don't know about you," I said, "but I'm starving. Have they got room service in this joint?"

She shot me a cool look and then called downstairs and ordered the special.

"When we left off this morning, you were telling me that you sent some money here, addressed to me, for safekeeping, I guess.

You and Pauley Domo had kidnapped a bootlegger, but he managed to get loose and contact his thugs. You got the money and escaped in a hail of gunfire. Pauley was seriously wounded and succumbed in an Ohio tourist court. Is that right?"

She gripped her glass hard. Her hands didn't shake. Neither did her voice. "Yes, that's right."

"I heard another story today. I won't bore you by going over the whole thing, but it ended with a woman driving out of a little Colorado town one night about a year ago with two suitcases full of money—a hundred thousand dollars is the figure I heard—and it was meant to ransom Benny Numbers for Jacob the Wise. Does that mean anything to you, Signora Sophia?"

The stiffness left her body. She leaned back, looked up at the ceiling, and said to no one in particular, "Damn, you think that just one time, the pieces are fitting together nice and neat, and you think you can see how it's going to end, and then it goes all screwy."

"Tell me what happened."

"Listen, no matter what Jacob said, nothing has changed. We can still handle this, you and I, we can do it."

"Tell me what happened. I want to know."

She got up and added another shot to her drink.

"First, you need to understand that the story I told you about Pauley Domo, that was true. Well, part of it was true. We did kidnap that drunken son of a bitch Livingston from his party, only Hildy and I had to be a bit more persuasive to get him out to the garden. And, like I told you, we made arrangements for the payoff, but he got himself loose *before* we got the money. Hildy, Pauley, and I waited for the money for hours and hours before we realized it had gone bad. We went back to the farm empty-handed that night and saw the lights from the cars. We could tell they were beating on Vaughn and Hildy's family, and we heard shots, so I guess they killed them. I hope to hell they got the idiot brother.

"And the three of us ran, without the money, to Wapakoneta."

"And Pauley wasn't wounded?" I said.

"Not then. Two weeks later I caught him and Hildy having a little fun in the sack one afternoon. He was wounded then all right. Hildy yelled and ran into the bathroom, and I went after Pauley. And you know what's funny? It wasn't the first time. Back when we first got together, before I knew you, I caught him. Like a sap, I believed him when he said it would never happen again. The second time with Hildy, he tried to tell me that it wasn't what I thought it was. Can you believe that? And him talking to me like that made me as mad as catching them. I went nuts and grabbed the first thing I could find. It was just a cheap little cheese knife. Who'd've thought you could cut off a couple of fingers with it?"

So, Three Fingers was Pauley Three Fingers. Figured.

"Anyway, I stormed away and took the car. Hildy was still crying and yelling and Pauley was bleeding all over the place, saying, 'When you calm down we'll talk this over and you'll see that I'm right.' Hah!"

She said that she understood then that she had no life and no future with Pauley, so she headed west, back to her hometown, Grindstone, Illinois. Now, I know she made that part up. I checked and there is no Grindstone in Illinois, or in Ohio or Indiana, but I guess that's not important. She said she went back there because that's where her grandmother was. Anna had no use for the rest of her family, but she could trust her grandmother.

The two of them sat down together and came up with a plan. Thus the widow Signora Sophia was born. Anna sold the car and combined that money with the old woman's savings. In Chicago, they bought fashionable, flattering clothes, dyed Anna's hair black, and headed for Saratoga Springs. Grandma stayed close in a rooming house while Anna made herself visible at the resort but kept apart from the floozies and debutantes who were there for the same reason she was—to catch a rich guy. She'd been looking for someone in legitimate business, but she knew who Jacob was, and hell, maybe it was just some kind of fate that she always wound up with guys who were on the wrong side of the law.

She knew Jacob wasn't the perfect answer to her problems. He'd never leave his wife for her, but for a while at least, he'd provide for them. She could have done a hell of a lot worse.

Anna didn't mention the child then, the little girl I'd seen in the car with her that afternoon, but it was easy enough to fill that gap. It seemed likely to me that Anna might have been in the family way while Pauley was dipping his wick in Hildy, and she went to "Grindstone" to have the baby. She wouldn't have wanted to advertise the fact that there was a kid in the picture while she was at Saratoga, and as I'd figured, it explained the secretive angle she played when she and Jacob moved back to New York.

She'd got to about that point when the room service guy knocked on the door and brought in a tray. It had sliced apples and cheeses and strange little sandwiches without crusts. I found out later they were cucumber and watercress. There wasn't much to them, but I ate about a dozen while she talked. They took the edge off.

"So after you met Jacob at Saratoga Springs, he moved you into that place up on Fifth Avenue."

She nodded her head. "Everything was just dandy until Jacob decided we all had to take a goddamn vacation and see the West."

I finished a tiny sandwich. "You know that a lot of people have been saying that you and Benny ran off together. You seduced him and hatched this scheme to get Jacob's money."

"Sure," she sneered, "me and Benny, right."

"And some people said you cooked up the scheme to have somebody else snatch Benny and then demand that you deliver the dough. But from what Jacob and Weeks said about what happened out there, they didn't think you were in on it, and they should know."

She slugged back her drink and got up to make another. Her voice was angry.

"I didn't want anything to do with it from the beginning. I was packed up and ready to get on the next train back to New York the morning we found out he was gone, but no, Jacob said we had to stick together. What a goddamn sap."

"OK," I said. "What really happened?"

She sat back down beside me. "What really happened was . . . " She stopped and thought for a moment. "Did you ever see that movie 'Phantom of the Opera'? Yeah? I guess that's what happened to me."

Now, I wasn't there in that room in the mountains that she talked about, so I can't swear that everything Anna said was absolutely true. Knowing Anna, it wasn't, but it was close. And maybe I've added a few details that she hinted at but didn't come right out and say. You can be the judge of that. I'll explain by and by.

CHAPTER FIFTEEN

It was about midnight when Anna left the Hotel Colorado, and it took her fifteen to twenty minutes to drive to the crossroads they called Miner's Camp No. 3. Not long after she stopped, a car came up on her right. The driver slowed and an arm appeared from the window and waved for her to follow.

They drove for what seemed like an hour on rutted gravel roads. At the end, they went down a series of hairpins on a steep slope, crossed a one-lane wooden bridge over a loud creek, passed a small shed, went halfway up a hill, and stopped in front of a dark structure.

The driver of the other car got out and lit a lantern and beckoned for her to come along. So scared her knees felt weak, she got out of the car, keeping one hand in her bag so she could grab her pistol, and followed him. She heard a door open, and the lantern revealed a doorframe and a shadowed room. She climbed uneven stone steps to the door and stopped outside, afraid to go in, thinking she should go back to the car, toss the money out, and drive away. She waited too long.

The guy, or somebody else, came up behind her and got an arm around her neck, elbow forward, and a hand locked behind her head in a chokehold. She grabbed at the arm and kicked at his shins but knew it was useless. Within seconds, she blacked out. Her last thought was anger at her own stupidity, letting somebody get her like that. She hated being helpless more than anything else.

She had a sense of being moved, and when she woke up, she was in a cold dark room, still wearing her coat and dress. She had her hat and her bag, but the gun was gone. She could tell that he—whoever he was—had handled her and her clothes. Some buttons were undone and her slip and bra weren't right, but nothing south of that. At first, she was more scared than angry, but by the time the first faint dawn light revealed the place, she was just angry.

She saw the building was a cabin with well-worn floorboards and rough log walls patched with some kind of stucco. There was a crudely built stone fireplace on one wall, open rafters overhead, and one small wavy glass window that wouldn't open. She was on a low pallet made of straw and ticking. Near the pallet, a four-by-four vertical post was bolted to the floor and a rafter. Like the floor, it was worn smooth. At the bottom was a round eyebolt. A chain about fifteen to twenty feet long was attached to the eyebolt. The other end of the chain was a metal band that was locked around her right ankle. As soon as she saw it, she knew she wouldn't be leaving with Benny Numbers.

In the middle of the room was a lever-action water pump over a metal sink in a waist-high counter. On the other side of the room beyond the reach of the chain, were a table and chair and a door with heavy iron hinges and a simple latch. Beside the pallet was a mound of stuff that appeared to have been thrown into the corner. She went through it with a growing feeling of dread as she saw that most of the things were women's clothes. It chilled her to the core to realize that she wasn't the first woman to be chained up there. Her knees buckled, and she sat on the floor. She saw a chamber pot under the pallet and immediately had to pee.

That, she said, was the most terrifying moment she spent there, because she didn't know anything. She'd been in tough situations before, lots of them, but she could always see what she had to do to get out. But that morning, all she knew for sure then was that she was alone in what appeared to be a one-room cabin high in the mountains. She had to assume that the guys who kidnapped Benny Numbers decided that they wanted her, too, or they were afraid she'd lead Jacob's guys back to them. More likely, they wanted to screw her, like the other women they'd chained up there.

She checked the chain at her ankle and saw that there was a leather cuff inside the metal bracelet or anklet or whatever the hell you called it. The lock that held it shut was heavy and solid. The other end of the chain had been welded directly to the eyebolt in the post. There was no give when she tugged on it. The heads of the screws that held the eyebolt had been filed down. When she walked, it rattled and scraped across the wooden floor.

She got up and tried the pump. She had to lean in and put both her hands and her shoulders to work to get it started. The pump squealed but produced a stream of mostly clear well water that smelled and tasted of minerals. There was a gallon-sized leather bucket in the sink. She filled it, scrubbed her face, neck, and hands and felt better. She also felt hungry.

Kindling and firewood were stacked next to the fireplace. Two hinged irons that could support heavy pots were bolted to the stone chimney, and there was a box of wooden matches on the narrow mantle. She used a piece of the kindling to push the ashes back and broke up the smallest pieces of kindling to start a fire. It took four matches. When she snapped one stick over her leg, it broke in half and both pieces had sharp ends. She tucked one behind the pallet and kept the other up her right coat sleeve. Looking out the window, she could see cloudy morning sky, trees, and a bit of ground that sloped down.

She got as close as she could to the table and saw a metal plate and an empty Mason jar. Dragging the chain, she walked back to the other side of the room and went through the clothes.

They were mostly dresses. One was a long, old-fashioned, high-necked heavy piece made of green velvet. There were also two dresses that looked more modern, shorter and lighter, and a blouse and skirt. There was a blue silk robe with wear at the elbows, a pullover sweater, and a long coat. Two simple long skirts and blouses were made of homespun wool. They looked like the clothes she'd seen Indians wearing, and they were made for smaller women. Some of the clothes were clean, some dirty. No blood stains. There were also some towels, rags, and wash-cloths, a wire coat hanger, and her small bag with some hairpins, perfume, lipstick, rouge, and powder.

It was after noon, she thought, when she heard scuffing noises outside, and then the door opened. She waited, crouched on the pallet with the sharp kindling still hidden in her sleeve.

Sunlight through the open door silhouetted a man. Her first impression was of his height, but when he stepped inside, she saw that was wrong. He was a medium-sized guy, maybe thirty years old. It was hard to say with all the scars. His hair was black and straight. His face was dark. The first thing she thought was "half-breed," and that's the only name she ever had for him.

He walked over to the pump, set something down on the counter, then went back to the table and sat where he could watch her. He gestured toward the thing by the pump and said, "Eat." His voice sounded hoarse and painful.

The thing was a frying pan. She forced herself to stand and walk to it. It held clumps of cold fry bread that smelled of bacon grease. She took a piece and chewed. Her stomach lurched at the smell, but she was still hungry and ate it all.

When she finished, she said, "What do you want?"

"A squaw," he answered, and left.

That evening, he brought in a stew pot, a ladle, and a kerosene lantern. He left the lantern out of reach on the table and hung the pot on one of the fireplace irons.

He turned and she got her first good look at his face. His cheeks and half his forehead were a shiny welt, like he'd been burned with fire or acid, or scalded by steam. It was the same with the skin she could see on his hands and wrists. One eye teared and blinked almost constantly. The other was set so deep in the smooth flesh she couldn't see it at all. A sharply pointed nose and receding chin made him look like an evil turtle. He wore plain black pants and a red shirt that looked to be made of the same homespun she saw on the short women's clothes, and a heavy lamb's wool vest that was tied at the waist and the neck with two lengths of rawhide. It had been a long time since he'd been close to bathwater, and he reeked of wood smoke, old sweat, grime, and something long dead and rotten.

"You can't kill me," he said. "Nobody can. I am immortal. This is the stew pot. You tend it. I bring meat in the morning." He said all that in a level tone, not sounding at all crazy. He picked up the lantern and turned to leave.

She yelled, "Wait a goddamn minute! What's going on here? Where's Benny? I brought the money! Let me go."

He threw back his head and laughed and did a little spinning, hopping dance that took him out the door.

Wonderful, she thought, *I'm going to have to fuck a lunatic to get out of here.*

The next day, he came back with more wood, the poorly skinned, hacked-up carcasses of several small animals, a couple of potatoes, and some other things she took to be vegetables. He took out the chamber pot and brought it back empty, along with some small rags.

Later that morning, she thought she heard some kind of distant activity, the sounds of automobile engines, men coming and going, buying and selling. At least that's what she guessed or hoped since the sounds were so faint. She pulled out a piece of the stucco that chinked the log wall by the chimney and found that she could see a worn footpath and part of another building up the hill.

Since she still didn't know what was going on, she spent the rest of the day examining the clothes and straightening them up. The Indian clothes looked to be the same color and style as his outfit. The other dresses, skirts, and blouses had probably belonged to three women, judging by the sizes and styles. That evening, he brought more fry bread, tasted the stew, and scooped out a big bowl for himself. He pulled a spoon out of a pocket and sat down at the table to eat and stare at her.

Again, she asked where Benny was and why he was keeping her locked up. He ignored the first question and said, between bites, "Squaws don't talk."

When he finished eating, he dropped the plate and spoon in the sink, took the lantern, and left.

What the hell did he want from her? Did he want her to cry, to beg, to seduce him? She decided to hide her fear as much as she could, keep herself looking presentable, and eat the nasty stew to stay strong so that when the moment came, she could kill him. Even if it turned out that she couldn't escape, she would try to kill him. *I am immortal*, my ass.

During that first week, she mulled over what she knew and what she could assume, and she figured out one arrangement of facts and assumptions that made sense. It also made her sick to her stomach.

First, she knew that it took more than one guy to snatch Benny

Numbers. He was no tough guy, but there had to be more than one man involved to knock him out or to keep him quiet while they moved him out of the hotel. The half-breed clearly wasn't the brains of any outfit. It was more likely that he owned this place way out in the high mountains where they could keep Benny. She and Pauley Domo did the same thing, using Hildy's family farm to stash their bootlegger.

So, since she had not heard any sounds of human activity, she assumed that the rest of the gang was gone. They got the money she brought and either released Benny Numbers or they killed him. Then they left. The half-breed stayed. He got his cut, and he got her.

She remembered the second note where someone had scrawled at the bottom *Send the Woman*. Maybe the half-breed had been their lookout or the eyes of the gang in Glenwood Springs. He spotted her when she was out walking and decided that's what he wanted.

All right then, she thought, there was a chance they had returned Benny Numbers. If he was still alive, Jacob the Wise would do anything he could to get her back. She knew that, and the thought gave her a scrap of hope to hold onto.

Then it started to snow.

The half-breed wore snowshoes. She heard the noise of his taking them off outside the door. There were fewer small animals for the stew, and the vegetables were softer and moldier. When he came to eat in the evenings, he didn't speak. She didn't either. Squaws didn't talk.

Once when he gestured for a second helping, she got as close to the table as the chain would allow, and he stretched to hand her the tin plate. She went to the stew pot, and when her back was turned, he banged his fists on the table and let out a loud roar to scare her. It worked. She dropped the plate, and when she turned back around, he was giggling and rocking in the chair. Part of her wanted to fling the hot stew in his face. A stronger, smarter part told her not to react. Sure, he startled you. Leave it at that. Cold anger settled.

She woke up that night and found him squatting on his heels by her bed, staring at her. He'd got through the door without making enough noise to wake her, but when he got close, the pungent smell of him was enough. In the faint light of the fireplace embers, she saw him lean in until his face was inches from hers.

She was on her side, facing him. She kept her eyes mostly shut and her breathing slow and even. The slender stick of kindling, even sharper since she'd worked it on a hearthstone, was in her hands, and her hands were between her knees, as she was curled beneath the thin blanket and the coat, desperate to stay warm. He sniffed at her, like a dog. He licked his lips, and his good eye teared and blinked. With his arms wrapped around his knees, he rocked on his heels, slowly at first and then faster, and moaned painful animal-like sounds. When she opened her eyes wide, it startled him, and he scuttled away.

Most days began with the half-breed bringing more crappy stuff for the stew and eating a bowl while he stared at her. Then he'd take out the slops, throw his bowl into the sink, and leave. She ate out of the frying pan with her hands, never when he could see her. He would stay away all day. Sometime after dark, she'd hear him taking off his snowshoes. She served up more stew and handed it to him. The chain wouldn't let her reach the table. He always stood at its limit, making her stretch to hand him the bowl. Then she sat on the bed and watched him watching her.

The routine went on for days and weeks and months. She wasn't sure how much time passed. With the snow, the faint sounds of outside activities ended. It was just the two of them in the pump house.

The fire didn't keep the place very warm, and she wore all of the heaviest clothes she could find in the pile. She wondered who the women were who'd worn them before. There were no name tags on any of the garments. One light summer dress had a label from a clothing store in Denver. Were they the girlfriends and wives of the other gang members, the ones she'd never seen? Girls the half-breed had brought up here or kidnapped? Were they alive or dead?

Out of boredom and the realization that she had nothing to lose, she decided to spice it up. She knew that even if the mis-shapen shit hadn't touched her since the first night, he wanted something to do with sex. That, she could deliver.

When he came in that evening and set the lantern on the table, she was wearing the heavy green velvet dress. She'd pinned her hair up as best she could without a mirror and hoped that she had the distant buxom look of a Gibson Girl. Instead of sitting on the bed, she stirred the stew and cleaned her fry pan in the sink and tended the fire. She was slow, languid, graceful, and superior.

It worked.

He couldn't sit still while he ate. Instead, he fidgeted and rubbed his thighs together and stared at her much more intently, his good eye blinking almost constantly. He jumped up without finishing and hurried out the door. He didn't even give her his plate. It remained just out of reach on the table. That's when she got the first ideas of how she could kill him, and by then, she understood that it wasn't a matter of choice. To get out of that cabin, she would have to kill him. Even if she could get loose from the chain, she was at least twenty crooked snow-covered miles from nowhere. She'd need to take a car, and he wasn't going to hand her the keys. So she accepted it. She hadn't killed anybody before, but she didn't doubt that she could kill the half-breed. Either that or he was going to kill her.

The next night, she gave him nothing. He found her wearing the heaviest clothes. She filled his plate, handed it to him, and sat on the bed. He didn't say anything or do anything, but he was disappointed. She could tell.

The next night, she was a Gibson Girl again, an unmoving Gibson Girl. She served his plate and stood by the fireplace where the flickering light was most flattering and stood as still as she could until he finished. More leg rubbing, more blinking, more agita. It was hard to figure out how to play him, even though she had plenty of boring hours to work on it. She spent the time obsessively going over what she thought of as her weapons, the things she could reach, the things she'd use to kill the bastard.

Everything changed the night after that. He showed up drunk. She could tell something was different from the sound of his approach. He banged against the wall outside and came in with snow up to his knees. He carried the lantern and a Mason jar mostly full of something clear, yellowish, and oily-looking. He fell into his chair and hunched over the table. Breathing hard through his mouth, he stared at her. The familiar smell of the homemade rotgut wafted from the jar. It was on his sour breath and in the sweat that beaded on his forehead. It looked like he was one of those drunks who didn't touch the stuff for weeks or even months at a time and then went on a bender that lasted for days. She'd seen it many times.

How far should she push him? Drunks could be unpredictable. Finally, what the hell—nothing ventured . . .

She was wrapped up in warm clothes again. She turned her back to him and shrugged off the heavy coat. Next came the jacket, still with her back to him. Strolling away, she took off the sweater and tossed it on the bed with the rest. She turned around, hip cocked, one leg extended. No smile, no anger, no emotion, just a level stare. She still had on two blouses. Standing where the light was best from the fire and the lantern, she undid the first one, taking care with the buttons down the front and at the cuffs. He was breathing faster, she thought, as she got out of one sleeve and then the other. The second blouse was too small for her, too tight across her breast. Good.

One of his boot heels drummed a fast involuntary tattoo on the plank floor.

She stood where she was, shoulders back, tits out. He stared and drank until he raised the jar and found it empty. He hauled himself up and blundered out the door. A moment later, she heard him howl.

She wasn't surprised when he came back hours later.

She was in bed by then, with most of the clothes back on. She had both little sticks of sharpened kindling in her hands. He had a fresh jar, and he still carried the lantern. He'd stripped down to a tattered red union suit and his boots. He came close to the bed and immediately backed away. He seemed to be trying to work himself up for something, advancing and pulling back. She tightened her grip. The next time he brought the lantern close, she sat upright, the heavy coat around her shoulders.

He stopped and lowered the light, and she saw his body through the torn front of the union suit. It was worse than she could have imagined. The shiny mottled hairless scar tissue continued down his chest and belly and groin. His dick was a useless little stub of flesh.

He stood there, swaying on unsteady legs until something made him stumble back out the door.

She stayed in bed and tried to tamp down her excitement. She didn't have to worry about "a fate worse than death" from that piece of equipment, but that meant nothing. In the lantern light she had seen, as clearly as if it was in the noonday sun, a leather thong around his neck, and hanging from the thong, a small leather pouch—small but big enough to hold a key.

He stayed away for four days. The morning he came back, he looked like seven kinds of hell, the bad booze still seeping out of every pore, leaden body, roiling stomach. She did nothing to make it worse for him. Not then. He started slowly on the stew but finally gulped it down. He tossed the empty plate to her, took the slops pot, and came back an hour later with wood for the fire and a bucket

It was important for her to keep herself clean and attractive.

She didn't know what fantasies the half-breed had about her, but he saw something he wanted. That's why he had her deliver the money. Maybe he wanted to kill his fantasy, she couldn't be sure. If he was anything like the other men she'd known, though, he'd lose interest fast if she let herself go. She kept the bed and the clothes as neat and orderly as she could. Washed every day and used a little of the perfume when the loneliness and hopelessness of the situation overwhelmed her.

He never changed clothes and stank more as the days went by. She worked out her plan to kill him. It wasn't complicated, because it had to happen in the cabin and there wasn't much to work with. The sharpened sticks were too flimsy to trust.

The pump was in the center of the square room. Her bed was on the east wall. The door and the table where he sat to eat was opposite, on the west wall. The fireplace was in the middle of the north wall. She could easily reach the pump and the fireplace, but the table was a foot and half behind the end of the chain and her outstretched arm. As long as he was sitting at the table, she couldn't reach him. To escape, then, she had to do two things. First, she had to get close enough to touch him. Second, she had to kill him. The way she had it figured, the second part was actually easier. If she could get right behind him, she knew what she could do. Getting close—that was tougher. She thought she had a way though.

On a morning soon after he ate and left, she took the wire coat hanger out from under the stack of clothing. She pulled it and bent it straight so that the crook was at the end of a double piece of wire about two feet long. She moved as close to the table as the chain would allow, got down on the floor, and stretched out on her stomach. Hooking the end of the extended hanger around the bottom of a table leg, she pulled, slow and gentle. It didn't work. The single crook wasn't strong enough and began to give before the table moved.

She went back to her bed and unwound the wire where it was twisted at the neck. Again, she straightened it into a double length of wire and bent a new crook at the other end where it was twice as strong. At least, she hoped it was.

Again, she got down on her stomach and stretched out with the bent wire that was then a couple of inches shorter than it had been before. At first, it wouldn't reach around the leg. She sat up, pushed the iron ring around her ankle as far down as it would go, and stretched her arm until the shoulder joint stretched and popped. The hook barely reached around the leg, but when she pulled, it held, and that end of the table moved about half an inch toward her. She did the same with the second leg at the other end and waited for dinner.

He didn't notice.

She waited a day, then moved the table another half inch. He didn't notice that either.

She suspected that mornings were more dangerous than evenings, but the cabin was dark then, too, and he was more interested in the food. Evenings, he was interested in her. She didn't tease him very often, only once every seven to ten days, and never very much, not like the night he was drunk.

Most nights, she was prim, modest, neatly buttoned. Some nights she smiled. The important thing was not to get too close to the table. By the time she'd got it about six inches from its original spot, she kept a half turn of the chain around the post to shorten it. Since the night he'd come to crouch by the bed, he hadn't been on that side of the room, and he couldn't see the base of the post from his seat at the table. The pump blocked it from his view. The shortened chain kept her farther from the table, but he didn't notice that, either.

Four weeks after he showed up drunk, she sensed he was getting restless, distracted. His morning visit was brief. He brought only a few spongy root vegetables for the stew. She did nothing with the table that day and dressed severely with the heavy coat. By evening, it was bitter cold and snowing again. When he kicked open the door, he was drunker than she'd seen him. She went to the stew pot. He shook his head and took a long pull on the

Mason jar. She sat on the bed and draped the blanket over her shoulders.

Before long, he began some kind of rhythmic chant or song accompanied by a measured tap of one foot. It was nothing like the tattoo he'd drummed out when she stretched the tight blouse. This was a lament, slow and sad. His good eye was closed. It went on for an hour or more, she thought, and was broken only when he drank. He left when the jar was empty and was gone for five days.

She had moments of panic during that stretch, thinking that he'd passed out and frozen to death in the snow, and she would freeze or starve chained to the goddamned post. Don't think about it, she told herself, conserve the wood and the stew. Make them last. That's what she did, and she hated to admit that she felt a wave of relief and gratitude when she finally heard him outside. But she didn't let it show, not even when he came in with fresh meat for the pot and more wood and another blanket and a second chamber pot. She acted like nothing had happened and kept her face as impassive as his. It was going to feel so good when she killed him.

After he left, she moved the table another half inch.

To keep herself from going crazy as the table made its painstaking way to her side, she became more animated in the evening, adding more movement back and forth across the floor and the odd wink. Even though he still seemed to enjoy her captivity, she knew he'd tire of it, just as he'd tired of the others before. So she tried to keep him interested. With the spring thaw, her clothes became more revealing, but he was gone longer. He seemed to come earlier in the morning and later in the evening. The faint sounds of activity outside returned, too. One morning when he opened the door, she saw that he had a wooden box on the step outside, a box with dividers that held twelve-quart jars of the oily moonshine. She realized then that he was making the stuff. He had a still nearby, and the sounds she heard were from his customers. Better vegetables and meat appeared for the pot.

She remembered that she'd passed a small shed when she crossed the creek at the bottom of the hill, and from the pump house, she could see part of another building up the slope. So, maybe he sleeps up there, she thought, and sells 'shine from the shed down the hill. That explained how he lived, but it didn't help her. She couldn't make enough noise for anyone down there to hear, and if they did hear her, the half-breed would say it was his squaw.

By late summer, she had the table where she needed it. The next step was to get him there at the proper level of drunkenness. She'd worn all of the outfits many times, except for the home-spun Indian skirts and blouses that were too small. But nothing was doing the trick, and she was afraid that this could be her last chance.

Three weeks after his last drunken visit, by her count of days, she started getting ready, pulling stitches out of the homespun clothes, trying them on in different combinations, unsure of how she looked without a mirror. She reasoned that all the clothes reminded the half-breed of other women he'd held there. The green velvet dress, at least at first, seemed to fascinate and excite him more than the others. When she wore tight clothes or left off her bra, she got what she thought of as the "flared nostrils" reaction. He might dig a greasy paw into his crotch for a little while but nothing more.

Maybe the Indian clothes belonged to the first woman or women he brought there. Maybe they had been something more than squaws. Maybe the clothes would keep him there.

When he turned moody, frowning, ill at ease as he picked at his food, she could tell another bender was close.

He was late the next night, and he rolled in with a full Mason jar. It wasn't his first of the day. She shrugged off the coat, walked into the light, spooned up a bit of stew, and brought it to the table. He turned up the wick on the lantern, and she heard his sharp intake of breath.

She was barefoot. The long black skirt was tight around her

hips and came down to her calves. The blouse was so short on her that the sleeves barely reached her elbows, and it left her stomach bare. She'd torn it at the neck so she could move her arms freely. He stood, swaying, but didn't move past his usual place at the end of the table where he sat. When he didn't accept the stew, she put the plate on the counter by the pump and stood facing him.

Something was working. He was breathing hard, and his good eye blinked twice as much as it normally did. He took a long messy drink that spilled down his shirt. She walked to the fire and pretended to mind the stew.

She came back to the pump and drew water. She filled her frying pan and drank from it. He watched every movement and drank from the jar again, right after she did. He seemed almost to be mimicking her, so she sat cross-legged on the floor by the pump. He sat in his chair and did not need to be coaxed to drink more.

As the level of booze in the jar fell, he began his moaning chant again, beating out a slow rhythm with his foot. She nodded her head. He nodded. Some time after the jar was empty, he crossed his arms on the table and his head sank down. She waited until the ragged breathing evened out. His face was turned away from her, and it was several minutes before she was sure he was asleep.

Quiet and deliberate, she got to her feet. She picked up the chain to muffle the sound of it as best she could and went back to the post where she had taken three turns around it to shorten the length. *You will do this. You will do this. You will do this*, she repeated to herself as she unwound the chain and padded back to the table. Now she could reach him. She stood right behind his chair and took a deep breath.

She grabbed his hair and pulled his head up with her left hand. Her right arm snaked around his neck. She locked her right hand on her left biceps, got her left hand behind his head, and squeezed as hard as she could in a strong chokehold.

I never found out if Anna knew exactly what she was doing,

but when you grab somebody like that, you cut off the blood to his brain and he'll pass out within a few seconds. That's what he did to her the night she brought the money. If you keep the pressure on his neck for more than a few seconds, you can kill him.

Anna hung on tight when he reared up out of his seat and tried to claw at her. She tucked her head against his grimy neck, and as he stumbled around, she locked her ankles around his waist. He yelled, not very loud since she was strangling him, and flailed and spun, wrapping the damn chain around both of them. They banged against the pump, and he was reaching for the stew pot to brain her with it, but the taut chain brought him up well short. All the while, Anna kept her arms locked around his neck and remembered every goddamn boring, terrifying, humiliating, shitty day she spent as his captive, his slave, his squaw, and she squeezed harder.

When finally he fell, he landed on his side and knocked the wind out of her, but she didn't let go. She hung on, gagging at the foul smell until she felt the last breath go out of him and his muscles went slack. Scared that he was trying to trick her, she didn't let go until her arms cramped, and she released him.

Then she had to disentangle herself from the chain. She pushed and pulled, frantic to get away from him, and once she was free, she tore at the lamb's wool vest and found the pouch around his neck. She tried to yank it off him, but the leather thong wouldn't snap. She wound up pulling it over his head and then ripping with her teeth at the cord that held the pouch closed. She crawled over toward the fire, where the light was stronger, and emptied it onto the floor. Some kind of animal claw, a smooth pebble, a bullet, something moldy that smelled of tobacco, and three steel keys on a ring.

Her hands shook so hard it took several tries, but the small one fit, and the lock popped open. She collapsed and cried.

At first, she was afraid to go out. She hesitated at the door, then went back and locked the chain around the dead man's ankle. Better safe.

The night was full of buzzing insects that bumped against the lantern as she made her way up the footpath. The house where the half-breed had lived was dug into the side of the mountain. His car, an old Model A, was parked beside it. The place looked to be older than the pump house. It had two windows and a porch with a rocking chair. Inside, it was a mess, as cluttered as the pump house was spare, and the smell was even worse than the half-breed himself. He'd slept in a small room on a rough pallet that was no better than the one she'd used. In the main room, she found a fireplace and wood-burning stove, a pile of hides, and material for tanning them. Stacked up next to them on shelves were a dozen or so fifty-pound bags of sugar and wooden crates of Mason jars.

There was a cabinet he'd used as a pantry where she found some canned goods and a loaf of stale, moldy bread. She tore away the green part and wolfed it down.

Also on the shelves were old rifles and guns, most of them rusty, pots and pans and dishes, bags of beads, boxes of mineral water, bolts of cloth, canning supplies, kegs of nails. She guessed it was all taken in trade for his 'shine. The two suitcases of money were on a bottom shelf, near the back, with the ledger books and her pistol. As best she could tell, nobody had even opened the suitcases.

When the sun came up, she went through everything to get a better idea of what was in the place and how she was going to get out. She found cans of coffee and a coffee pot, and the memory of the taste overwhelmed her. She hadn't had a hot drink in months. She had to go back down to the pump house for water. He hadn't moved. She brought back a full bucket and brewed a pot. She filled a clean cup, took it out to the porch, and sat with full sunlight on her face for the first time since she left the hotel in Glenwood Springs. She put together the first parts of her plan.

"Wait a minute," I said. "What about Benny? The gang of kidnappers?"

"I don't know," she said, and I thought she was lying. "I know the half-breed didn't have the brains to plan and pull off a job like that. The way I see it, he had a partner who came up with the idea, and the two of them took Benny and left the first note. But something went wrong when they brought Benny back to the place in the mountains. Maybe after they got to the hideout, Benny tried to escape or grabbed a gun, I don't know, but it ended up with him and the first guy dead.

"By then, the crazy half-breed had decided that he wanted me. By the look of his place, he didn't care about money. He just wanted his liquor and his squaw. That's all I can tell you." I knew there was more to it, but I couldn't understand why she wouldn't tell it.

As she'd said before when she spun the little story of the kidnapped bootlegger, she knew that it was dangerous for a woman to travel with that much cash. So she used what she could find to disguise it. But first, how was she going to get out?

All she could see around her were steep slopes, trees, and rock. She saw that the path between the house and the pump house went on in the other direction. She followed it through the woods to the still, a fragrant haphazard collection of tanks, coiled tubes, and car radiators. The fire had gone out, so she thought it wouldn't explode. She went back to the house and walked a quarter of a mile downhill to the shed by the creek. It was an open-sided structure, little more than a lean-to, with a handwritten *Gone Fishing* sign hanging from a nail. Later that day and the next, she heard cars approach the place. Sometimes they'd stop, wait a while, and leave. She guessed it was nothing unusual for the half-breed to disappear, and his customers understood it.

She found the car she'd driven hidden behind some brush on a side road off the rutted track that led up to the house. The forlorn thing was already overgrown with weeds and wildflowers.

Back at the house, she ate a can of beans and a can of peaches, savoring every bite, and studied the money. If she even thought of getting it back to Jacob, she didn't mention it to me. Instead, she concentrated on making the money not look like money.

She couldn't keep it on her or carry it herself. She'd be too nervous. She'd give herself away. No, the best way was to have somebody else transport it. Not the mail. Railway Express was about as reliable as she'd find. All she had to do was get it back to Glenwood Springs. No, not there. Even though it had been so long since she'd been there, she might be recognized. Denver. Take it to the office in Denver. But suppose some guy along the way wasn't as reliable or honest as he ought to be and got curious. What then? Make the box hard to get open, and seal the stuff up in a good wrapper, and finally, disguise it so that if a box should break open, it wouldn't look like anything particularly valuable.

She went through the stuff on the shelves again. The boxes of mineral water were a convenient size. What if she put the money in bottles of water? No, too hard to reseal. Seal. Wax. Paraffin.

She fired up the stove, tore open the boxes, and put tablets of paraffin into a big pot. They melted quickly and turned a clear milky-white. She didn't want the wax to seep between the boards of the crates, so she lined the box with a piece of oilcloth and poured in a layer of hot melted wax. She covered it with bills and poured in more wax. When she'd almost filled the box, she added some molasses to the last layer, giving it an ugly, chocolate-brown color.

She filled four boxes before she realized that she'd embedded all the cash and had to pull the last one apart to separate some traveling money. She'd need it to buy some clothes right away.

She packed the few clothes that were wearable, Benny's ledgers, and some money in a suitcase and loaded the boxes next to her in the Model A. A day after she killed the half-breed, she drove away and made her way to Denver. She got lost often and nearly ran out of gas, but she made it.

Now, this part of her story wasn't over, but I've got to interrupt for a moment. As I said, I wasn't in that pump house with Anna and the half-breed, so I can't swear to the truth of everything she said, and I admit that I have filled in some details, maybe more than I should have, so you may be thinking that she made it all up. But, a few years later—the how and the why and the when aren't important—I found myself in Glenwood Springs in a bar in the Hotel Denver, a smaller joint across the river from the big spa. I struck up a conversation with the proprietor, since we were in the same line of business. In the course of it, I asked if he happened to know of a half-breed Indian who used to operate a still and sold home-brewed liquor someplace close by.

Right away, he drew back and asked why I wanted to know. Was this guy a friend or relative? I replied no, just the opposite. A woman of my acquaintance, a woman I cared about, had some trouble with this customer. Saying it like that was true enough, and I left it at that.

After giving me a long serious look, the guy said, "There was a man like that, a man by the name of Johnson Hat. He worked construction on tall buildings. He was burned real bad in an accident on one of them when a bucket of hot charcoal and rivets fell on top of him. The way I heard it, he was such a mean son of a bitch that it was other Indians working on the building that did it to him. He was in the hospital for a long time.

"After that, he took a place up north of here. Only guys who'd buy from him were desperate. Bad things happened up there. There were stories of Indian children and women disappearing. I don't know, you always hear stories. But it doesn't matter. He died, and not long after that his house and his still and his pump house and his shed burned down. Everybody's glad that he's gone, and nobody showed up at the funeral. That answer your question?"

"Yes it does. The next round is on me."

CHAPTER SIXTEEN

By then, I'd eaten all the little crustless green sandwiches and was looking for something else. I made another drink instead.

"OK, it still comes to this. Why me? Even though I haven't seen this money," I lied, "I believe what you say. But why send all this money to me instead of your dear old grandmother?"

"Because my dear old grandma is more than halfway senile on her best day. It wouldn't be safe with her."

She had to be talking about the old lady I'd seen giving me the evil eye outside the Chrysler Building. The same old lady who'd been in the car with Anna a few hours ago. I wondered if she and the baby and the kid were in another room of the suite.

I turned from the booze when I heard scratching at the door followed by the sound of the lock snapping open.

Mercer Weeks stepped through and slipped the lock picks back into his coat pocket. His eyebrows rose in surprise when he saw Anna. She stood up and held herself straight and square-shouldered, looking pretty damn terrific in that red dress. The two of them traded long stares like fighters sizing each other up. Though Weeks probably had eighty pounds on her, they were evenly matched.

"Long time, no see, Signora," he drawled.

She said, "How the hell did you get in here?"

What followed was one of the strangest conversations I ever heard. I'm not sure there was a single moment when all three of us understood exactly what the other two were talking about. At least, that's how I saw it.

Weeks sat in one of the classy chairs, took his works out of his breast pocket, and rolled a smoke. "Marie Therese. I called Quinn's place, and she told me he was here with a woman named Anna. I didn't expect to find you."

He struck a match on the sole of his brogan and said, "Where's Benny? Where's the money?"

Her voice gave nothing away. "What are you drinking, Mercer? Gin? Jimmy, fix something for the gentleman." She sat facing him, one arm stretched across the back of the sofa. A corner of her mouth lifted like she was trying not to smile. "You want to know about Benny. Let's see, what can I tell you that you don't already know?"

Weeks stared at the ashtray on the table in front of him. Why wouldn't he look at her? I put his drink down and sat where I could watch both of them.

"Benny is dead. I was just telling Jimmy about it. I'm sure you remember how it went that last night in Colorado. I didn't want to have anything to do with the ransom, the money, any of it. I was ready to leave. You and Jacob insisted that I deliver it. Do you remember that?"

He didn't respond. She repeated, louder, "Do you remember that?"

He looked up and nodded, poker-faced.

"I followed a crazy half-breed Indian to a place way the hell up in the mountains. He knocked me out and kept me chained in a cabin for ten months. Ten months!"

"How did you get away?"

"I killed the son of a bitch. I strangled him. He was crazy, Mercer. If he'd been around normal people, they'd have been measuring him for a straitjacket. But he was up in the mountains. Like I told Jimmy, he must have had a partner, somebody to plan it out for him. Did you find anybody to fit that description while you were out there?"

"No," he said, sounding more confident. "And I did look for you. All of us did. Right after you disappeared, Jacob brought in more of the guys. We drove so many miles and asked so many questions the cops got suspicious. We even hired the Pinkertons to look for the car. Then it snowed and we really couldn't do anything. Jacob had to come back here to tend to business. I went back in the spring and searched again."

"Since you were part of the Denver Mint job, you knew something about that part of the world."

Weeks stubbed out his smoke. "Not enough. You and Benny and the money just disappeared."

They stared hard at each other, and I realized that there was something else going on behind the words. They were testing each other.

Weeks said, "You're sure Benny is dead?"

"Yes."

"Then where is the money?"

"I don't know," she said, which was, I guess, true enough.

"Two people told Jacob that Quinn has it," Weeks said. They both turned and looked at me. It pissed me off that they knew something I didn't, something important.

"A lot of people have been saying things and doing things," I said. "Planting bombs and killing other people. Mercer came to my assistance this afternoon when I was waylaid by a pack of Krauts. Later on I saw this kid jump a guy in a bus station and run out in the middle of the street." Anna narrowed her eyes at me. "It's all getting complicated because I don't even know who these guys are. Actually, I do know one name. My friend Detective Ellis found out that a guy who broke into my room this morning is Saenger, Justice Saenger. Does that mean anything to either of you?"

Weeks didn't react. Anna gasped and said, "Where is he?"

"Cops put him in Bellevue. If he's still alive. He didn't look good the last time I saw him."

"Good. One less to worry about," she said.

"One less *what* to worry about?"

Weeks said, "Wait a minute. Is Quinn in this with you?"

I ignored him and focused on Anna. "One less *what*?" I repeated.

She glared at me and Weeks. Finally, she muttered, "My family. My goddamn family."

Without mentioning the money, Anna said that she drove to the Denver train station. The next eastbound train was going to Chicago. She took it. She was tired, spooked, and dirty for the entire trip. By the time she reached Chicago, she couldn't stand herself. She went directly from the station to the Palmer House. That's where she had a long hot bath and slept in a real bed.

"I tried to stay out of sight," she said. "There are people in Chicago I'd rather not associate with. One of them found me. The Saengers are cousins on my father's side. They're Reds—dyed-in-the-wool 'Death to the Capitalist' oppressor types."

"And they found out that you've got—"

She shook her head a little, not wanting Weeks to see.

I said, "He knows. Hell, half the population of New York thinks that I'm holding a fortune."

"Are you?" said Anna.

"Yeah, are you?" Weeks wanted to know, too. I let 'em wait.

"Let's go back to what we were talking about before Mercer joined the conversation. Why did you send the money here?"

Anna folded her arms across her chest and shot me an icy look. Weeks was intrigued.

I said, "Working with what you've told me and what I've seen, I figure that when you first set your sights on Jacob at Saratoga

Springs, you had a kid. You brought your crazy grandmother along to take care of the kid. Jacob told me that while you and him were together, you were up to something, something you admitted to him without spilling any details. That was the kid and the grandmother who, I'm guessing, you had stashed somewhere in an apartment that was close but not too close. Am I right?"

She narrowed her eyes and didn't need to say anything.

I continued, "And that's why the money is here and not in Paris or Brazil or wherever the hell it is that people run away to. The whole time the half-breed had you chained up, you were going crazy worrying about how the kid and grandma were getting by. Or had Jacob been so generous that they were well set up?"

Anna said, "Nana and her landlady get along. I knew she wouldn't kick them out onto the street, but I wired money the first chance I got."

"That was in Denver?"

"No, I wanted out of Colorado as fast as I could. I waited until Chicago. That was my mistake. The first thing the crazy old bitch did was tell my family I was alive."

Even though she had registered under a false name, the Saengers found her. As she explained it, she was the only girl who survived past infancy in her generation. She had two brothers, and the whole family shared a house with the Saengers. Of her six Saenger cousins, only one of them was worth a damn. That was the youngest, Edification, known as Eddy, the kid I'd seen a couple of times. The others hated her, and she hated them right back. They were Justice; Knowledge, known as No-No; Fortitude; Deliverance; and Harmonious. At one time, Justice had been tight with the Wobblies and other Reds, but sometime while Anna was out of the picture, he took up with the local branch of the Free Society of Teutonia. He was so taken with Hitler and the Nazis that he really did want to donate Anna's money to the party and move back to Germany, where the Saengers and Gunderwalds were from.

I chewed that over and said, "Do any of them have any experience with explosives?"

"Yes, No-No. The cops tried to pin a bomb that was set during a miners' strike in Montana on him, but they couldn't make it stick."

"Did he do it?"

"If they paid him enough."

"And he knew about this money, and he knew my name?"

"Yes, I suppose so. When Nana told one of them, she told all of them."

Weeks said, "What are you getting at?"

"Guy found himself killed near my place the other night about the same time that a little stick of dynamite went off. Detective Betcherman was hanging around, too." Anna asked who Betcherman was. I ignored her. "It seems to me it's possible this guy was trying to knock down my gate at the alley. But if he didn't know the city and he didn't know my address, maybe he was in the wrong part of the alley, which brings up Benny Numbers's ledgers. There was a problem with the address on them, too. How did they find their way to me?"

Weeks said, "What the hell are you talking about? This is making no goddamn sense at all. How do you two know each other, anyway? This is looking like some kind of setup."

"I met Anna—what was it, six years ago, seven? We had some laughs for a little while until she left town. I didn't see her again until last night."

Weeks had his eyes locked on Anna's, and something was going on between them that I didn't understand.

"I was just a kid then," she said. "So was Jimmy. I trusted him then and I still trust him to help me out of this jam."

"She trusted me enough to send me the ledgers, even if she wasn't sure where my place was."

Her lips twisted into a self-mocking ghost of a smile. "I should've paid more attention when Jacob brought me there. When I heard there was a speak named Jimmy Quinn's, I was curious. You weren't there the afternoon that we dropped in, and I wasn't sure it was the same Jimmy Quinn, but I guess I was sure enough."

"But why put the ledgers in the mail? Why not hold onto them?"

"Because they broke into my room at the Palmer House."

The books were valuable to Jacob. She knew that. If everything else fell apart, he'd pay to get them back. So she kept them in her suitcase, and after she checked into the hotel, she bought another bag big enough to hold them and carried it with her when she left the room. She also carried her cash, most of it anyway.

She spent the first days in Chicago sleeping, eating, regaining her strength and sanity, and working out her possible moves. The clothes she was wearing made her look like a crazy hobo woman. She called the hotel dress shop and ordered some suitable outfits. She didn't leave the room. They sent up girls with underwear, dresses, suits, blouses, skirts, and shoes in her size. She made her choices, signed the bill, and felt wonderful.

Given the circumstances of the past ten months, it didn't take long for cabin fever to set in. She took a stroll over to Michigan Avenue one afternoon and came back to find that the twenty and two tens she'd left in a drawer were gone and somebody had been through her underwear. That's when she knew that Nana had talked, and the Saengers and Gunderwalds were onto her. She could have used Railway Express for the books, but she thought that she remembered my address, and the hotel was happy to follow her mailing instructions.

"OK then," I said, "let me see if I've got this straight. There you were in Chicago with your cousins who were trying to steal your money . . ."

Weeks said, "Where the fuck is the money?"

"Yeah," Anna said, "where the fuck is the money?"

" . . . And they knew it had been sent to one Jimmy Quinn in New York, so they hotfooted it here. Somewhere along the way,

you picked up the youngest, the one you like—what's his name—
Eddy?"

She nodded.

"Then that explains everything except your husband."

That got their attention. Both of them nearly spilled their
drinks.

Mercer said, "What husband?"

"Pauley 'Three Fingers' Domo."

"Oh, shit," Anna said. "He's here?"

"He was in my place last night. Gave me a ten-spot that had
some kind of crap all over it and a key that he wanted me to hold
for him for twenty-four hours. Made it all sound as mysterious
as hell."

Anna laughed. "God, that's Pauley, all right. I'm sure it's part
of some brilliant plan he cooked up."

Weeks said, "I'm starting to get steamed. What the hell are
you two talking about? Where's Jacob's money?"

They stared at me.

I said, "Let's go take a look at it."

Anna cut her eyes at Weeks. He was suspicious.

"It's close. We can walk or take a cab."

Anna said, "Let me check on Nana and the baby," and went
through the door to one of the bedrooms.

A second later she screamed.

CHAPTER SEVENTEEN

While Anna and Weeks and I had been yakking away, Nana had decided to take a powder with the kid. She left a hand-scrawled note that didn't even look like writing to me.

Anna pointed out the words: Worry Not We See Paul Baby Need You Husband.

It made no sense to me. Anna translated. She said that despite everything they'd done together, Nana thought that she, Anna, was still Pauley Domo's wife and should be obedient and respectful to him.

"I told her he was dead," she said, "and when the son of a bitch learned about the money, he tracked her down."

"How'd he find out about the money?"

"The Saengers. He's practically another brother. That crazy old woman, I do not understand her. For years, she's afraid to touch a telephone. Now she's calling Pauley, she's calling Jacob, she wants me to give the money to the church. Jesus Christ, why did she do this *now*?"

It was strange, watching her then, half-focused on the money, half on the kid.

"All right," she said out loud to herself, "she's safe enough with Nana." Then she turned to me. "Where's the money?"

Weeks demanded the same thing, and that did it. I'd had enough. As you've figured out, I am an even-tempered, good-humored guy. Unless provoked, I don't set out to make trouble or anger people. Bad for business, bad on general principle. But by that time that night, I'd heard so many crazy stories and been bombed and punched and shot at and Mickey Finned, and lied to and threatened and had two of my best suits ruined that I was well pissed off.

I stood up, grabbed my hat, and said to her, "Where's your kid?" and to Weeks, "Where's Jacob? Why don't you two straighten out whatever it is that you're not telling me. Find Jacob and meet me in a couple of hours at 405 Lex, top floors, and we'll work this out." They didn't know what the hell I was talking about. Like I said, there was hardly a moment when each of the three of us completely understood the other two.

I went back downstairs, had the doorman hail a cab, and went back to the speak.

Fat Joe unlocked the front door. He had a sawed-off double barrel in his big mitt.

He said, "You took your sweet time. It's been a fucking parade out there."

"Anybody you know?"

"The fat fucking Kraut who was in the other night with the gent. He's been driving and walking by. Got a fucking big bandage on his nose. Malloy says there's action in the alley."

"Anybody try to get in?"

"Only regulars. Read the fucking sign and went away."

"OK, we're going to move the stuff later. It's probably going to get rough. Expect you'll be able to shoot somebody."

Fat Joe smiled. I went to the back door.

Malloy had made himself comfortable on the landing with a couple of barstools. He sat on one and had a drink and his Luger on the other. He was reading a book.

"Good evening, sir," he said when he saw me. "I hope you don't mind my borrowing one of the books from your office. Even with the savages circling our outpost, it gets boring." He'd taken Will Durant's *The Story of Philosophy*, and it looked like he'd made it farther than I had.

"Not to worry. What's going on outside?"

"This being my first night on the job, it's not really my place to say, but this does seem to be an uncommonly busy alley. Couple of times I've heard guys rattling the gate and trying to climb over it. Can't tell how many of them. When they hear me open the door, they fly on winged feet."

"Fine. In a couple of hours we're going to move the money. Be ready."

The kitchen was a mess. There were wax shavings and dirty towels and pans of milky water all over the worktable. Somebody had strung up lengths of cotton string like clotheslines. Wet dripping tens and twenties were paper-clipped to the string. All four of the boxes had been opened, but it looked like they'd only been working on the first one. The oilcloth had been peeled back on the other three, revealing more solid brownish wax.

Marie Therese said that it took too long to scrape away the stuff with knives. That's where the shavings came from. They put the block in a big wash pan, boiled up a pot of water, and poured it slowly over the block. That softened it up enough for them to pry loose the first six inches or so and work with those bills, the ones that were hanging up to dry.

I asked what the count was, and Frenchy answered too quickly, "Two hundred and sixty dollars, with that much more in the pan. Now that we've got the block cut down, it will fit in the oven and we can melt it. Marie Therese thinks we should keep it down to two hundred and fifty degrees. Don't want the wax to catch fire."

I told them not to bother with it. "There's still some question as to who's got the most legitimate claim on this nasty stuff, but since Jacob the Wise is one of the interested parties, we're going to move it out of here and let them settle things. Like I said earlier, none of you signed on for anything like this." I was looking at Connie when I said it. "And I think it's likely that somebody's not going to be happy at the way this turns out. Any of you want to stay here and get ready to open tomorrow night, you're being smart."

Everybody said no. Connie was the most bright-eyed and excited of the bunch.

"All right, then, I've got to make some calls. Shut the boxes back up and take them back to the cellar. And let's spruce up a little. We're going to take all this up to the Cloud Club, where the interested parties will make their case. We should have the joint to ourselves, but if somebody questions us, we need to look like we belong there. "And could somebody make me a sandwich, a *real* sandwich? I'm starving."

Back in my office, I called Ellis's precinct and asked for him. The sergeant who answered said he was busy. I told him who I was—he knew me—and said it was really important for Ellis to talk to me. I had information on two cases he was working.

Connie came in with a ham and swiss on rye, a glass of milk, and a thermos of coffee. She was the most wonderful woman in the world.

The most wonderful woman in the world stretched out on my divan and said, "I guess all this got started when we were here the other night, when the bomb went off."

I nodded while I chewed.

"But," she said, getting to her point, "it really started when you met that woman, your 'old girlfriend.'"

"That was five, six, seven years ago, I don't remember exactly and it's not important. She and I . . . " I stopped. What were Anna and me?

"She's Jacob's mistress. Or she was. She's got a kid who's about three years old, I think. And she's got a husband, the guy who was part of all the commotion at the bus station this afternoon."

Connie sat up quick. "Three Fingers is her husband? That's what Marie Therese calls him, says he gives her the heebie-jeebies. He's been in for the past three nights, nursing beers, acting strange but not doing quite enough for Fat Joe to throw him out. What's he got to do with this?"

"It's a really involved story. What it comes down to, I think, is that this is money Jacob paid to get Benny Numbers back after he was snatched out West. Three Fingers seems to think it's his. So do a lot of other guys."

Connie asked if I knew why the cash had been sealed up like that, and I admitted that I did.

"That's another involved, crazy story. Crazy as hell. When there's time, I'll tell you all about it, but here's what it comes down to: Anna, my 'old girlfriend,' delivered the money, and she was held captive in the mountains by some kind of hermit. She thinks he saw her in this little town where she and Jacob were staying and he became—what's the word—obsessed with her and decided to lock her up for his own. Does that sound possible to you?"

Connie seemed to pull inside herself on the sofa, knees and feet together, arms clasped around her chest. "Oh yes, it's possible. It's . . . never mind. Believe me, it could happen."

I thought she had another story to tell, but she didn't say anything more about it. That night wasn't the time. She said they needed her in the kitchen.

I guess I'd believed Anna from the beginning. She lied to me with things she didn't say and things she left out, like a husband in the Tombs, but I didn't doubt what she said about the months in the cabin. She didn't make that up. I still wasn't sure why she sent the money and the books to me, and what she was holding back about Benny, but I thought the story about the half-breed was true, because the girl who'd challenged me to race in the street would have done just what she did. She'd be patient, she'd think it through, and when she got the chance, she'd kill him.

As for me, I think it was while I was sitting there by myself that I finally understood just how important the speak had become to me. It was my place, our place. I may have lived at the Chelsea, but this was home. And I knew that Marie Therese and Frenchy thought of it as home, too. Connie hadn't been there long enough for me to know what she thought, and nobody knew what Fat Joe thought. I just realized then that I needed the place, and as long as I could hold onto it, I wouldn't sell out.

It was a little after eleven when Ellis called back. I asked if he'd set it up for us to get back into the Cloud Club.

He said, "Yeah, I know one of the supervisors on the janitorial crew. He'll help us out, but what the hell's going on? Why the Cloud Club?"

"For the same reason you took me there, to impress people," I said. Actually, I didn't really know what I was doing, but it seemed likely that things would get rough, and I didn't want anybody shooting up my place. Didn't want to clean up either.

"The situation has changed a little. And I'm not sure it really makes a difference, but now I am certain that this money everybody is so interested in is Weiss's ransom for Benny Numbers."

"How did it get here?"

"I can't tell you that. Not now, maybe later. As near as I can tell, it has nothing to do with Betcherman's killing. Sure, he was looking for it when he got killed, but Jacob didn't rob a bank to get it. He just did what he does every day, and you're not interested in that."

"So, the money is clean, that's what you're saying."

"Well . . . Yes, it's clean. Jacob and another interested party are going to join us at the Cloud Club. Our friend Herr Klapprott has his guys keeping an eye on my place, so they'll follow us. He'll bring along his number one thug, a guy named Luther who killed Betcherman."

"You know this?"

"Yes, I do."

"How will I find him?"

"That's easy. First, he's going to be coming after me, and second, he's wearing a big bandage where his nose ought to be."

I finished my coffee, checked to see that I hadn't left any of my sandwich on my shirt or tie, and went back down to the cellar. I collected Malloy along the way.

The rest of them were waiting with the four crates. Marie Therese and Connie had dolled up. Connie was wearing a man's duster to hide the gun she was carrying. The gents, even Fat Joe, had put on ties. He and Malloy started to load the crates onto the hand truck until I told them to wait.

I knew guys had been watching us when we brought the stuff down from the Railway Express office. Maybe they'd been close enough to see that we had four crates. So we'd have to take four crates back uptown, but they didn't have to be the same four crates.

It had been years since we'd used the storage space behind the false wall, and it took me a while to find the spring latch. When the door popped open, it smelled even more strongly of raw excavated dirt than the rest of the cellar. I told Frenchy and Fat Joe to stow the third and fourth crates of Yampah Hot Springs Mineral Water inside and took two wooden boxes of Gordon's Gin from inventory. I was probably being too cautious, but if anybody had been watching carefully, they'd see that we had four wooden crates on the bed of the truck, and all six of us were along for the ride. Nobody was staying behind to guard anything. I can't say that I had any sort of plan in mind. I didn't know what was going to happen, but I figured that splitting up the money couldn't hurt.

As we took the crates up to the truck, Fat Joe said to Malloy, "Sometimes he ain't as fucking stupid as he looks."

CHAPTER EIGHTEEN

Fat Joe and Malloy stayed on the bed of the truck as Frenchy eased out into the alley and I locked the gate. Connie squeezed into the cab with Frenchy and Marie Therese. Since she was more comfortable with rifles and long guns, Fat Joe gave her the riot gun he'd carried that afternoon. It was loaded with birdshot, but I hoped like hell that she didn't have to use it. That thing really made a mess. Marie Therese had the little Spanish .25 automatic she always carried in her purse. Fat Joe pulled me up and I sat on a crate of money.

As we drove toward the streetlights, it seemed that everyone on the sidewalk was paying extra attention to us. I told myself that was just nerves, that it was odd for people to see three guys riding on the back of a truck on Third Avenue in the middle of the night, and that nobody was really paying attention. Right. About then I heard the rumble of a V-8 and saw the big bright headlights coming up behind us, and there was Klapprott's Phaeton pulling up alongside. He was smiling in the backseat as he touched the brim of his hat with a gloved hand. Luther wasn't with him. I think it was the same driver who'd been in the car that morning.

The Cadillac stayed even or ahead of us until Frenchy turned on Forty-Third Street and then went into the service entrance. I got down and banged on a metal door. A guy in coveralls with the name FRANKIE stitched on the chest answered. I told him Ellis sent us. He pointed us toward the hall that led to the lobby. Frenchy asked if it was OK to leave the truck there. I gave Frankie a buck, and he said he'd watch it.

While the guys unloaded the stuff, I asked Frankie if he had a phone line to the Cloud Club. He said that he did, and I gave him a five to let us know when anybody else showed up.

Nothing had changed on the sixty-sixth floor. I still couldn't get over how small the place was. Sure, they'd done a great job with the fancy ceilings, and the bar had a gentlemen's club feeling, but the selling point of the place was the elevation and the view, and the windows weren't that big. Maybe it meant enough to the members that they were up there above it all and the rest of us unwashed hoi polloi weren't bothering them.

Not that I was really worried about such things that night. Like I said, I didn't really have a plan, so first I had to figure out how we'd spread out and where we'd set up the dirty loot. Seemed to make sense to me that we act like we actually worked there. That meant Fat Joe stayed at the door. Frenchy and Marie Therese were behind the bar. Connie took the little coatroom and found the telephone switchboard there. We put the cases of Gordon's on the floor and the two boxes of waxed cash on the bar. Frenchy pried open the first box again, and we left the chunks of wax that they'd separated on top of the bar. Malloy and I went up to the top floor of the restaurant and checked to see where the doors were, which ones were locked, and where they led.

The stairs and elevators were in the center. We couldn't find any doors on the exterior walls, but there were odd-shaped little closets and cabinets, some locked. We also found buckets and wet spots on the floor from all the leaks in those weird windows, I guess. They made the footing treacherous in places. Malloy and I took the stairs up through the kitchen to the observatory. Not much light was coming through the narrow triangular windows. Malloy found the switch and turned on the screwy fixtures that looked like planets and stars. Again, there didn't appear to be anyplace a guy could hide up there, but some of the windows could be opened.

I was ready to leave when Malloy said he wanted to look around.

"You know, we came up on one elevator to the fifty-seventh floor, I believe it was, and we took another to this overweening farrago they call their Cloud Club—'Cloud Club' my bleeding ass—but if we are to be having visitors who might wish us harm, I'd like to know more about the floors directly below us, particularly the one with the gargoylian eagles at the corners."

It was a good idea, but with my leg it would take too long to get down the stairs. "OK," I said, "make it snappy."

He zipped down the stairs.

Gargoylian—what the hell was that?

Back in the Cloud Club, Connie said, "Frankie called. There's a guy on his way up."

There was no place I could sit where I could watch everything, so I took a four-top in a corner where I could see the bar and one set of elevators. Fat Joe was watching the elevators and stairs on the other side. I took out the little Smith and checked the load. Like me, Fat Joe kept an empty chamber. I cocked the pistol to put a round under the hammer and laid it on the table close to my hand. It was in plain sight. Just wanted to let everyone know that I was taking this seriously. It's been my experience that a pistol in a holster or a pocket makes a damn poor defensive weapon.

I heard the elevator working and felt the vibration of it through the soles of my shoes. It stopped, the doors opened, and Fat Joe grunted. Johann Klapprott, cool as you please, strolled around the corner. Fat Joe patted him down and said he was clean. The German glanced at the pistol and a tiny smile lifted the corner of his mouth. He checked his hat and Malacca with Connie and nodded to Frenchy and Marie Therese, taking an extra moment to check out the crate and yellow oilcloth. He turned to me and said, "May I join you?"

I nodded to the empty chair. He sat, glanced at the crates again, and said, "First, I must apologize for what went on this morning. I was told by the party that responsibility had been transferred to the Chicago organization and I was to introduce you to them. I had no idea that Luther intended to do you harm, and I am reconsidering my association with them."

"And you had nothing to do with dosing the coffee."

He shrugged as if it meant nothing. "A simple precaution, but not, I understand, an effective one. I advised against it, but the people from Chicago insisted. Do you suppose they stock Stein-häger in this establishment?"

"Try the Gordon's." I nodded to Frenchy. He poured gin over ice in a short glass and brought it over. I wasn't buying Klapprott's story and the way he was making nice, but I figured it was good to have him right there where I could see him.

Klapprott sipped, crossed his legs, and leaned back. "The young man who claims to be the rightful owner or, I suppose, inheritor of the money in question will be here soon. I have seen—" He stopped and appeared worried. "What is that object?" waving toward the messy waxy oilcloth.

"If your young fellow can explain that, it'll go a long way toward supporting his claim, but I doubt that Justice Schilling or Justice Saenger will be joining us."

"Is that Klapprott?" I hadn't heard or seen Ellis approach, but there he was by the bar. He handed over his hat and overcoat to Connie and sat with us. I gave Fat Joe the high sign, and he poured another gin for the detective.

I made the introductions. "Johann Klapprott, Detective William Ellis. Ellis, Klapprott." They didn't shake hands. Ellis didn't waste any time.

"What is your connection to the 115 warehouse on the wharf off South Street?"

"My firm represents the owners, Herr Schmidt and Herr Watts, in matters involving real estate and investments."

"What do you or they know about two murders that took place there Tuesday night?"

"Nothing." Klapprott was unruffled. "I do know that my clients own those properties, but even if they are suspected of any involvement in the incident, my firm does not handle criminal cases."

About then it came to me that nobody had called to say that Ellis was on his way up. I interrupted and asked if he came in through the Forty-Third Street entrance and saw Frankie downstairs. Before he could answer, the elevator doors opened.

Jacob the Wise and Mercer Weeks walked in.

It was a strange moment, seeing how the four of them reacted to one another.

You had Weeks and Ellis, a strong-arm enforcer and a cop. As I saw it, they did the same job on opposite sides of the street. The few times I'd seen them in my place at the same time, they avoided each other without making a point of it, and I had the idea they respected each other.

With Weiss and Klapprott, it was the opposite. The German's back stiffened and his normally bemused expression twisted into naked contempt. Jacob Weiss read it right away. He was looking at a guy who hated Jews and didn't care who knew it. You could tell they'd be after each other soon enough.

Jacob was wearing a decent suit, and he had a big Havana fired up. Weeks cased the room quickly, establishing where everybody was. He noted the pistol on the table in front of me and took a longer look at the crate on the bar. He and Jacob went over to it. While Weeks read the Railway Express label, Jacob picked up one of the wads of waxy bills. You could tell it was money if you were looking for it. After a few seconds he put it down, frowning around the cigar and sniffing at his fingers. He cleaned them off with his pocket square and muttered, "What the hell is this?"

"That's what we're here to establish," I said. Then I asked Connie, "Have you heard anything from Frankie downstairs?"

She shook her head. I asked Ellis again if he'd seen Frankie. He said no. I heard fast footsteps on the stairs, and Malloy, breathing hard, ran into the room. He had his Luger out.

"We have company," he said between breaths, "a lot of company."

Malloy had gone down four or five floors, where they had normal offices. He didn't see anybody working in any of them. At that hour, all of them were dark. But he heard somebody, at least two groups of guys.

The first were men's voices close and distinct. They were on the far side of a corner and Malloy ducked into a men's room. He heard at least two guys who'd taken the elevator up to the fifty-seventh but didn't understand where they were and couldn't figure how to get to the other elevator. They were arguing about what to do, and it sounded to him like they'd decided to take the stairs, if they could find them. Then they shut up because they and Malloy heard somebody else. Mind you, Malloy didn't actually see any of these guys, but that didn't matter.

The second group got off the elevator, and even though one of them was trying to quiet the others, Malloy could hear enough.

"They're Krauts," he said, "and I'm certain they're some of the same schnitzel-eaters who frequented the 115 warehouse late on moonless nights, the same ones who set upon Mr. Quinn this morning."

His voice chilly, Klapprott said that they might be his colleagues. I asked how they knew to come to the Chrysler Building.

He shrugged. "Who can say? They have been talking to people on the telephone at my office all afternoon and evening."

Jacob the Wise snorted. "This guy says it's his dough?"

"No, I am simply here to warn Mr. Quinn that my former associates mean him harm."

Jacob turned back to the bar and said to nobody in particular: "What the hell did you do to my money?"

I said, "Is it your money? How do you know?"

Weeks said, "Label says it came from Denver. That's enough for us."

I heard the elevator doors on the other side open, and there was some commotion. A few seconds later, Fat Joe shoved two guys into the room.

I'd seen one of them a couple of days before on street level when he followed me up Lexington from my place. It was the gaunt guy in the gray canvas jacket and black cap. The other one looked a lot like him and was also wearing tradesman's clothes. I was pretty sure their last name was Saenger. They took one look at Ellis and saw that he was a cop right away.

I said to Ellis, "I think you're gonna find these two are related to the guy you've got at Bellevue, the guy who broke into my room. They might also have something to do with the dead guy who set the bomb."

They started squawking that they didn't know anything about breaking and entering or bombs. Ellis cut them off and demanded to see identification. Each of them handed over a thin wallet. Ellis went through their pockets and found several others. He sat them down at a two-top.

"What the hell are you doing here?" he asked.

They looked at each other, trying to figure out what they could get away with. Finally, the one who'd followed me said that Pauley Domo told them to come there. He said he had a job and offered each of them twenty bucks. All they had to do was carry some boxes.

They were interrupted by a ringing telephone in the coat closet. Connie answered, listened for a moment, and said, "It's Frankie from downstairs. He says there's a guy, an old woman, and a baby on the way up."

Klapprott leaned back and laughed. "This really is becoming quite a production. I can't wait to see what happens next."

"Ain't it the truth," I said.

We heard the next batch before we saw them. I guess they were one floor below us, and there were enough of them that they split up. The first ones came out of the stairwell, the second from the elevator. They rushed into the room together and stopped. There were six of them, and I don't think they expected to be outnumbered. Luther was in the lead, and he looked worse than he had the last time I saw him. He had a square gauze bandage stained rusty-red with dried blood in the middle of his mug. It was held in place with a big *X* of adhesive tape. His eyes were dark and swollen, and he gulped air through his mouth like a fish. The rest of them looked to be some of the guys who worked me over in the warehouse.

By then, the little place was far too warm and crowded. I slipped my knucks onto my left hand.

Like the Saengers, Luther made Ellis for a cop PDQ and ducked back between two of his fellow thugs. He went for the stairs with the detective close behind. His thug pals tried to stop Ellis. Mercer Weeks waded in to assist him, and things got lively.

From where I sat, it looked like a couple of the Germans turned tail and three stayed to fight. Neither Mercer nor Ellis messed around, and two guys went face-down in the first seconds. They were brawlers, not professionals. The third guy charged down the stairs with Detective Ellis right behind. Mercer Weeks went back beside his boss. I looked over at the two-top and saw that the Saengers had taken the opportunity to make a quiet departure.

I sensed movement nearby, turned, and saw the boy, the boy who'd slipped me Anna's note and gone after Pauley Three Fingers in the bus station. He was standing right next to my chair, and it was almost spooky the way he just appeared there. He leaned in and whispered, "Anna says you should come with me."

I shook my head. "Not now."

The two downed Germans got to their feet, and one of them

was so damn stupid he made another move on Mercer Weeks, who backhanded him with a sap across the cheek and then broke his right arm with it. You could hear the bone go, even with all the noise in the place. By then, Marie Therese was yelling something, and Frenchy was coming around from behind the bar. Connie racked a load of birdshot into the shotgun.

Jacob watched it all without disturbing the ash on the end of his cigar.

The smarter German tried to help his friend who moaned and cradled his arm. The smart guy made the mistake of pulling a nickel-plated pistol, but before it cleared the shoulder holster, Weeks was on top of him. He smashed the guy's wrist with the sap. As he twisted the piece from the numb fingers, it went off.

Everybody got quiet as the report echoed away. But the noise coming from downstairs got louder. I could hear banging and thumping and yelling, like several guys in a fight. Weeks scooped up the nickel-plated pistol and put it on the bar by the crate.

Klapprott got up and retrieved his hat and cane from Connie. She put the gun down long enough to get them. He walked to the elevators and pushed the button.

"Ladies, gentlemen," he said looking at me and ignoring Jacob, "I believe it's time for me to say good evening. I've done what I came here to do. Mr. Quinn, again I apologize for what happened earlier today. It was unnecessary. I am, however, still interested in purchasing your establishment. We shall talk of it another time."

The elevator doors opened and he left.

Jacob the Wise, who would not be moved off his point, asked me again what the hell I did to his money.

That did it. I was tired of him. "First, I don't know what it is. I only got the stuff this afternoon. Look at it. It's a big chunk of brown wax. They tried to separate the banknotes from the wax, and it didn't go so well. It's going to take a while to do that right, and, when you think about it, if this really is *your* money, I should be asking you what the hell you did with it."

He snorted. "Don't get smart with me, you—"

"Fuck off." The cigar drooped. "You'll get a chance to state your case."

Damn, it felt good to say that.

Jacob cut his eyes to Mercer Weeks like Weeks was going to lay into me for mouthing off. Weeks paid no attention. I wondered what he'd told his boss about his talk with Anna and me that evening. Or if he'd even told him that Anna, aka Signora Sophia, was back in town.

Jacob and Weeks messed about trying to pull a bill out of the smaller block of wax for a few minutes. A familiar face peeked around from the corner of the stairs. I said, "Come on in, Pauley, you're invited to this party, too."

Pauley Three Fingers edged in slowly, like he was ready to rabbit at the first sign of trouble. That sign turned out to be Jacob. He looked up from the money, saw Pauley, and said, "That's him. That's the guy who tried to tell me you'd bought my money for a penny on the dollar."

Pauley flinched. He wanted to run, but by then he'd seen the money on the bar and he wanted it bad. You could tell that by the way his remaining fingers twitched as he scanned the room. If he'd thought that he had half a chance, he'd have grabbed that box and gone straight to the stairs. But that wasn't in the cards, not then, so he straightened up and said, "I guess I got part of the story wrong, but Quinn did have the money, didn't he? I shot straight with you. And I know more now than I did when I talked to you. That's not your money. It belongs to my wife."

The older woman, Anna's grandmother, came up the stairs. She had the baby in her arms, and she hung back, away from Pauley Three Fingers. I don't think Jacob or Weeks noticed her. They were focused on Pauley as he edged closer to the bar. Sweat beaded on his forehead and upper lip.

"He is *not* my husband."

Anna must have come in from the elevators. Her voice was loud and cold, and everybody in the room turned to look at her.

She was wearing a long black coat unbuttoned over that tight red dress. She shrugged the coat off as she strode across the room and gave Pauley a scornful glare. He tried to meet her eyes but really couldn't. I had the feeling that maybe he had never seen her looking like she did then, hair blonde and bobbed, expensive beautifully fitted clothes, heels that made her legs look even better than they always did. All I can say is I'd seen her at her best, and I hadn't seen anything like that.

It was hard for me to read exactly what Jacob was thinking. He stood up and kind of smiled when he first saw her, but that turned into a calculating suspicious frown in two heartbeats. She turned from Pauley to him and said, "Good to see you, Jakey."

He said, "You too, Soph."

More confusion spread across Pauley Three Fingers's face. He had no idea what was going on between them.

Jacob said, "Weeks told me I was in for a surprise. He knew what he was talking about. I never thought I'd see you again. Everybody said you ran off with Benny, but I thought you were dead. Tell me what happened."

She crossed her arms across her chest. "I followed the instructions that night and drove to the place on the map, Miner's Camp Number Three. Another car met me there, and I followed it a long way up into the mountains. We ended up at a little cabin that the gang had been using as a hideout. There were three of them—two white men and a half-breed, the one I followed. All of them had guns. They'd tied poor Benny to a chair. He looked like hell, and right off they started arguing about how they were splitting up the money and whether they should let us go or kill us. They locked me up in an outbuilding, and I heard them arguing and fighting all night long, and finally, I heard shots. A lot of shots.

"The next morning, the half-breed came into the outbuilding and locked a chain around my ankle. He said they were all dead. They'd killed each other, and he didn't care because they'd just been renting his place. Now I was going to stay there and be his squaw."

"Do you mean he . . . "

"Do I have to spell it out for you, Jakey? Yeah, he did everything you think he did, and he kept me locked up for ten months before he got careless and I found a knife."

The best lies are almost the truth. She must have rehearsed the story to herself a hundred times because she delivered it with the right anger and bitterness.

Jacob bought it, I think. He looked at Weeks.

Weeks shrugged and said, "It's screwy but it squares with what happened and what we know."

Jacob said, "But that doesn't explain all this," waving his hand at the waxy mess.

Pauley found his voice and stepped up. "She doesn't have to explain anything. She'll take care of this, and I'm here to help her."

Laughing, Anna said, "You son of a bitch, you broke into my room and stole every dollar you could get your hands on. In a pig's ass you'll help me with anything."

Without my noticing, the grandmother had joined the group. She reached out and slapped Anna and called her something in a language I couldn't understand, but I knew it was a curse. She tried to slap her again, but holding the baby on her hip, she couldn't move her free arm very well. Anna blocked the slap and muttered something to her grandmother.

The old woman spat more curses back at her and finally said in English, "A woman does not like this talk to her husband which is the father of her only child."

The only child bawled, and it seemed like everybody was yelling at everybody else to shut the hell up. Pauley was sidling over to the money. I noticed Ellis coming from the stairs. He heard the raised voices, walked into the middle of everything, and yelled, "Pipe down!"

Nobody did. This was turning into a four-alarm Chinese fire drill.

When Ellis realized that the Saengers had tiptoed away, he really got pissed. Pauley Three Fingers being close at hand, the cop slammed him down into a chair.

"All right," Ellis said in his big cop voice, "somebody explain this. Seems to start with you, Quinn."

Following Anna's lead, I explained that I had received these two boxes from Railway Express. Anna didn't give anything away when I said "two." All the people who worked for me examined their fingernails or found something fascinating to look at up near the ceiling. I told Ellis I couldn't be sure who sent them. Over the past couple of days, several parties had approached me and said that they were the rightful owners.

"Actually," I said, "the first one was Detective Betcherman. Right after that bomb went off, he put the arm on me. He said that he knew an item had been delivered to the speak and he was part of the deal. Those were his exact words. The next night, somebody plugged him in a warehouse on the East River. You remember, there was another dead guy in the warehouse, and he had papers made out in my name. From the way he was dressed, I'd say there's a good chance he was one of these Saenger fellows from Chicago."

I explained how one of the Saengers had thrown in with the Free Society of Teutonia and the Nazis and the other Germans, while other parts of the family, probably including the guy who planted the bomb, were in it for themselves and hated the Krauts.

"Can it," said Ellis pointing at the stuff on the bar. "Maybe that's true and maybe it ain't, but it doesn't tell me what this is or who it belongs to."

Without dwelling on boring details, I said we'd picked it up that afternoon and found that the crate contained a big block of sticky brown wax. There appeared to be something inside, so we did a little work using this and that and discovered that paper money was embedded in the wax. Since so many people, including the deceased detective, claimed a piece of this, I decided to invite them here to make their case.

"Johann Klapprott bowed out early on, but his associate Luther and his fellow thugs, some of them anyway, are still around."

He scowled. "I've got more people on the way. Who are you?"

he said to Pauley Three Fingers. "You look familiar. I've seen you somewhere before. Where was it?"

I gave him a hint. "Did you catch the attempted stickup of a mail truck about, what, five, six years ago?"

Pauley said, "I did my time."

"That's right, I was in uniform then. You wrecked the car, you and that other guy."

"Yeah," Anna said. "One of the highlights of his extensive criminal career."

"You don't have any room to talk," he answered. "You were there. If you hadn't distracted me, it would have been perfect."

"You are a lying son of a bitch. Go back to that skinny bitch, Hildy."

He jumped up and got right in her face. "Don't say that. You know it isn't true. I explained that."

"You didn't explain shit, you slimy little weasel. Now just get the hell out of here. None of this concerns you."

She hauled off and hit him with her fist. He slapped her back. Until that moment, I hadn't understood how much they loved each other. Ellis waded in to break it up and shoved Pauley into the bar. The bastard whirled back around with the German's nickel-plated pistol in his three-fingered mitt. In the same motion, he grabbed Anna around the waist, pulled her in front of him, and stuck the muzzle into her ribs.

In a calming tone, Ellis said, "Don't be crazy, son. Put it down."

Pauley looked around until he spotted the older woman and said something to her in her language. She smiled and said something in agreement and hurried over with the squalling baby, shoving Weeks and Jacob out of the way. Anna struggled against him. He tightened his grip, leaned down, and whispered something that made her stop. I picked up the Smith. Anna saw what I was up to and shook her head. The old woman moved in so close I didn't have a clear shot at him anyway.

The boy who went after Pauley at the bus station slipped through the crowd and glared at Pauley with pure anger.

His voice breaking, Pauley Domo said, "The money belongs to my wife, so it belongs to me, too. Isn't that right, darling?"

She nodded.

"And Quinn is going to loan us his car."

I didn't say anything. Anna said, "Please, Jimmy, I can straighten this out."

Jacob said, "The hell you can. That's my money."

She said, "Let me handle this. You don't understand. She's *your* daughter."

Jacob's mouth opened in surprise, and he almost dropped his cigar. Either he hadn't had a good look at the baby or he was even worse at judging kids' ages than I was. I didn't think the lie would last. He was figuring it out already.

There were too many guns in the small room. I could see that Ellis and Weeks were unbuttoning their coats to get at the holsters on their belts. Malloy had his Luger hidden under his jacket, and Connie had the riot gun at her shoulder. Too much could go wrong there.

I stood up and said, "Frenchy, Malloy, take the crates. When you get downstairs, give him the keys."

Everybody looked like I was nuts.

"It's all right." I got up and made my way through the crowd to the bar. Pauley turned, keeping Anna between us.

I said to Frenchy, "You and Malloy take the crates. Remember, we've got to change elevators on the sixty-first floor."

They all started talking at once. Pauley's voice came out louder than the others. "You heard the man. Just stay out of the way." The boy faded to the back of the crowd and scurried for the stairs.

I held the elevator doors open as Frenchy and Malloy got on, followed by the grandmother and the baby and Pauley Three Fingers and Anna. She looked as angry as I'd ever seen her.

The doors closed. I pushed *61*, and the car lurched down. When the doors opened, I was the first one out. I saw two guys were ducking out of sight behind corners. Yeah, my brilliant plan just kept getting more and more brilliant.

The offices were dark, and only a few of the hallway lights were turned on, so the open area in front of the elevators had a dim, shadowy look. You could catch a little reflected light off the shiny stainless steel eagles out on the balcony where Ellis and I had been. A hard wind thudded against the wide glass doors.

Pauley still had a tight grip on Anna, and the old woman with the baby stayed right at his side. The little girl had stopped crying by then and sucked her thumb. Frenchy and Malloy shifted the heavy crates they held and moved away from the others. Pauley Domo turned when he heard me walking toward them.

"That'll do, guys," I said. "You can put them down there by the doors."

Pauley's head looked like it was on a swivel as he tried to watch me and see what Frenchy and Malloy were doing. They dropped the crates and stepped back smartly. Malloy pulled his Luger but kept it at his side.

I got the Smith out of my pocket and cocked it. "Do you want me to shoot him?" I asked Anna as I aimed at his head.

She started to say something but stopped.

Pauley said, "I thought we had a deal. I'm serious about this." He twisted around behind her, giving me no clear shot.

I said, "You've got two choices and you better make up your mind fast because we're going to have more company soon. You can let Anna go and take a crate and scram out of here on your own. Or you can keep dancing around here and either Malloy or I will shoot you. Malloy is the guy behind you with the Luger aimed at your spine. What's it going to be?"

He never had a chance to answer. I heard running footsteps from somewhere close, and Luther and three of his pals barreled around a corner behind Frenchy and Malloy. They knocked my guys to the ground and swarmed over Pauley and the women. Luther stopped and tried to pull the lid off one of the crates.

I took a slow breath and shot the closest thug in the center of the chest. For the second time that night, the sound of the gun-shot made everyone freeze for a short moment. Everyone but me.

I cocked the pistol and took aim at another Kraut who turned and ran before I could pull the trigger.

Then Luther was on me. He knocked me on my ass. Both the gun and my stick clattered away. I rolled as Luther tried to kick me in the ribs. I guess he was still so angry about his nose that he tried too hard. The toe of his shoe hurt like hell where it caught me, but it didn't hit square. He either hit a wet spot on the floor or the momentum of the kick pulled him around and his other foot slipped out from under him. I was on my feet before he was, and my knucks were still on my left hand. The big bandage in the middle of his ugly mug was much too tempting to resist. He howled even louder than before when I pasted him.

The bastard didn't stay down. I found the gun and my stick on the floor. By the time I'd collected them, he was getting to his feet. Pauley and Anna had disappeared. Frenchy and Malloy were mixing it up with Luther's guys. On my way past him, I clipped Luther across the ear with my stick. It barely slowed him down.

Frenchy was half as big as the Kraut who'd jumped him but was pounding the guy against the wall. Malloy was getting the worst of it, so I came up on his guy and caught him on the back of the neck with my knucks. Malloy pushed him away and he collapsed. I turned back to Luther. He was on his feet and reaching for his gun in a big shoulder holster.

Ellis came up behind him and said, "Don't touch it. Hands behind your head."

Luther did as Ellis said and then spun around and took a swing. He tagged Ellis on the chin. That really made him mad. He slugged Luther in the midsection, and the big shit went down to his knees again. Ellis got out the cuffs and ratcheted them on Luther's wrists none too gently behind his back.

I tried to find Anna and Pauley Domo. The old woman and the baby were still standing close to Frenchy and the crate he'd been carrying. The other box of money was gone. Somebody yelled something I couldn't understand. Through the glass doors, I saw figures moving out on the balcony.

When I got out there, I saw it was Pauley, Anna, and the boy. The crate was on its side near the doors. Waxy chunks had spilled out. The top had come off, and Pauley held it in front of him like a shield. The boy was going after him with a knife. Anna was trying to calm them down. The kid's blood was up, and he was having none of it. Pauley Domo had a queasy look. He backed away from the kid but kept an eye on the low barrier at the edge of the balcony. It was about two feet high, and I guess he could tell how easy it would be to go over. The gusting wind didn't help.

The kid held the knife low and level and kept it moving back and forth in a narrow arc. He feinted at Pauley Domo's legs, and the older guy backed away toward a corner where one of the eagles jutted out. They danced side to side, each giving a little ground, but the kid was more aggressive. He attacked with the blade. Pauley Domo retreated and then came back swinging the wooden lid. They didn't have much room to work with. The balcony was no more than ten feet deep.

Anna came up behind the kid and said, "Eddy, stop it, leave him alone, this is wrong."

The kid paid no attention until she grabbed at his shoulder, and he shoved her away without looking.

Anna stumbled back toward me, hit the box, and stepped on one of the waxy clumps of bills. She staggered back toward the edge. It caught her just at the knee, and she went over onto the shiny back of an eagle gargoyle. The red silk slid across the smooth steel, and it made a muffled, hollow rattle. She twisted and before I knew it, her legs were dangling over nothing, and she got one hand onto the lip of the square cutout on the back of the thing. It was sixty-one floors down to the Lexington Avenue pavement.

Pauley saw her, but the kid didn't know what had happened and kept slashing. I got right up to the edge and knelt down to be level with her, but I couldn't reach her with an outstretched arm. I glanced down for a dizzying, terrifying, gut-churning second at the car lights on Lex so far below us. At first, she didn't even see me; she was concentrating so hard on her hands where they gripped the metal edge. The wind whipped at her dress. It tore at her shoulder, and I could see the muscles of her arms clenching. She pulled herself part of the way onto the flat top, but her hips slid back as she fought to keep her grip. I reversed my stick, yelled her name, and held the crook end out to her.

Her knee caught a narrow ledge that ran along the side of the eagle's neck, and she was able to raise herself up enough to let go with one hand and reach for the stick.

"Go ahead, I've got you," I said. She got one hand around the crook and then the second. I pulled. Her knee slipped off the ledge, and I took all of her weight. For an awful moment that lasted forever, she slid back and almost pulled me over the edge. I was able to brace myself against the low wall, but I couldn't get the leverage to pull her in.

"Don't look down!" I yelled. "Look at me, look at me."

I don't know how long we stared at each other, but my shoulders were screaming when Pauley Domo and the kid got their arms around me and pulled both of us back up.

Anna wound up on her stomach, flat on the back of the eagle. Then I was able to tug her across with the stick.

As we caught our breath, we were too spooked by what had happened to stand up while we were out there on that narrow, windy balcony, so we crawled back inside.

Jacob, Mercer Weeks, and everybody else from upstairs were waiting for us.

CHAPTER NINETEEN

They didn't know what had just happened. The way the light inside reflected off the glass doors, it was hard to tell what was on the other side.

Ellis took Jacob and me and Mercer Weeks to one side and said we should move everything back upstairs. "Look, this place is going to be packed with police in a few minutes. You," he said to Jacob, "are not going to be mentioned in any of the reports. If anybody asks, the Cloud Club is off-limits." Jacob and Weeks left. Frenchy and Malloy took the crates to the elevator. Anna and everyone else followed them.

"Have you got a good story?" I asked when they were gone.

"I got a tip when I was at your place earlier tonight that a suspect in the warehouse shooting would be here."

"You won't have to worry about pinning it on Luther," I said. "Bring him over here."

Ellis dragged Luther to his feet. I opened his coat and pulled the broom-handle Mauser out of his shoulder holster. I handed it to Ellis. "He killed Betcherman with this."

"How do you know that?"

"Because it's a machine pistol. Has a fully automatic setting. You'll be able to match the bullets, and you're going to find that Betcherman was in this up to his eyebrows with Luther."

"Yeah," Ellis said. "He was in that Teutonia Society. We didn't have to dig very deep to get that."

"OK, then, one of the Saengers from the Chicago chapter learned that some money had been sent to a Jimmy Quinn in New York. He came here with a bunch of brothers. Anna told me there were six of them. They've got funny names. One of them was called No-No. He was the explosives expert. Some of them made the mistake of getting in touch with Betcherman and Luther, who agreed to throw in with them. One guy blows himself up. Luther and Betcherman take care of the other one in the warehouse. Then Luther cuts Betcherman out of the picture."

Ellis said, "We know there was one Saenger in your room at the Chelsea. One of the dead men might be a Saenger, too."

"Right, the one who came in from the hall. The one who busted through the window was a Kraut."

"Where does Klapprott fit in?" he asked.

"I'm not sure, but I think he's not really the big cheese he made himself out to be. Luther here didn't seem to pay him much mind."

The big Kraut knew we were talking about him, but it was hard to tell how much he understood or what he was thinking with all that blood on his face.

"That leaves this one." I nodded to the dead thug on the floor. "I shot him."

Ellis said he was sure it was self-defense and told me again to go upstairs. As it turned out, the department did bang-up work on the rest of it. There were only a few short notices buried in the back pages about the swift arrest that was made in the case of the slain detective, and they made no mention of anything else. Luther was convicted and sent to Sing Sing, where somebody stabbed him.

As the elevator door opened, Ellis said, "That blonde, what's her name?"

"Anna."

"Is she really married to that guy?"

I shrugged.

"But you and her . . . "

"Yeah."

"She's something."

"Ain't it the truth."

In the Cloud Club, Frenchy had elected to lubricate the proceedings with a round of Martinis.

Jacob knocked his back but was still sounding pretty steamed at Anna. "What the hell do you mean she's my daughter?"

The old woman, the baby in question, and Pauley Domo were at a four-top near the back. I think he'd realized that the only chance he had of getting anything now was by laying low.

Anna was sitting in my chair. The kid was beside her. She ignored Jacob's question. She said, "These two boxes are what's left of the ransom ten months later. I know you're wondering why I packed it like this. Maybe it was a little crazy, but it worked. Cash attracts attention. A lot of cash attracts a lot of attention. I wanted it to look like something else, and I used what I had at hand."

"I guess that makes sense. Anyway, it's here now. I'll take care of it." Jacob was comfortable on a barstool, drink in hand, back against the bar. He grinned around the Havana.

"No." Anna's voice stayed level. She wasn't mad. She wasn't arguing. "I did exactly what I said I'd do. I did what you and Mercer asked me to do. I delivered the money. Those guys killed Benny, then they killed each other. I didn't have anything to do with it."

"I still don't understand what you're talking about. We all agree. This is *my money.*"

"Have you forgotten what you said that night? I think it was just about the last words you spoke before I drove away. You remember, I know you do, I can see it in your face."

I could see it, too. Jacob took a drink, rattled his ice, messed with his cigar, and mumbled, "I don't know what you're talking about."

"Think about it. The last note said, 'Send the Woman.' I knew it wasn't kosher. So did you, but you didn't have any other choice, so you made me a promise, 'as an honorable man'—your words, Jacob. You said that if I did this thing for you, you would be in my debt and I could ask anything of you. Anything. Mercer was your witness."

She turned to him, "Isn't that right, Mercer?"

It was his turn to bob and weave. "We said a lot of things that night. We had to get Benny back."

She stood and stepped up to the bar. She got right in front of Jacob, her face level with his. I saw that she was barefoot. I guess her shoes were somewhere down on Lex. "That's right and I did my part. I took that money, and I tried to get Benny back, and I was locked up for ten months, ten months, because of it. And now it's time for you, as an honorable man, to live up to your word. You said I could ask anything of you. I ask for this money."

Jacob tapped his glass. Frenchy filled it. Jacob pondered the gin for a long time. Then he shook his head.

"I cannot do that. You don't understand. Ever since we lost Benny and the money, we're fighting just to stay even. If I can put this back into the system, we'll be fine, I know we will, but without it, the way things are going, a year from now Schultz will take over my operation. I can't let that happen. I won't. This is my work. This is my life."

He got up and slapped the top back on the first box. "Weeks is right. We said a lot of things that night. I don't remember them all. You say that Benny really is dead and that breaks my heart, because he was so important to me. He was my son, my true son."

Jacob was making excuses, but there was truth to what he was saying.

"You've got to understand, I can't let you have it. I need this."

"You promised that—"

"No!" He spun around to face her. "There's nothing more to say. This is my money. I'm taking it. Weeks, get the boxes."

As Mercer Weeks stacked the crates, Anna turned and glanced at me. I nodded so that she was the only one who could see it. But Connie caught it, and maybe Marie Therese, too.

Weeks held the two boxes like they weighed nothing. At the elevator, Jacob turned back to Anna and started to say something but just stood there.

As the elevator doors opened, Pauley Domo jumped up and said, "Hey, wait a minute, this isn't supposed to be happening."

Anna cut him off, "Shut up, Pauley. We're leaving. Help Nana. Eddy, don't hurt him."

She slipped into her long black coat and as she was leaving said, "See you around, Jimmy. Thanks for nothing."

After they were gone, we loaded up our cases of gin. My guys were asking all sorts of questions, and I didn't have any answers.

Back at the speak, we unloaded and they set about cleaning up Vittorio's kitchen. I went down to the cellar. The other two crates were where we left them. I wrestled them out and loaded them into the dumbwaiter. Back upstairs, I found Connie waiting on the divan in my office. There was a cheese sandwich on my desk. She was working on a sandwich of her own and had a glass of beer. I sat at the desk and wolfed mine down.

When she'd finished she said, "Are you going to go with her? Joseph says you're going to sell this place to Herr Klapprott and take off with Anna or Soph, whatever her name is."

"Fat Joe doesn't know shit from Shinola, pardon my French.

I'm not interested in selling. I'm not interested in leaving. What about you? Are you going back to California?"

"I don't know. Nothing that's happened since I left home has been what I thought it was going to be, and then there's you and all this, and today has been stranger than anything else. We saw a couple of fights and went for a walk. We visited a neat place. Then we made mud pies with money and it ended with me holding a gun on a guy. What more could a girl ask for?"

I'd missed the part about the gun, but I guess it had been a busy day, and I could see that she might be having second thoughts.

"When you put it that way, it sounds different, but I hope to high hell we don't have another one like it."

She laughed and picked up the empty plates and glass. On her way out she said, "Do you want to know about the money, I mean the box we started to separate?"

I said we'd see to that tomorrow.

Sometime before dawn Marie Therese came into my office and said they were finished. "I expect you'll want me to leave the front door unlocked for her," she said, sounding snippy and pissed.

I told her to leave it as it was and followed her out the back door with Frenchy and Connie. I held the gate open as Frenchy drove through. Before she climbed up into the cab, Connie turned back, grabbed me by the neck, and gave me a hard kiss. She pushed away quickly and said, "Thanks for everything, Jimmy." She might have been saying good-bye, I couldn't tell.

Back inside, Fat Joe and Arch Malloy were waiting for me in the bar. Fat Joe asked for the short Smith. I told him I was going to need it for a while longer.

He snorted. "Hell, she's coming here and you're going to give her the fucking money. What a sap." He shook his head in disgust and left.

Ain't it the truth.

Malloy said, "You should know there's been a town car parked on the street for the past half hour. Driver and two people in the back, maybe more. Is there anything else you'll be needing me for, and what time do you want me to report this evening? Some of the fine points of my employment have yet to be defined."

We settled on eight o'clock. I went behind the bar and poured a couple of greasecutters.

After a toast to nothing in particular, he said, "We've not known each other very long, but these have been eventful days, so I don't think you'll mind my making an observation about the young lady we met up there."

I shook my head.

"I'll venture that you and she have a long and uneven relationship."

"That's a fair way of putting it."

We drank. After a time he said, "I've known women like that, two of them, and I was not able to hold on to either of them. I believe that is part of their nature and allure. We're blessed to enjoy them while we can. Someday, you must tell me about her."

I agreed to do that. He left by the front door. Anna knocked moments later and hurried inside as soon as I unlocked it.

She'd brushed her hair, fixed her makeup, and found some high heels. The red dress was still ripped at the shoulder. She wrapped her arms around my neck and kissed me as hard as she could. She was shivering, and when she pulled back she brushed tears off her cheeks. This time, she wasn't working on me. She was close to wrung out.

I poured another whiskey. She drank and said, "I guess I was naive to think Jacob would keep his word. He should have, goddammit, he owed me."

"Yes, he did."

She gave me a sharp, sudden look. "The rest of it's here, isn't it?" She sounded hopeful and almost angry. "You're not going to try to keep it."

"Yes, it's here. It's your money. Maybe I'm putting my head in a noose taking what Jacob thinks is his. Maybe the next time I see Mercer Weeks, he won't be so accommodating."

She shook her head. "You don't need to worry about that."

"No, I didn't think so, but before we go any farther, I want to be sure that I understand how we got here and why. Let me start. You can correct the things I get wrong."

"All right," she said, sounding skeptical and suspicious.

"First, you had to come back here for the little girl and your grandmother. And you knew that once you were in the city, there was a fair chance you'd run across Jacob and Weeks, so you decided you could use some help, and that was me. Why?"

"Because we were always square with each other. That night in the Taft Suite, it was nice. Yeah, I enjoyed it, too, but you know what was more important? Remember that night we ran into that crazy angry guy and you shot him? That stayed with me. Then later, when I came here with Jacob and saw Jimmy Quinn's Place, I knew you'd turned out all right."

She may have been buttering me up, but I didn't mind.

"And when that crazy half-breed had me chained up, I remembered what it was like with you, that spring when we went out to all those funny places, that was one of the best times of my life, maybe the best, but you don't want me to get all sappy."

"And if everything had worked out perfectly, you'd have cooked up some Jimmy Quinn identification for some other guy to use at Railway Express."

She shook her head. "No, I was going to take care of it myself. I bought Jimena Quinn papers in Chicago. That's probably where the Saengers spotted me."

"And some of the Saengers and Pauley went after it for themselves, and we know what happened to them. And that brings us back to you and Mercer Weeks."

"What do you mean, me and Mercer?"

"Come on, Anna, up there in your suite, I could tell there's something between you. At first I thought you'd been two-timing Jacob with him, but that's not it."

MICHAEL MAYO

"Mercer and I have an understanding, leave it at that. Let's get back to the money. Is it here, the other two boxes?"

I nodded.

"Why didn't you bring them earlier?"

"A hunch, I guess. When you told me about the talk you had about delivering the money in Glenwood Springs, you made a point about Jacob saying you could ask anything of him. I figured you'd use it if he balked at letting you have it."

Hesitant, she agreed.

"Did you really think he'd let you have it? I didn't. Hell, I knew he wouldn't. He wasn't lying up there. That money *is* his business. It was bad enough when word got out that he'd paid a fat ransom for Benny and got nothing for his trouble. If anybody found out that he had a chance to get the money back and let it get away, he'd go under in a month."

"I didn't think of it that way," she said.

"But you say that I have nothing to worry about with him and Mercer. Why's that?"

"I told you, Mercer and I have an arrangement."

She was starting to piss me off. "Then straighten out something else. You've told some pretty wild stories, some of them true, I guess. For instance, I will buy that while you were at that resort in Glenwood Springs, the half-breed spotted you and decided that he had to have you. That makes sense to me.

"And I'll buy that he had a place set up to keep a woman locked up all for himself."

She didn't say anything.

"But I don't buy that that he and his 'gang' just happened to have everything else in place for a professionally planned kidnapping when Benny happened by. It doesn't wash."

"How would I know what they had planned?" She tried to sound unconcerned.

"Can it, Anna. There's something you're not telling me. What is it?"

Now she was getting pissed. "How to tell it?" she said. "How to tell it . . . OK, I know there are some people who thought that Benny and I cooked this up to run off together."

"Yeah."

"Well, they were half-right."

I waited for her to explain. When she didn't, I said, "I don't get it."

"Benny wanted to run off, but not with me. It was him and Mercer."

"You mean . . . "

"Yeah, they're a couple of crumpets."

It took a while for the idea to sink in. Benny and Mercer . . . son of a gun. I've got to admit, it was something I'd never have thought. I mean, Benny was no he-man tough guy, but he wasn't what you'd call a pouf, either. And Mercer was the last guy anybody would make for lavender. Sure, there were plenty of guys down in the Village who were pretty open about who they were, but that was the Village. You couldn't get away with it in the rackets.

Anna said, "I knew they were fey the moment I clapped eyes on them. I think they knew I was onto their secret, and maybe it's why Benny decided they had to get away from Jacob."

She said that after I left them in her suite at the Lombardy the night before, she and Mercer had a talk. Mercer didn't tell her everything, but she could fill in the details easily enough.

It was Benny's idea for them to take off, and I guess when I think about what it must have been like for them, I can see why. They couldn't let anybody they worked with know what was going on, and it must have been hard as hell for them to find a time and place to be alone together. Must have been a tough act to keep up every day.

Still, Mercer would have lived with the situation but Benny said no. They could go west to California, change their names, and start new lives in a place where they'd be left alone. They both knew that was a pipe dream drawn from the sweetest opium fumes. But then Jacob started talking about a western vacation.

That's when Benny came up with a half-formed idea. When Jacob told him where he and the Signora wanted to go and insisted that Benny and Weeks accompany them, it took shape.

Benny asked if Mercer knew anybody in Colorado who could provide a hideout. Mercer said it had been more than ten years since he'd set foot in the state.

But surely he knew somebody who's still in the business and might know somebody else.

Well, yeah, said Mercer, and he gave Benny the name of the guy who'd handled the local arrangements in Denver for the mint job.

It took several stacks of nickels and long distance calls made from phone booths late at night before Benny found what he needed. The guy Mercer suggested couldn't help, but he knew another guy who might know somebody. Four connections later, Benny was talking to a guy who said that sure he could help. Benny said he needed somebody for a simple job, a job that wasn't even illegal, but he needed somebody who'd keep his mouth shut, somebody who was not too tight with the local crooks.

For the job itself, all this guy had to do was pick up another guy late at night near the Hotel Colorado, take him to a safe place to hide for a week or so. He also had to keep an eye on the hotel during the day, deliver a note or two, and then lead another guy to the hideout. Some people might be asking questions later, but there was no chance that the cops would be involved. Could it be any easier?

The guy on the other end of the line said it sounded strange to him, but what the hell. Wire him the money and he'd get in touch with a half-breed Indian moonshiner who lived in the mountains north of Glenwood Springs. He was a little on the strange side himself, so he'd fit right in with this.

After that, it played out just like Benny predicted. The simple note and the apparent professionalism of the snatch led Jacob to believe he was dealing with fellow crooks who wouldn't hurt Benny unless he, Jacob, refused to pony up.

When Jacob called Weeks and explained what had happened, Weeks was relieved and terrified. Until the phone rang and he heard the hardness in Jacob's voice, he hadn't believed that Benny could pull it off. But it was happening, so he went to work, digging up the cash they had stashed here and there, and damn near tapping out their loan bank.

From then on, things clicked into place too neatly. Mercer and his guys took the train to Denver, where he bought a used car, and they drove to Glenwood Springs. That's where the final steps in the plan should have been easy. They get the note telling them to go to Miner's Camp No. 3. Mercer is chosen to deliver the money. He drives away, and neither he nor Benny is ever seen again. By the time Jacob begins his search for them, they're on the way to the California coast.

But the guy—a guy Mercer does not know—didn't show up, so he sent the next note, *Send the Woman*. What the hell did that mean?

He told Jacob it was too dangerous to send her alone. He'd hide in the backseat. She agreed right away, but Jacob said no. The guys who snatched Benny probably had people on the staff watching everything we do. He said, "Soph, you've got to do this for me. I swear to you, with Mercer as my witness . . . "

After she finished, I chewed it over and said, "I gotta say, Benny came up with a good plan. Right up to that point, but then the half-breed took a shine to you, and when Benny objected, he killed him? Is that it? What happened?"

"I don't want to talk about this," Anna said. "He's dead, leave it at that."

"No, there's more. What is it?"

She glared at me. "All right, but you can never, never tell anybody, especially Mercer Weeks."

"All right."

"The first night I was there, the night he chained me up, I heard screams, terrible screams from the house up the hill. It was Benny. He was alive when I got there, but the half-breed killed him. I say that because Benny would not have let him do what he did to me, just like you wouldn't. It was wrong, and he wouldn't allow it. And finally . . . "

She searched for words. "Finally, I found evidence, oh hell, not evidence, I found Benny's head. The goddamn half-breed killed him and cut off his head and put it in a glass jar full of that foul home brew he made. I found it the morning I escaped, on one of the shelves. If I hadn't known Benny, I wouldn't have recognized him. Looking at it made me sick, even more when I thought about some of the meat I put in that stew.

"You understand why you can never say anything to Mercer. I told him that Benny was trying to save me. It's probably true. Let him believe it."

"So how do things stand between you two?"

"The way we left it, his business is his business and my business is my business, and they don't have much to do with each other. He and Jacob are rebuilding the policy game and their bank. I'm leaving town."

I hit the button for the dumbwaiter. The cage rumbled up from the cellar. "Where?"

"West. California, Mexico, someplace to start over. Want to come along?"

When the lift stopped, I pulled on the strap to open it, took out the first box, and put it on the bar. Her eyes brightened.

"Let's see, you've got your grandmother, your daughter, your little brother, and your husband."

"He's not my husband, and he's not in this, not anymore."

She ran her hands over the top of the crate and then the other one after I put it down. Maybe she still loved Pauley Domo, but she'd be a damn fool to allow him to get anywhere near that much money.

She cut her eyes at me, and I could tell that she thought I was going to pull something. She'd gone through a lot to get where she was—more than I could imagine—and I wasn't about to get in her way.

"Here you go," I said. "Take it away."

She hurried out the front and whistled to the hired car. The boy and the driver got out and came down the steps, following Anna back inside.

The kid honed right in on the crates, stepped up on the rail, and pulled a box to the edge of the bar. The damn thing must have weighed half as much as he did, but he was tottering out the door with it before the driver, an older gent with wiry gray hair, had picked his up.

Yeah, every guy who met Anna fell for her a little, some of us a lot more.

I watched as she made sure they got the crates into the trunk of the car. Like her, I kept an eye on the street, but that early, there wasn't anyone else around. Still, I kept the Smith down by my side until they were finished. I put it back in my coat pocket when she came back. She wiped away more tears, and her voice caught when she spoke.

"Thanks, Jimmy. I know this has been pretty crazy and I know . . . I know . . . Hell, I don't know anything. Half of me says I ought to stay right here with you."

"I know. I want you to."

"Then come with me, dammit."

"No, you've got people to take care of. So do I."

She kissed me again, slipped a waxy folded bill into my hand—a hundred as it turned out—and got into the car.

I went back into the speak and checked all the locks again before I walked back to the Chelsea. They wouldn't have finished cleaning my room, so I figured I'd have to sleep in that room up on the fifth. I hoped like hell I'd find Connie there.

ACKNOWLEDGMENTS

First, apologies to Dashiell Hammett, Murray Burnett, Joan Alison, Howard Koch, Julius Epstein, and Philip Epstein for the liberties I took with their excellent plot.

At Mysterious Press, associate publisher Rob Hart made excellent suggestions, specifically concerning the first few chapters. Lauren Chomiuk and Lisa Kaitz at Open Road Media tried to correct Jimmy's questionable grammar and his many insensitivities. They did their best to make this a better book.

My agent, Agnes Birnbaum, is invaluable.

Several historical figures are mentioned in this fiction, among them Arnold Rothstein, Meyer Lansky, Charles "Lucky" Luciano, Abner "Longy" Zwillman, Dutch Schultz, Otto "Abbadabba" Berman, and Louis "Diamond Jack" Alterie.

The descriptions of the Wall Street bombing, the Denver Mint robbery, and "Gentleman" Gerald Chapman's mail-truck heist are accurate. Pauley Domo's kidnapping scheme is loosely

ACKNOWLEDGMENTS

based on George "Machine Gun" Kelly's disastrous snatch of Charles Urschel.

Rachel Warren read an early version of the manuscript and gave excellent advice. Ernie Linger and Shelley Hachman helped to spread the word.

Reginald Marsh, Berenice Abbott, Rian James, Gordon Kahn, Al Hirschfeld, and William Seabrook showed me their city in the early twentieth century.

Nick Carr at Scouting NY (ScoutingNY.com) spends his time looking beyond the surface of things in the city and was as intrigued as I was by the bus terminal beneath the Hotel Dixie.

Finally, special thanks to publisher Otto Penzler for his support of crime fiction.

THE JIMMY QUINN MYSTERIES

FROM MYSTERIOUSPRESS.COM
AND OPEN ROAD MEDIA

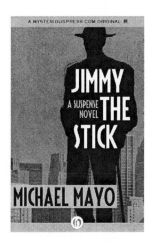

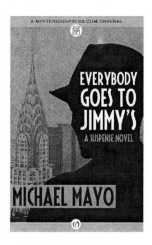

Available wherever ebooks are sold

MYSTERIOUSPRESS.COM

Otto Penzler, owner of the Mysterious Bookshop in Manhattan, founded the Mysterious Press in 1975. Penzler quickly became known for his outstanding selection of mystery, crime, and suspense books, both from his imprint and in his store. The imprint was devoted to printing the best books in these genres, using fine paper and top dust-jacket artists, as well as offering many limited, signed editions.

Now the Mysterious Press has gone digital, publishing ebooks through **MysteriousPress.com**.

MysteriousPress.com offers readers essential noir and suspense fiction, hard-boiled crime novels, and the latest thrillers from both debut authors and mystery masters. Discover classics and new voices, all from one legendary source.

FIND OUT MORE AT

WWW.MYSTERIOUSPRESS.COM

FOLLOW US:

@emysteries and Facebook.com/MysteriousPressCom

MysteriousPress.com is one of a select group of publishing partners of Open Road Integrated Media, Inc.

THe MYSTeRIOUS BOOKSHOP, founded in 1979, is located in Manhattan's Tribeca neighborhood. It is the oldest and largest mystery-specialty bookstore in America.

The shop stocks the finest selection of new mystery hardcovers, paperbacks, and periodicals. It also features a superb collection of signed modern first editions, rare and collectable works, and Sherlock Holmes titles. The bookshop issues a free monthly newsletter highlighting its book clubs, new releases, events, and recently acquired books.

58 Warren Street
info@mysteriousbookshop.com
(212) 587-1011
Monday through Saturday
11:00 a.m. to 7:00 p.m.

FIND OUT MORe AT:

www.mysteriousbookshop.com

FOLLOW US:

@TheMysterious and Facebook.com/MysteriousBookshop

INTEGRATED MEDIA

Open Road Integrated Media is a digital publisher and multimedia content company. Open Road creates connections between authors and their audiences by marketing its ebooks through a new proprietary online platform, which uses premium video content and social media.

CPSIA information can be obtained at www.ICGtesting.com
Printed in the USA
BVOW07s1207080115

382499BV00001B/11/P

9 781497 662728